Cursed

Cursed

by Karol Ruth
Silverstein

Charlesbridge
TEEN

At the time of publication, all URLs printed in this book were accurate and
active. Charlesbridge and the author are not responsible for the content or
accessibility of any website.

Published by Charlesbridge
9 Galen Street
Watertown, MA 02472
(617) 926-0329
www.charlesbridgeteen.com

Library of Congress Cataloging-in-Publication Data
Names: Silverstein, Karol Ruth, author.
Title: Cursed / by Karol Ruth Silverstein.
Description: Watertown, MA : Charlesbridge, [2019] | Summary: "Depicts
young teen Ricky Bloom's struggles with her recent chronic illness
diagnosis, which comes amid family upheaval and challenges at
school."—Provided by publisher.
Identifiers: LCCN 2017055928| ISBN 9781580899406 (reinforced for library
use) | ISBN 9781632897992 (ebook)
Subjects: | CYAC: Rheumatoid arthritis—Fiction. | People with
disabilities—Fiction. | Family problems—Fiction. | School—Fiction.
Classification: LCC PZ7.1.S544 Cu 2019 | DDC [Fic]—dc23 LC record available
at https://lccn.loc.gov/2017055928

Printed in the United States of America
(hc) 10 9 8 7 6 5 4 3 2

Display type set in Hoosker Doo by Chank
Text type set in Amasis Regular by Adobe Systems Incorporated
Printed by Berryville Graphics in Berryville, Virginia, USA
Production supervision by Brian G. Walker
Designed by Joyce White
Jacket design by Joyce White

For the Disaster-Formerly-Known-As-My-Parents,
aka Mom and Dad, with love

the me i am now

I have a perfect mouth. That is, according to my dentist, aka my dad, aka *Dr. Dad.*

Straight white teeth. Healthy pink gums. Zero cavities. Perfect.

The rest of me is *anything but.* It's irregular. Damaged. Cursed.

Here's the basic info on me (the me I am now anyway):

1. I currently live with my dad in his one-bedroom bachelor pad, aka Dr. Dad's Batch Pad. He obviously wasn't thinking about me—or my older sister, Dani—when he rented this place. All there is for us to sleep on when we visit is the lumpy pullout couch in his poor excuse for a living room. Right after Thanksgiving, the Disaster-Formerly-Known-As-My-Parents decided I should live here. For my own good, they said. Now I'm riding the Sofa-Bed-From-Hell full time and Dani's so busy at college studying every second she's not burning up the basketball court, she hardly ever visits.

2. I'm fourteen and I'm in middle school. I kid you not. I was in high school, like a normal fourteen-year-old, back at the beginning

of the year, before I got shipped to my dad's. Now I'm enrolled in Glorious Grant Middle School, the only seven-eight-nine school left in Philadelphia, maybe the only one left in the country. It was the only school close to the Batch Pad that the Disaster-Formerly-Known-As-My-Parents could get me into midyear.

3. Speaking of Glorious Grant Middle School, I haven't actually attended classes since the last week of December, which was about six weeks ago. No one knows. Not Mom. Not Dr. Dad. Not even Dani. Soon enough my secret will be out and, if I'm lucky, my parents will just kill me. If I'm not, they'll force me to go back to Glorious Grant Middle School, where I may or may not still be able to pass ninth grade.

4. My life seriously sucks (in case you haven't picked up on that yet). And it's not just living with Dr. Dad and going to middle school even though I'm fourteen or some other bullshit, like the boy I'm crushing on isn't crushing back. Trust me, my particular *life suckage* is on a whole different level. (For the record, the boy I was crushing on *was* totally crushing back—until I got sick.)

5. About that—I have this pathetic disease. Never mind what it's called. If I told you, you'd laugh and think I was joking. That's what Crush Boy did—right before he ghosted me. I did an internet search three months ago when I was first diagnosed, and what it turned up was so depressing I decided the less I knew, the better. Worse yet, pretty much no one gives a crap about this boring-ass disease. It's not something that would prompt my classmates to shave their heads in solidarity or have a bake sale for me. I doubt it's ever trended on Twitter. It's just this embarrassing, painful, fucked up *thing* I have.

6. And, yeah, I curse. Deal with it.

That pretty much sums up life here in Rickyville, as I call it. Technically, my name's Erica, but everyone calls me Ricky, except Dani, who calls me Roo. (She was obsessed with playing Kanga as a kid and wanted her own Roo. Dani marches to her own badass drum.)

2

my going-to-school charade

Here's how The Charade goes: It's simple, really. While Dr. Dad gets dressed for work, his bedroom door shut, I go through the motions out in the living room, pretending that I'm getting ready for school. Pretending everything's rainbows and unicorns.

I tug on a pair of jeans. I say *tug* not because my jeans are butt-flatteringly tight, but because my knuckles are so stiff and sore, I can barely bend my fingers.

I have to stand to pull the jeans up, of course, and that means pain. My feet are probably the worst part of my body. Ever see one of those skeleton illustrations of a foot? It has a stupid number of bones and they're little bones, all connected with joints. That's the key to my misery—*joints*. A joint is basically anywhere one bone meets another, and all of my joints burn with pain. Like I'm on fire. Think about that skeleton illustration again, but zoom out for the whole-body view. See all those bones-connected-to-other-bones? Now imagine each of those joints ablaze with hot, red flames. Yeah.

Now you're getting it. Plus, an added bonus of my delightful disease is that I'm tired all the time. Like, can't-keep-my-eyes-open tired. All the time.

Even so, I usually get ZERO sleep on the Sofa-Bed-From-Hell. It seems to be getting even more hellish, if that's possible. Last month, Dani stayed over one night, and pulled a muscle in her back sleeping on this thing. Her basketball coach had to sit her for a week. The Temple Owls went 1–4, and Dani hasn't slept over since.

I barely slept at all last night, so it's a good thing I'm not really going to school. Of course, Dr. Dad *thinks* I've been going to school all this time. And really, he's made it *way* too easy to ditch. Once he's gone, I go right back to sleep (in his bed because it's loads more comfortable than the Sofa-Bed-From-Hell, which he folds up before he leaves anyway). Trust me, if you were in my too-tight shoes, you'd do the exact same thing.

I struggle into a sports bra (*much* easier than bras that close in the back) and pick out a T-shirt—color doesn't matter (for the record, today's is dark blue). Most of my clothes are still back home (back at Mom's anyway), but it's not like that matters either. Even if I had access to every piece of clothing I own, I'd still never look all put together like the girls I dubbed the Center City Barbies at Glorious Grant in their trendy clothes from Teen Heaven or wher- ever the hell it is they shop.

I could never look like them. Ever. I'm not like them.

I hurt, and they don't.

I'm weird, and they're not.

I push that from my brain. It's whiny, and I can't change it. So . . . *whatever.*

I check myself out in Dr. Dad's gaudy mirror with the swirly- gold frame. It's hideous but it does its job as a reflective surface, so it works for Dr. Dad.

My hair's a spiky catastrophe, like Albert Einstein and Edward Scissorhands had a baby and she's having a bad hair day. I do my best to make it presentable—for The Charade. My aching fingers struggle to hold on to the brush. I take a few stabs at the sides, my elbow doing a jolt-of-pain thing with each brushstroke, and manage to get the hair to lie flat against my head so at least I don't look like a punk-rock porcupine. When I try to lift my arm and get at the back, my right shoulder just plain refuses. So I make a pathetic attempt with my left arm and quickly decide to just face forward when Dr. Dad breezes through, which will be any minute now.

Later, after I sleep, I'll take my heavenly/hot bath. The hotter, the better. I can wash my hair then.

The only useful piece of advice Dr. *Blech*-stein (not his real name) has given me is to take baths, which I do daily. Sometimes more than once a day. If I wouldn't end up looking like a giant raisin, I'd spend all day soaking. In the water things are different—almost normal. *Almost.* My joints loosen up, and I can move a little bit. I can pretend I don't feel like I'm ninety years old.

As I cram my swollen feet into my too-tight Converse Chucks, I decide today will be a giant-fizzy-bath-bomb day. Even my greasy/gross hair is excited.

I hear the bedroom door handle jiggle, and Dr. Dad comes out. "Good morning, Ricky Raccoon!" he chirps—his nickname for me since I was two. Never mind that I'm *not fucking two* anymore.

I grunt something like *hey* back. (Not that he really notices.)

He's wearing a suit, like he always does. Only the tie changes. Today's is burgundy with dark-green diamonds.

"How are you feeling?" he asks, as he folds up the Sofa-Bed-From-Hell with one seamless tug. "Having much pain?"

"I'm fine," I tell him quickly, automatically, because I don't want him to know that every bone in my body hurts and that I miss Dani terribly and that I'm terrified about what'll happen when he and Mom find out I've been cutting school, because I know they'll find out eventually, probably soon, and then, and then . . .

Screw him. He's not worthy of knowing any of that.

Dr. Dad accepts my answer, no questions asked. I wait for him to try to tousle my hair or make some other classic dad move, so I can flinch away from him, just to hurt his feelings. But he doesn't give me the chance.

He gathers a few of his things, says, "Have a great day!" and then there's just the door slam. Breakfast at the office, I guess.

I slump back down on the Sofa-Bed-From-Hell, (sofa mode) and wait to make sure he didn't forget an umbrella or a bag of dry cleaning he meant to drop off. I give him three minutes. Statistically, that'll mean I'm in the clear.

I let the minutes pass. *Tick, tick, tick*—there's no sign of him. He's left for sure now, on his way to drill teeth and tell people to spit.

After a quick pee, I kick off my too-tight Chucks, grab the extra pillows from the Sofa-Bed-From-Hell, and crawl onto his bed.

Dr. Dad always leaves the blinds closed—says the brick wall view of the building next door is too depressing—so it's nice and dark in here. The bedspread is soft and warm and smells like the lemony-fresh laundry detergent I made him buy when I moved in so it would smell like home—my former home, anyway.

I shift my body around, trying to find a comfortable position, propping up the most painful parts of me with pillows. My right ankle is stinging like crazy, but I'm out of pillows. So I hang that foot off the side of the bed an inch, letting it dangle. That does the trick.

I close my eyes, exhale.

Relief. Alone. All alone.

In the yummy/comfy dark, I wonder what's happening at school today. Will that guy Julio with the wild corkscrew curls be jamming in the music room after school, like he was that first day I spotted him and all the days after that, when I casually cruised by the music room, hoping to get a glimpse of him? Did he even notice me? Would he notice me if I started going to school again?

I managed to learn a few facts about Julio in my brief time at Glorious Grant: He plays the drums (I'm not sure anything else really matters), he's best friends with a guy named Lex (who's in all honors classes and is some kind of guitar genius who started playing while he was still in diapers), and they both live in one of those fancy buildings on Nineteenth Street, off Rittenhouse Square.

Julio's last name is Sánchez and he has beautiful light-brown skin. He's tall and lean, like maybe he'd be a good basketball player if music weren't his first and only love. (I'm guessing at that last part since, even in English class, he always has a pair of drumsticks sticking out of his back pocket.) But his crazy corkscrew curls are the most delicious part of the whole package. They're dirty blond and frame his gorgeous face in a way that makes me simultaneously weak in the knees and tempted to run my fingers through his hair without an invitation.

That's all I know for sure. The rest is a fill-in-the-blank scenario. But my blanks are exceptionally fun, like . . .

I start going to school again, after some doctor cures me, even though they said I couldn't be cured, and Julio is all, "Hey, I remember you. Where you been?" And I'm feeling good and strong and pretty and normal, and I say, "Miss me?" with a shrug, like "I'll bet you missed me!" And I walk past him and down the hall, all straight and slick, but slowly, so he can check out my butt, which looks exceptional in my new jeans from Teen Heaven. And he searches his brain, trying to remember if we have any classes together and when he'll get to see me again. Because he really wants to see me again. He can't wait. We have English together third period. I know that, but I don't tell him.

I let him suffer.

It's a nice filled-in-blank, but I'm still not going to school. Not today, anyway. Not until I get caught and they force me to go back and I have to face the possibility that my mostly As from West Mount Airy High might not be enough for me to squeak by and pass ninth grade. Have I mentioned that I consider having to repeat ninth grade the Absolute-Worst-Imaginable-Fate-In-The-Known-Universe? Considering that, I should really *force* myself to go to school—the jerks at Grant be damned—and just get through it.

But I can't. I just . . . *can't.*

My brain's restless with all that dread swirling around and I can't get to sleep, even though I'm tired. So tired.

On the bedside table, Dr. Dad has a picture frame with us in it, most of us anyway. I'm there next to Dad and beside him is Dani and her girlfriend, Noland. They've been dating since high school and both got basketball scholarships to Temple University. Now they live together off-campus. Noland's basically family since Dani's being gay is No Big Deal for us, but Noland's parents are still "working through their feelings" three years later. Totally our gain, because she's awesome.

I pick up the frame and stare at the picture. I remember when it was taken. We'd all gone out to Dani's favorite restaurant in Chinatown to celebrate her seventeenth birthday. It was a couple years ago, before everything went to hell. Before Dad decided he didn't want to be married to Mom anymore and my parents started hating each other. Before the vicious fighting began anytime they shared the same space, which I had to listen to but was powerless to do anything about.

Then it dawns on me—Mom's supposed to be in the picture.

I grab the frame, open up the back. He's folded the picture, folded her out of his life. I smooth the crease on my mom's side of the picture and fold him away instead.

Take that, Dr. Dad.

I'm tempted to fold them *both* out of the picture. Mom's really no better than Dr. Dad. They both decided to banish me to the Batch Pad. Mom said living in our three-story house had gotten too hard and that I needed to go to a smaller school, one with an elevator, now that my body doesn't work right anymore (not her exact words but it's basically what she meant).

No one bothered to ask me how I felt about it. The Disaster-Formerly-Known-As-My-Parents just *decided.*

UGH. Don't think about them. Shut that out, shut down, shut off.

Focus on sleep. Sleep so I can dream about Julio with the wild corkscrew curls. Sleep until the afternoon when I don't hurt as much.

Sleep it away.

Sleep.

we interrupt this glorious nap . . .

The phone jolts me awake after *who-knows-how-long*, several hours by the height of the sun peeking through the cracks in the blinds. I lie there, not hurting so much, not at the moment anyway, listening as Dr. Dad's ancient answering machine picks up. That thing's so old it has one of those tiny cassette tapes in it.

After the beep, I hear:

"Um, yes, Dr. Bloom, it's Patricia Perdanta calling from Grant Middle School. Again."

I attended classes long enough to learn her nickname—*Principal Piranha*.

"The work number we have on file for you doesn't seem to be correct. . . ."

My handiwork. Serves them right for leaving me alone with my school records file, even for a millisecond.

"We really must discuss your daughter Erica. Please call me at your earliest convenience."

She leaves her number and then the machine clicks off.

I roll onto my side (ignoring my throbbing shoulder), reach over the picture with Dr. Dad folded away, and fumble for the right button on the answering machine.

"Message deleted," a robotic voice reports. I smile.

If he only knew. Open wide. Spit, please.

At some point, she'll figure out that I added letters after Dr. Dad's name, that he's not a PhD but a DDS, and then she should be able to find him online. Honestly, I'm surprised she didn't figure it out and track him down weeks ago.

And don't judge me. I tried going to school. I went for close to a month when I first started living here with Dr. Dad.

Glorious Grant Middle School is nine blocks away from the Batch Pad. Nine blocks there and nine back. I took the bus the first few days, but it was always crowded and I had to stand. I kept losing my balance, falling into people, getting glared at. So I started walking, moving slowly through the cold winter air—past never-ending happy holiday window displays that made me want to gag—through snow, through slush.

Nine blocks there and nine back.

It felt like I was wearing bags of broken glass on my feet, with all those little bones jabbing into one another, a thousand tiny stabs cutting into me with every step, a thousand times worse than any pain I ever thought I'd ever feel—ever.

I knew absolutely NO ONE and spent my days shuffling from class to class, my eyes glued to the gray-green linoleum floors, trying not to limp too much, trying not to whimper like some kind of wounded dog, trying to be invisible. At lunch I'd steal peeks at the Center City Barbies, who, for the record, aren't all white, blond, and perfect. Actually, they are a mix of sizes and races. It's just that they all seem to possess this confident I'm-better-than-you-

and-I-know-it air. Like they got some sort of instruction manual on *How To Be Hot And Happening* that I certainly never got. I was equal parts fascinated and horrified by them. I tried to imagine ever feeling that comfortable in my skin but I couldn't.

Then, the week before Christmas break, the Barbie with the flowing red hair came up to me after lunch and said she wanted to talk to me after school, that I should meet her outside. I was suspicious—why not just talk to me now?—but also curious. So I decided to show up.

Once school let out, I spotted the Redhead Barbie with a bunch of her friends at the far corner of the school grounds. I should have trusted my instincts and gone home but I headed for them instead, walking slowly so I'd limp less. When I was just a few feet away, two boys suddenly crowded into my personal space. One was short with kind of a pug nose, the other tall and lanky.

Behind them I saw the Redhead Barbie snicker. Another Barbie—busty, blond, and supermodel pretty—shook her head and said, "Ronnie, you're a pig."

I wasn't sure if the Redhead Barbie had lured me here on purpose or not, but it was pretty clear she and her friends weren't going to come to my rescue.

The shorter boy stepped even closer to me. "We just were wondering," he said. "What's wrong with you?"

"Nothing's wrong with me," I lied, but my heart was instantly pounding.

"Then why do you walk funny with your face all weird?"

Wait. My face is weird? What the hell?

I watched as he imitated me—hobbling with his face twisted in pain. I turned to walk away, but he grabbed my arm.

"Gross. Don't touch her," the lanky friend snorted. "You may catch it." (For the record, I'm not contagious.)

I yanked my arm free and lost my balance, falling hard onto the cold concrete, which was still damp from a light snowfall the night before. I heard laughing but I didn't look up to see who it was. From the volume, it seemed like a small crowd had gathered.

Getting up would be a struggle and I certainly didn't want to do it in front of these jerks. But my pants were getting wet and I was cold. So I scrambled painfully onto my knees—which fucking *killed*—and crawled a couple feet toward the wall so I could brace myself on it and pull myself up.

The laughter grew louder and louder.

That was my last day at Glorious Grant Middle School.

After some rest, now that I'm not so tired that my head feels like it's going to explode, it's time for my heavenly/hot bath. I sit up on the side of the bed and test my feet. Anytime I've been off them for a while, my feet get all relaxed or something. Standing up generally sucks to some degree. Usually my feet calm down after a few steps, but those first few can be Pure Hell.

I press down on my feet, lightly at first, and see if they hurt—or rather how *much* it hurts. Then I press a little harder and rock each foot, ball to heel, and see how much *that* hurts. I usually try to rock for a while until my feet toughen up or until I have to get up—even if it's going to hurt like hell—because I'm late for something or people are staring or I have to pee or there's some other stupid emergency.

Today, after only a few rocks, my feet are decent.

I stand, wobbly but with only some minor jabs of pain, and head back to the living room for my *American Idiot* CD, which I picked up about a year ago when Dani and I were at the South Street Goodwill. Yes, I collect CDs. I know they're old-fashioned, but I love having something *physical*. I'd always liked Green Day's sound and the cover art for *American Idiot* is amazing, so I grabbed it on a whim, not knowing it would basically become the national anthem of Rickyville.

In the bathroom, I put the CD in the stereo—another old-fashioned thing I love, because I can blast the volume and sing along to the music. I match Green Day's Billie Joe Armstrong note for note as I wrestle with the hot-water knob, turning it on full blast. While the tub fills, I look through my supply of fizzy bath bombs. I decide I'm in a green-apple kind of mood and drop the little green ball into the churning bathwater. It fizzes and fumes, as I struggle out of my T-shirt. Getting out of my jeans isn't nearly as hard, thanks to gravity. I just unbutton, wriggle a little, and let them drop.

Using the toilet tank to keep myself steady, I step out of my jeans and into the tub. I ease myself down into the heavenly/hot water, immersing myself in all its glorious glory.

Ah . . . floating. Not hurting. No stabbing pain. No anything. Heaven.

And then the damn phone rings. I mute the music and listen.

Could it be another call from Principal Piranha? But no—

"Rick-eey, it's Mo-om!" She uses this annoying, sing-song-y voice when she's trying to pretend that things don't suck with a cherry on top. *"I tried your cell. No answer. Where are you? Hopefully, on your way to CHOP . . ."*

(CHOP=Children's Hospital of Philadelphia.)

"You have an appointment with Dr. Blickstein today." (Dr. Blech-stein's real name.) *"At four o'clock, remember?"*

Um, nope.

"The Uber I ordered for you has you down as a no-show. Thought I'd try you here in case you stayed home sick. I can order

you another Uber, honey, just let me know. I'm getting nervous. It's twenty of."

I look down at my naked, green-bath-bomb-tinted-and-not-at-all-ready-to-bolt-out-of-the-apartment body.

Crap à la mode!

(groan) do i have to?

Another dreaded Blech-stein appointment.

I (very reluctantly) drag myself up out of the blissful water, dry off, and give my teeth a thorough brushing (I *never* skimp on that). Getting my clothes back on is a tiny bit easier, now that my bones aren't grinding quite so much. My Chucks still protest when I squeeze my feet in. I grab my backpack (I'm supposed to be coming from school, remember?) and glance at the clock on my way out the door. It's 3:54. I'm toast.

I leave the Batch Pad and start down the long hallway to the elevator, struggling into a sweater. The throbbing in my left shoulder, which I probably made worse by lying on that side, is still bad. The pain doesn't stop after I get the sweater on. I try holding my arm stiff against my body, but then my neck starts feeling wonky.

Something I didn't realize until my body started malfunctioning is that, when you walk, you move almost every part of your body —ankles, knees, hips, arms, and yes, even your neck. If you favor one part, like holding your arm stiff against your body, for example, then some other part is going to make you regret it.

I decide it's better to have my shoulder hurt than my neck, so I release my arm and keep going.

Throb, throb, throb.

I rest in the elevator, leaning against the back wall. Down in the lobby, the doorman on duty, Gus, greets me with a big smile.

"Afternoon, Miss Erica," Gus says.

He's an older dude, with a Santa Claus vibe—big gut and an overgrown white mustache. He gets on my nerves, but I can't bring myself to be rude to him. He's too damn cheerful. It'd be like yelling at, well, Santa Claus. Even though technically I'm Jewish, that still doesn't seem right.

"Haven't seen you in a long time," he says, minding my damn business. "I was getting worried."

"Could you flag down a cab for me, please?" I ask as politely as I can manage, completely ignoring his nosy concerns.

To his credit, Gus doesn't push the issue. He just flips on the taxi light and opens the front door for me.

A cab pulls over the moment we hit the street, and Gus opens the cab door for me, too. The man takes his job very seriously. I grunt my thanks and fold myself, slowly, painfully, into the back seat of the cab, convinced that whoever designed taxicabs must have hated people over four and a half feet tall.

"Children's Hospital," I tell the cabbie, who gives me a nod and then zooms into traffic. I root around in my backpack for my phone and turn it on. It's two years old, so the screen's small and the camera's chintzy. Plus it's snail-slow. When the home screen finally loads fifteen minutes later (okay, two—but it feels like fifteen), I clear the *storage space low* message it's been giving me since the last system upgrade and start a text to Mom to let her know I'm on the way. But then I have the brilliant idea to tell her my phone battery died and I couldn't contact her. I delete the text I started and I have the whole ride to come up with an excuse for why I missed her Uber. Plenty of time.

To torture myself, I open Instagram and check out what my former friends are up to. Meghan and Jenna posted photos from some party they went to last weekend. Crush Boy was there too. The captions describe how awesome it all was. Rage and loneliness and *I-don't-know-what* burn in the pit of my stomach. I go back to my home screen and my phone gives me the annoying *storage space low* message again.

So I delete Instagram. And Snapchat. And Twitter. Screw it. The stupid social media apps are just painful reminders of my former life and I have enough pain without them. Besides, now I won't keep getting the stupid message about my storage space.

The cab stops at a red light and I glance out the window at the throng of people going about their business in Center City Philly. Watching people walk never used to amaze me but now it does. It's so effortless for normal people, with all their body parts moving in perfect harmony. I watch a woman rise from a bus stop bench, *effortlessly.* Her brain just tells her muscles to engage and up she goes. I can barely remember it being that way for me. Now every movement's a struggle.

I rest my head on the back of the seat—inconceivably, I'm still tired—and close my eyes. . . .

A sharp rap on the taxicab window jolts me awake. I'm disoriented, probably drugged by the sickly-sweet smell of the cabbie's Little Tree air freshener.

We're stopped. Mom points at her watch and gives me a frowny face. Children's Hospital looms behind her. I haven't seen her since my last Blech-stein appointment, a month ago. She wanted to take me out to dinner last week but I lied and told her I was too busy with homework. Just didn't feel like dealing with her—or anything. Now she looks so relaxed and upbeat—showing shades of her pre-Disaster self—that I'm wondering if being rid of the burden of being my full-time mom was the best thing in the world for her.

She opens the cab door and immediately asks, "What happened?"

"Sorry. I missed the Uber. I would have texted you but my phone's dead."

While Mom digs through her purse for cab fare, the cabbie tries to help me out of the back seat by grabbing my arm, my *furiously aching shoulder* to be exact.

"Get off!" I scream, and the guy jumps away, like he's worried about a lawsuit.

"Erica!" Mom barks. She hands some bills to the cabbie, smiling apologetically, and then turns back to me, not smiling. "Let's go," she says.

I force my legs out of the cab, which isn't easy because my left foot gets caught on the stupid doorjamb and I have to wrench it free, which totally burns. I must have had it bent up funny against the divider thing, because my leg nearly buckles beneath me when I stand on it.

"You okay?" Mom asks, reaching out to steady me, reaching for *my shoulder*.

I flinch away and she looks genuinely hurt, like she thinks I don't want her touching me, which I don't, but not for the reason she thinks.

Great. Now I've hurt her feelings.

"I'm okay," I grumble. My ankle toughens up after a few steps anyway.

In the hospital elevator, Mom says, "Hope they can still see us. We're nearly thirty minutes late."

I don't bother mentioning that I'm the one being seen, not "us," and that Dr. Blech-stein's made us wait way more than half an hour plenty of times.

I'd fallen asleep before coming up with my why-I-missed-the-Uber excuse but an impromptu one rolls off my tongue: "Sorry. I went to the library to kill time. I was doing Spanish homework. I checked the clock when I got there and then again a while later, but it said the exact same time. So obviously, the clock was broken or something. You know how I am with Spanish. I get into it and time flies. I had no idea how late it had gotten. And like I said, my cell was dead, so I couldn't let you know what was up." I check Mom's face and it seems like she's buying my bogus story. "I could really use a better phone, you know."

"Yes. You've mentioned that a few times," Mom says with a wry smile. "I hope you let the librarian know about the broken clock."

I nod and we ride in silence as the elevator climbs. I spend an awful lot of time on elevators these days.

What happens if, some day, I can't walk up stairs at all?

What happens if, some day, I can't even walk?

What happens . . . ?

I plunge into a chair in the waiting room while Mom checks in at reception. She sits beside me when she's done and says, "It's fine. He's running behind anyway."

"Hooray!" I fake-cheer.

"Oh, Erica, try not to be so morose," she says, which is a really stupid thing to say because it's not like morose people choose to be morose, right?

Just to mess with her, I say, "I got an A on a geoscience quiz today."

"That's great!" my clueless mother says, her face lighting up at the tiny morsel of information about my life I've so graciously shared (never mind that it's fake). She's like an exhausted polar bear drowning at sea who's finally spotted land. And I'm like the Worst Daughter Ever.

I'm saved from elaborating on the geoscience quiz I supposedly aced because Nurse Vampire (not her real name) calls for us and ushers us into an exam room. She's wearing Hello Kitty scrubs that are almost half-cute. She takes my blood pressure and my temperature and jots down the figures. Then she grabs her little plastic tray full of needles, gauze, and Band-Aids.

"When did you last eat?" she asks me. *Um, yesterday.* But I know I should have had lunch at school, so that's what I tell her.

She ties a tourniquet—a long strip of rubber—around my upper arm and gives me a smiley-face squishy ball to squeeze so my veins pop out. Then she says maybe it's better if I don't look, like she always does. But I do look, like I always do. If I watch as the needle pierces my skin, I can brace myself for the prick.

My blood's red, proving I'm a normal human being (even though I feel like *anything but*).

Nurse Vampire selects a blue stretchy wrap to match my T-shirt and wraps my arm up like I've had major surgery. Then she tells us to sit tight, the doctor will be right in—medical-speak for *it could be another twenty minutes.*

Once the nurse is gone, Mom says to me, "You're a brave kid, Ricky."

"What am I? Five years old?" I say, exasperated. She and Dr. Dad are always telling me I'm brave these days. It's nauseating.

"Sorry. You're a brave young woman," she says, thinking I meant what I said instead of what I *really* meant, which is *leave me the hell alone!*

"Whatever," I growl under my breath.

Still completely missing the point, Mom asks, "Okay, if you're not a kid and you're not a young woman, then what are you?"

I'm nothing. Absolutely nothing.

I climb up on the exam table to get away from her (it's where I'll end up anyway), and I'm wondering whether it'd be rude for me to lie down while I wait—since I'm *still* deathly tired—when Dr. Blech-stein comes in. He's nearly a foot shorter than Dr. Dad and has dark, wiry hair and a permanent look of superiority on his face.

"So, how's she doing?" he asks *my mom*. He talks only to Mom, *never* to me, like we're at a veterinarian's office and I'm the family pet, panting and wagging my tail while they decide whether the most humane thing to do would be to put me to sleep.

Dr. Blech-stein and Mom chat away as he feels my joints and moves my body parts around, checking for changes in my range of motion. While they're busy ignoring me, I glance at the pain scale chart on the wall with its color-coded stages of misery, wondering why they even bothered with the no-pain/bright-green smiley face at the top. It's not like it would ever apply to anyone in this exam room. Is it just there to mock us?

"How long have you had this node?" he asks.

It takes a minute to realize he's talking to me, since he so rarely does. He squeezes the knuckle of my right pinkie, making it burn.

I yank my hand away from him. It's a tiny thing, but it looks gross, like there's a macadamia nut under my skin where the knuckle's supposed to be. It's embarrassing enough. I certainly don't want anyone *touching* it.

"What about it?" I say.

"How long has it been there?"

"I don't remember," I tell him. But I do remember. It was last Thursday morning. I was brushing my teeth and I saw it in the bathroom mirror. It was only the size of a pea then. Now it's macadamia nut–sized. If it upgrades to cherry, I may have to wear gloves permanently.

"Why aren't you wearing the wrist braces I prescribed?" he asks next.

Because they're ugly. And I hate them. And I left them in my locker at school. I think.

I shrug.

"It's important," he insists, clearly frustrated that I don't adhere to his every command.

"Dr. Blickstein," Mom interjects. "What about her feet? She's still limping a lot."

"They're fine!" I huff, lying through my perfect teeth. Part of me wants to hear his answer, though. What *about* my feet?

He says, "Give the medicine time. It's only been a few months. Meanwhile, she can use a cane."

My eyes instantly burn, hot with tears. "I am *not* using a fucking cane!" I scream.

well, that was awkward

Mom and I ride the elevator down in silence. The appointment ended pretty quickly after my outburst. Dr. Blech-stein just said "suit yourself," told Mom I should make an appointment to see him in one month, and then walked out. Mom didn't even yell at me, probably because she's beginning to realize what a lost cause I am.

I should say I'm sorry, that I know I shouldn't curse in front of the doctor and be so difficult. What I say, calmly, quietly, is: "I am not using a cane."

"Yes. You made that super clear," she says back. Thankfully, it doesn't seem like she's going to argue the point, like maybe, possibly, she almost *gets it.* "Could you at least wear the wrist braces? Maybe just around the house and while you sleep?"

Ugh! She's being reasonable. That's so unfair!

I nod in agreement, even though there's no way I'm really going to wear them and it's not like she'll be around to check.

I wait by the front entrance while Mom gets her car.

She pulls up, and the moment I get in, she asks, "So how hungry are you?" Our post-Blech-stein appointment routine is to go somewhere to eat and spend time together. "You want dinner or just a snack?"

I'm starving. I haven't eaten all day. But I just shrug.

"We could go to Cush's Deli if you want something substantial." She makes a quick left turn as a traffic light goes from yellow to red. "Or just go to Coffeeland for bear claws and hot chocolate. Yum!"

Mom seems to *live* for these get-togethers ever since she shipped me off to the Batch Pad.

"I'm kind of tired," I tell her. "I think I just want to go back to Dad's."

She tries to hide her disappointment, but it's unmistakable. "Sure, honey. If that's what you want," she says quietly.

The truth is—I'm no more tired than I usually am and Dr. Dad will likely have zero to eat back at the Batch Pad. But this is too perfect an opportunity to hurt her feelings to pass up. Even though it's been three months since she sent me away, I'm still angry. It still hurts. I want her to hurt like I do.

Did I mention I'm the Worst Daughter Ever?

I check Dr. Dad's fridge, hoping to find leftover Chinese from the other night, but he must have eaten it at some point. There's a container of sushi (*yuck*) and an egg—a single, lonely egg. I shake it, gently, to see if maybe it's hard-boiled, since I've progressed to the level of *need-to-eat-right-now starving*. No such luck.

I settle for some old cinnamon rice cakes—like putting cinnamon on Styrofoam would make it taste any better. But I'm desperate, so I scarf a couple down.

It's nearly 7:30 when Dr. Dad rolls in. I'm parked on the Sofa-Bed-From-Hell (still in sofa mode). My laptop computer and some textbooks are in front of me on the coffee table so it looks like I've been studying, because that's what good girls who go to school do at night, right?

I see he brought groceries. *Thank God.*

I leap up . . . and instantly regret it. My feet are like burners on a gas stove when you turn the knob up all the way and the flame bursts out suddenly. I try not to cry out in pain but I can't help myself.

"You okay?" Dr. Dad asks, looking concerned.

"I'm fine!" I snap. I'm so sick of people asking me that!

The flames die down quickly and, after a moment, the pain's tolerable. I head over to the little kitchenette. "What's for dinner?"

He starts unpacking. It's the mother lode—cold cuts, rye bread from his favorite deli, cereal and real milk to go with it, barbecue potato chips, green apples and baby carrots, frozen mini-pizzas, coffee ice cream. All the stuff I like best, as if he's actually been paying attention and genuinely doesn't want me to die of starvation.

"This is awesome, Dad," I say.

He instructs me to park myself on one of the stools on the other side of the breakfast bar while he puts the groceries away and makes us corned beef sandwiches (plain for me, Reuben-style for him).

I'm a happy camper until he says, "So how was your appointment with Dr. Blickstein?"

I shrug. "All right, I guess."

"Your mom said he mentioned that using a cane might be helpful."

If you already talked to Mom about it, why bother asking me at all? But what I say is, "I'm fine. I don't need . . . a cane." It's hard to even say the word.

He slathers spicy brown mustard on a slice of bread. "They have some nice canes in the pharmacy downstairs at my building. I saw one with a pretty flowered pattern. They're not all horrible."

"Yeah, I'm sure the little old ladies in the neighborhood looove them," I say, rolling my eyes.

"Okay. No cane," he says as he serves up our sandwiches, placing them on the breakfast bar like a short-order cook at a diner. He comes around and sits on the stool beside me. "What about the wrist braces? Your mom said the doctor thinks they're very important."

"Sounds like you and Mom had a super great chat."

"Erica." He only calls me that when he's getting pissed, which I can tell by his face anyway—his suddenly harsh mouth, topped by squinty eyes.

"I left them in my locker at school." *I think.*

He swallows the bite of sandwich he has in his mouth and says, "Great. So tomorrow, when I get home from the office, you'll be wearing them, right?"

Uugghh. Walked right into that one. How could I be so stupid?

Well played, Disaster-Formerly-Known-As-My-Parents.

mission: (hopefully not) impossible

I'm headed to school. Yes, really.

My mission is to retrieve the god-awful wrist braces in order to get my parents off my back and then hightail it out of here without being seen. I'm not actually going to *wear* the wrist braces. I'll just put them on when I hear Dr. Dad's key turning in the front door.

This morning, I was getting dressed—not a charade this time, since I was actually planning to go to school—and I had this crazy idea to try on these super-sweet jeans I inherited from Dani. They're snug, so I usually get them up as far as my thighs before my fingers start to burn and I know they're going to be impossible to button with burning fingers so I give up. But my period ended two days ago, leaving me the least bloated I'll be for another twenty-six days, so I gave Dani's jeans a shot.

They slid up with a couple small tugs and buttoned with no problem, and then my fill-in-the-blanks started kicking in:

Julio does a double take when he sees me standing at my locker. "Who's that?" he wonders, intrigued. Then he realizes I'm that cool chick who only came to school for a few weeks and then mysteriously disappeared. "Hey!" he says. "How about a name before you disappear again?" I glance at him, like seeing him is totally minor. "What up, Julio?" I say. He grins, pumped that I know his name even though he doesn't know mine and says, "Man, I thought you transferred. I was so bummed!"

In my fill-in-the-blanks, I'm always mysterious and Julio's always intrigued.

Naturally, now that I'm dragging myself down Spruce Street, my head's crowded with *pain* instead of happy fill-in-the-blanks. I toy with the idea of walking by the music room to see if Julio's in there. I mean, I'll be at school, so it'd be a total missed opportunity if I don't at least see Julio—and have him see *me* in Dani's super-sweet, girly-girl jeans.

I limp the rest of the way there, daydreaming, hoping Dani's jeans will stand out more than my freaky walk, hoping I can avoid running into those asshole guys. Nineteenth Street. Twentieth. Almost there.

Finally, the wall around the school grounds is in sight. Sitting on it is forbidden. The guard barked at me for sitting there on my first day. My feet were killing me and I wanted to tell him to go screw himself. But I got up and kept my mouth shut. Now the stupid wall taunts me.

I lean against the wall—leaning is legal—and search the yard. I see a group of the Barbie girls off in that same corner—their territory, I guess—but they're in a tight cluster and don't seem to be paying attention to anyone outside their circle. No sign of those jerky guys, thank God.

No one's allowed inside the building until the first bell rings, so the place is swarming with bodies. Seventh grade punks run around me like idiots, coming too close to my furiously-burning-at-this-point feet. I tense my body, trying to prepare for one of them stepping on my foot or bumping into me or whatever, wishing I had an electric force field around me that would zing the piss right out of them.

Eventually the bell rings and everyone speeds toward the entrance. I take a deep breath and push off from the wall and walk, as straight as my feet will let me, up to the building's back entrance and through the door.

And now I'm inside, where I might see Julio and he might see me.

My locker's on the second floor, but there's no way I'm signing out an elevator key at the main office. I can't risk being spotted by Principal Piranha. Besides, the office is way at the far end of the hall, and guess where the elevator is? Just inside the main entrance. For the brief period I attended Glorious Grant Middle School, I did a lot of traipsing up and down the endless hallways because everywhere I needed to go (the office, my locker, all of my classes) always seemed to be the farthest distance from the stupid elevator.

Let me also point out that I had to get the key each day. The school wouldn't give me a key to keep—that would make too much sense. So *every day* I'd go to the office to ask for a key and have to stand there waiting, while the snots who got sent to the principal before school even began wondered why I couldn't take the stairs like a normal human being.

I wait for the horde of students to thin out before heading into the stairwell. I need to take the steps one at a time, using whichever knee hurts less and grabbing the handrail to pull myself up. It's certainly not something I want to do with a bunch of people staring and I'd really rather not get trampled either. So I wait. Once the second bell sounds, the few remaining kids bolt up the stairs. Perfect.

I slowly make my way up. My left knee stings a little, so I try taking a step with my right knee. That one stings a lot, so left it is.

I reach the second floor three hours later (okay, three minutes), heave my body against the heavy stairwell door, and walk out into the hallway, which is lined on both sides with long rows of green metal lockers. That's when it hits me—I have no idea which locker's mine. The combination is easy—it's left 4 (Dani's jersey number), right 43 (number of points she scored in her high school championship game, senior year), left 32 (number of wins her basketball team had that year to win it all). I inch down the hall, scanning locker after locker on the right side because I'm pretty sure I remember that much, hoping something will jog my memory. But the stupid lockers all look the same! At the far end of the hall, I'm debating whether to scan the left side or try my combination on every locker on the right side when I hear:

"You should be in class, Miss."

I look up. It's some dude. Doesn't look like a teacher. Maybe security.

"What's your first period class?" he asks.

"Public speaking."

I have no idea how I remember that. It's an elective, and the other choice that fit into my schedule was karate. So I wound up in public speaking, even though the last thing in the world I want to do is stand in front of a classroom full of jerks and talk.

I glance to my right and am shocked to recognize the teacher writing something on the board through the glass in the classroom door. Suddenly, I remember! *This* is my first period public speaking class and my locker is three down to the left of the door. All I need to do is get rid of the maybe security dude, and I'm home free. I motion to the classroom door, like *here it is. I'll just be going to class now.*

But the maybe security dude is no pushover like Dr. Dad. He smiles at me but stands there, waiting for me to go in the classroom.

I have no choice. I go in.

The public speaking teacher barks at me with a booming voice as I enter, drawing all eyes my way. "Ms. Bloom," he says. "What a surprise to see *you*." His tone is designed for maximum humiliation, and I realize I don't remember his name.

I pause there in the doorway, hoping my classmates, who're now gawking at me, will lose interest and look somewhere else.

Mr. Nameless stares at me too, waiting. "By all means, please do take your seat. It's that one there." He points four rows back. "In case you forgot."

I never should have paused at the door, because now my right ankle's locked up. I limp over to the seat he pointed out with everyone staring. I notice Supermodel Barbie a row behind my seat and a boy I believe is the lanky friend of the buttwipe who accosted me in the schoolyard way in the back row. Finally, I reach my assigned seat and slouch into the desk/chair combo, biting my tongue to keep from screaming.

I wait for Mr. Nameless to start teaching or something, anything to get the focus off of me. But I can feel his eyes drilling holes through the top of my head.

"Do tell us. Where have you *been*, Ms. Bloom?" he asks in a tone that says *I demand an explanation, you stupid speck of nothing*.

My brain files through possible responses, something that will shut him up, since I doubt he'll accept *no comment*. I'm not going to say I've been sick, even though it's the closest to the truth. There's no way.

Think, Ricky, think.

"I've been out of town," is what I settle for. It's vague and sounds mysterious.

Mr. Nameless finally turns his attention away from torturing me, announcing to the whole class that we should open our books to page *blah, blah, blah*. Of course, I don't *have* my book. I have no clue whether it's in my locker or maybe in a black hole under the Sofa-Bed-From-Hell.

"Ms. Bloom, share with Mr. Horn," Mr. Nameless says, his eyes narrowing to slits when he sees my empty desk.

He waves his hand toward the guy next to me and, from the back of the room, someone sing-songs in falsetto, "*Olivia.*" The whole class snickers.

"It's *Oliver*," the Mr. Horn–guy says quietly.

Great. The teacher's paired me up with some other loser: two for the price of one for the creeps in this class. I glance at my new partner. His stringy brown hair is long and not in any kind of style, like he hasn't bothered to get it cut in forever. He tucks a strand behind his ear and that's when I notice his eyes are an awesome shade of blue, like pictures I've seen of the Mediterranean Sea. Okay—hair 0, eyes 10. He has a nice smile too—sort of sleepy, sexy, and confident—which he flashes at me as he scoots his desk close to mine and positions his book so that it's half on my desk, half on his. It's not even a real book—just a bound collection of articles and speeches and stuff, all in different fonts and styles, some with pictures, most without.

Just when I'm thinking this guy isn't the worst dude I could be forced to share a book with, he takes a little bottle of hand sanitizer out of his backpack, pumps some into his palm, and then offers me a squirt. More snickers come from behind us. I decline his offer with a small shake of my head.

I pretend to concentrate on Mr. Nameless, who's in the middle of some subject I know nothing about that, apparently, the class has been studying for days. The fruity fragrance of my book-buddy's hand sanitizer makes me wish I'd eaten one of the apples I spied on the counter this morning. As the teacher drones on, I decide to scrap the idea of checking the music room to maybe "run into" Julio. Now that I remember where my locker is, I need to get those stupid wrist braces and get the hell out of here.

After class, Oliver packs his books into a backpack, which I notice has a tattered little bear clipped to one of the zippers. The bear has a nametag that says NED and a date that's too faded to read. He jumps up *effortlessly* and grabs a hoodie that was hanging on the back of his chair. It's a Captain America thing, like seriously. It has stripes on the lower half and a big red star in the center above the stripes. There's even a hood, with an A on the forehead part and cutout eyeholes. I gawk at him, not really sure if it's the coolest jacket I've ever seen or the dorkiest. Maybe both.

"Nice to meet you," he says. "Um . . ."

"Ricky," I say back when I realize he's fishing for my name. "Short for Erica."

He stands there, smiling, waiting—waiting for me, like a "ladies first" thing. But there's no way I'm heaving my aching body up and dragging myself to the door in front of the whole class.

I need to stall until the classroom's mostly empty, but it's not like I have books to pack up or anything.

"You okay?" he asks me. He'd been totally nice and normal (despite the hand sanitizer thing) the whole time we were sharing his book, but now he has that sound in his voice. That sound that means, *What's wrong with you?*

"Got a sheet of paper?" Dumb, but at least it's something. "I need to write something down before I forget it."

Oliver tears out a sheet of loose-leaf paper for me, and I'm horror-struck because then I realize I don't have anything to write with either. But he whips a chewed-up number 2 out of his backpack and hands it to me.

"Keep the change," he jokes.

The guy's kind of nice but tragically weird.

As I watch him head out, I grip the pencil he gave me, smiling at the bite marks in the wood because Dr. Dad would be horrified—chewing pencils is a huge no-no as far as dentists are concerned—and pretend to write notes from the class (what I'm really writing is the lyrics to "Give Me Novacaine," my favorite song on *American Idiot*, possibly my favorite Green Day song period). The students linger behind, chatting and flirting, but I focus on Billie Joe's poetry, determined to wait them out.

"Can I help you, Ms. Bloom?" Mr. Nameless says, startling me because he's standing right above me, peering down at my paper.

I fold it up and look around. There's just the two of us left in the classroom now.

"No. Sorry," I say, under my breath, sending him back to his desk at the front of the room, a smug look on his face.

No putting it off anymore. I swing my legs to the side of the desk/chair thing and my heart races. My feet are on fire with the slightest pressure. They're awful . . . they're just . . . awful.

A couple girls chat in the doorway to the classroom. This must be their homeroom. They'll come inside any second, and others will too.

I have to go. I have to get up. *Now.*

I push myself up, one hand on the desk, one on the back of the chair—carefully, or the whole stupid thing will topple. The glass shards cut at my feet instantly, catching me off guard. I grit my teeth (Dr. Dad be damned), fix my eyes on the door, and take a few steps, trying to imagine myself gliding across the floor like everyone else.

Don't look at that stupid teacher. Don't dare look up at all.

I can hear more and more students entering the classroom, can sense more and more bodies around me, more and more eyes on me. And I literally *feel* the nameless teacher's beady eyes boring through me. I can't help myself—I look up, right at him—and I see it in his eyes. Pity. Disgust. Then he brushes me off with the tiniest shake of his head, like my pain is no excuse.

"Fucking asshole!" It flies out of my mouth. Not under my breath. Not whispered.

I scream it at him.

7

mission: (tragically not) accomplished

The hardwood chair in the school office is not doing my butt any favors. It's actually my hips that are causing the soreness, but it radiates out to the general buttock region.

According to the clock on the wall, with its menacing *tick, tick, ticking*, I've been sitting here for two hours. Since the work number they have for Dr. Dad is wrong, I'm hoping they'll give up at the end of the school day and send me home with a note. With any luck, I'll get there in time to erase any messages on the answering machine before he gets home, and then everything will go back to normal, no harm, no foul. I'll just tell Dr. Dad I couldn't find my wrist braces. . . .

Great. Now you think of that!

It's a perfect plan, except it means I have four more hours to wait. I'm wondering if they'll give me bread and water around lunchtime. You know, like a prisoner. Before I have much time to ponder on that, I see Dr. Dad come in the office. He is *not* smiling.

Panic sets in. *How'd they reach him? How much did they tell him? He's for sure going to kill me!*

He storms over to me but before he can unleash a string of words that would get him in trouble too, Principal Piranha steps out of her office.

"You must be Dr. Bloom," she says. "Thank you for coming in." She has a gaunt face, with hollow cheeks and too-tiny eyes.

"Was this really necessary? I had to cancel a patient," Dr. Dad snaps at her.

That's when it hits me—he's mad at *them*. Maybe this won't be such a disaster.

"Why don't we go in my office, where we can talk," she says. She motions us into her lair. We're barely seated before she launches her assault.

"Erica shows no respect for our school," Principal Piranha tells Dr. Dad. "It's not just her language. She shows up late and unprepared—when she shows up at all."

My heart stops on a dime.

"I don't think that's fair," Dr. Dad says. "I haven't been notified that she's been late to school and Erica's attendance has been exemplary."

Poor, dumb, clueless Dr. Dad.

Principal Piranha looks at him like he's from another planet. "Dr. Bloom. Erica has not been in school since . . ." I look at the floor, while she flips some pages in my file and then a few more and then a few more. "December twenty-first—*last year.*"

The word comes out of Dr. Dad's mouth distorted and drawn out, like he's underwater—or maybe I just hear it that way: "Wwh-hhhaaaaaatt?"

"We've sent letters."

Letters I destroyed.

"We've left phone messages."

Like the one I erased yesterday.

I wait for him to scream at me, maybe even to slap me. But he doesn't.

"I'm afraid I didn't receive any of your communications. Perhaps you should have called my office, like you did today," Dr. Dad suggests, making it her fault. It's one of his special talents.

Principal Piranha opens up my file to the contact page, where I'd added the PhD to his name and changed the two sixes in his office number to eights, and shows it to Dr. Dad. "The work number we had for you was incorrect. I managed to track down Erica's mother and get the right one," she tells him.

Crap to the crapteenth power. I am so dead.

Dr. Dad's face twists up in a mixture of fury and embarrassment. He offers a vague apology and says he'll handle the problem. He tells her that I'm still going through an adjustment period and that some acting out is to be expected and some other stuff I don't pay attention to. Dr. Dad will say anything to get himself the hell out of here and back to the next rotting mouth that's waiting for him to perform his magic.

Open wide. Spit, please.

Principal Piranha removes her glasses and rubs her eyes, like she's had it with both of us. "At this point, it's clear that Erica won't be able to pass ninth grade. I think perhaps she should withdraw from school, take some time to rest and get better, and then start fresh next year."

"*What?!*" It's my turn to be shocked. "You mean you won't even let me *try*?"

"Erica," she says, "report cards don't come out officially until next week, but you must have some idea of what your grades will be."

"I am *not* repeating ninth grade!" I insist. My life is humiliating enough already, thanks. "My grades from West Mount Airy High were really good. They count toward my final grade, don't they? Can't I make up the stuff I missed?"

Principal Piranha comes out from behind her desk and perches on the edge right in front of me, so close I nearly gag on her perfume. "It's true your grades from the beginning of the year were outstanding. And your records from before that indicate you've always been a stellar student." She places her hand on my knee and I struggle not to slap it off. "What happened to you?"

"Are you kidding or just colossally stupid?"

Dr. Dad grips my upper arm *hard*, which I take to mean that if I don't stop embarrassing him this minute, he might just break my arm in two.

In my defense, it was a colossally stupid question. She knows damn well *what happened to me*.

Principal Piranha sighs deeply and retreats to her position of power behind the desk. "I'm suspending Erica for three days. The next time, she'll be expelled."

"Don't you think suspending her is counterproductive?" Dr. Dad asks, clearly exasperated. "She's already missed so much school."

"Zero tolerance," Principal Piranha says, a melancholy look on her face, like she's just so sorry I turned out so rotten. "When a student uses language like that, especially directed at a teacher, she has to pay the price."

Dr. Dad grunts something under his breath and gets up, pulling me up with him.

Out in the main office, the secretary gives him paperwork to sign, so I stand there, waiting. I don't sit, because my feet are decent at the moment. If I sit, I risk that changing once I get back up.

"Psst," I hear coming from behind me.

It's Julio!

A butterfly infestation hits my stomach. He's got on a vintage Led Zeppelin T-shirt and Levis, which hug his long legs deliciously. His crazy corkscrew hair is especially dreamy today and longer than I remember it.

"Heard about you and Jenkins," he whispers, shifting forward just enough for me to see the drumsticks sticking out of his back pocket. "That was righteous."

It takes me a moment to realize he means my public speaking teacher. At least now I know the jerk's name.

"You get detention?" he asks, flashing me a grin, his full lips slightly parted.

I swallow, wanting to kiss those lips so badly. "Suspended. Three days."

He smiles. "Three days of vacay."

"I know. Like, when are they gonna realize how stupid it is?"

"Never. Hopefully."

"What are you in for?" I ask, wanting to keep the convo going as long as possible.

"Some crap about English class," he says.

OUR English class!

Principal Piranha pops her head out and tells Julio to come in. He gives me a little wave that sets the butterflies in my stomach into hyperdrive and then heads into Principal Piranha's office. Before I can even revel in the moment for, well, *a moment*, Dr. Dad barks at me that he's ready to go.

Outside, after Dad had swung by my locker to get the hideous wrist braces, we head for the Batch Pad. Walking, of course. It doesn't take long for my feet to ignite. He walks in angry long strides, and I thrust my legs forward clumsily, one after the other, trying to keep up. He usually walks slowly when he's with me. But not today. Today he's pissed.

The thrill of seeing Julio is quickly replaced by a feeling of doom. I am seriously screwed. Not only might I have to repeat ninth grade, Dr. Dad may never speak to me again, especially after Mom gets through with him.

The burning in my feet is joined by a new kind of pain, like someone's jabbing a sharp knife into my right ankle. No jabbing-knife pain on the left—yet. Another step on my right foot and it gives out a little. I stumble but manage not to fall down. Dr. Dad must have sensed it, because he races back to me. At first, he seems startled, concerned, but then he remembers how pissed he is. He whistles for a cab—a sharp, piercing sound.

Inside the cab, both of us scrunched up in the back seat (he's over six feet tall, so he's probably almost as miserable as I am), I rest my head against the window. It's a bumpy ride over one pothole after another. My head smacks against the glass, but I don't care. Tears spill, silently, down my cheeks.

And Dr. Dad says nothing.

He waits until we're back at the apartment to lose his shit. It's the standard stuff: "Things are going to change around here" and "I expect you to do better" and "Any further misbehavior will not be tolerated." Then he throws in, "Let me handle your mother on this one," like he's doing me a favor, but I know he's just saving his own ass.

He has no intention of talking to Mom about this, *obviously*. If he wasn't so pissed and I wasn't so chicken, I'd say, "Oh, let me talk to Mom. I'm the one who messed up. She should hear it from me." But fantasizing about blackmailing Dr. Dad and actually having the guts to do it are two very different things.

"Do you have anything to say for yourself?" Dr. Dad asks when he's done laying down the new law. "Any explanation?"

I consider telling him how hard it was for me to get to school and how the school refused to give me an elevator key to keep for the year and how those boys accosted me and how I'm in *so much more* pain than I've let on. But I don't tell him any of that because *fuck him.*

He doesn't ask again. He just accepts my silence and then heads out the door, back to the dirty mouths he can do something about.

8

dani to the rescue

Dr. Dad and I are chowing down on Chinese takeout when he announces we're going to see Dani play tonight. I'm surprised, since I've been on lockdown since getting suspended, but I don't question his logic. I haven't seen my sister in weeks, and I don't want to say anything that might make him change his mind.

We ride the subway, rumbling toward North Philly, and don't talk much because it's loud and we don't have much to say to each other anyway.

As the subway approaches our stop, Dr. Dad leans in close to me and asks, "How are your feet?"

"They're okay," I tell him. And they are, kind of. "Mom's not gonna be there, is she?" She chewed me out royally on the phone right after I got suspended. I'm hoping she has lots of time to cool down before I have to face her in person.

"Dani says she doesn't think your mom will make it tonight," he says.

I hope Dani's right—for my sake but also because whenever the Disaster-Formerly-Known-As-My-Parents occupy the same space, the dot-gov guys have to raise the security threat alert up a level.

When we get off the subway, Dr. Dad drapes his arm across my shoulders, steering me in the right direction, protecting me from the swarming crowd. For a moment, I like feeling his arm there. But it's too hard to walk like that. My hip keeps bumping into him. So I twist away from his arm and tell him he's messing with my balance.

"Stay close," he says, and I can't tell whether he's hurt or couldn't care less.

We get to McGonigle Hall and the ticket girl says, her voice all sticky-sweet, "Hi, Dr. Bloom. Nice to see you." He goes to Temple games all the time. He went to college at Temple, too, and now that Dani plays for the Owls, he can't get enough.

We find our seats and I'm glad to sit down, even though my body's surprisingly decent today. We were early enough to get a program, which I scan and see that Dani and Noland are both starting. No surprise there. They've been killing it. It's still fifteen minutes before the game starts, and I'm excited, happy even, but then—

"Peter."

So much for Mom not being here tonight. I stare at the concrete floor, already sticky with spilled soda, and brace myself. Mom's like a totally different person when she's around Dad now—a total nightmare.

"I thought for sure Erica would be grounded during her suspension." Mom nearly spits this. I don't have to look at her to know she's *hair-on-fire ballistic.*

"I felt she earned a night out, Joyce." Dr. Dad puts his arm around my shoulder. "Ricky and I will be meeting with the principal next week and we'll come up with solutions to make things easier on her. Rather than just yelling and pointing fingers, I thought I'd try some problem-solving."

Oh, God. Did he have to say that last part?

The screaming starts. It's not like regular screaming. It's *whisper-screaming*, Mom and Dr. Dad's specialty. They think they're being quiet enough that no one around them notices, but eventually the hostility radiating off of them is too suffocating to ignore.

At first, people in the stands are talking and yelling because they're happy or trying to find their friends, and they don't realize that two grown-ups, who supposedly used to love each other, are hissing like angry possums battling over a trash can. But then people around us sort of stop talking and start staring. And I hope that Dani's busy in the locker room, that she doesn't come out early to look for us. I try to fold into myself, but I can't fold far enough or deep enough to get myself away from them.

Now everyone's staring, and I can't bear it one more moment.

"Mom," I say, trying to get her to stop for a minute. "Dad!" I say it louder, but it's still no use. They don't hear me or don't want to hear. So I scream, "YOU GUYS, WHAT THE FUCK?!"

That does it. They stop fighting and glare at me instead.

Anyone who wasn't staring before is definitely staring now.

I wriggle out of my seat and take off down the concrete steps, as quickly as I can with my feet not used to being feet yet, dodging people going up, looking for their seats. I assume one half of the Disaster-Formerly-Known-As-My-Parents will likely follow me, but neither half does. They just start *whisper-screaming* at each other again.

In a restroom, I splash water on my face. A girl comes in wearing a Temple sweatshirt, her hair in pretty cornrows. I remember seeing her in the row in front of Dr. Dad's seats. I stare down into the stained white sink.

She hits a stall without saying a word to me, but when she comes out, she says, sympathetically, "That was fucked up." I nod, because there's no use denying it.

She leaves and I'm alone again. I consider spending the whole game in here or maybe taking the subway back home (to Dr. Dad's anyway). But I really want to see Dani. So I'm back to spending the next three hours in the restroom, but then Dani walks in. She's wearing her Temple Basketball uniform, which looks great on her because she's tall and thin, like Dr. Dad, instead of getting Mom's curves, like I did.

"Hey, Roo," she says. "Pop said I might find you in here."

"What are you doing here?" I ask. "Shouldn't you be getting ready for the game?"

"I should. And you should be in the stands getting ready to cheer like crazy for the Owls—*hoot, hoot!*"

I laugh and realize she's right. I can't let cheering for Dani be one more thing ruined by the Disaster-Formerly-Known-As-My-Parents.

"Come on," Dani says. "I got Mom back to her seat on the opposite side of the court, so the coast is clear."

"I fucking hate them," I say, a lump instantaneously forming in my throat.

"No you don't." She wraps her strong arms around me and I don't care that her game will be starting any minute. I don't want her to let me go.

Ever.

After the game, Dr. Dad and I hover by the locker room door, waiting for Dani. Wherever Mom is, thankfully she's not here.

Public places ought to have separate waiting areas for divorced people who hate each other.

I shift from foot to foot, because my feet are starting up.

"Want me to find you somewhere to sit?" Dr. Dad asks me.

"No," I tell him, annoyed. *I just want Dani to hurry the hell up.*

The locker room door swings open and out come Dani and Noland. They're both in street clothes. Dani's long, auburn hair is wet and hanging loose around her face. Noland's rocking her usual all-natural afro. (She believes hair relaxer is a crime against nature.)

Dr. Dad hugs Dani with that *bursting-with-pride* look on his face.

"Ricky, where you been hiding?" Noland asks, giving me a huge hug.

"Not sure where your mother got to," Dr. Dad says. He looks around, warily.

"Relax, Pop," Dani says. "She texted me and said she was taking off. You're in the clear."

Dani leads the way out of McGonigle Hall. It's decided that victory sundaes are in order, so we walk the block and a half to an ice cream place. I struggle to keep up even though everyone's walking super slowly and pretending we're just taking a stroll and there's nothing at all weird going on. The burning in my ankles flames hotter with every step, but finally, we get there.

The place is packed with Temple students. Dani and Noland are greeted with loud *hoot, hoots* and congratulatory shouts about kicking ass and taking names. Dr. Dad finds an empty table in the corner and I plop down in a chair clumsily, not caring if I looked stupid. I need to get off my feet and nobody's looking at me anyway.

I watch my sister work the crowd, high-fiving and fist-bumping nonstop. She's as comfortable in her skin as the Center City Barbies are, minus the stuck-up vibe, obviously. Again I wonder what that must be like, but I can't even imagine.

"Dani, come sit with us," a skinny guy with sandy-brown hair says.

I'm nearly crushed with disappointment at the thought of Dani abandoning us. But she quickly says, "Raincheck, Spencer. I haven't seen my kid sis in forever."

The moment Dani and Noland sit down, Dani's phone makes the Snapchat *clink*.

Dani checks her phone, but Noland says, "D, honey, put the phone away."

"Good idea, Noland," Dr. Dad says.

"I do my best to keep her in line, Papa Bloom," Noland says with a wink.

"Okay, Roo. I'm all yours," Dani says, making me feel all gooey/warm inside, and it's not the burning in my feet either. "You wanna tell me what the hell you were thinking cutting all that school?"

Argh. So much for that gooey/warm feeling.

9

back in enemy territory

I was supposed to be free of this crappy school for three full days, but I'm here for the meeting with Principal Piranha that Dr. Dad mentioned to Mom. (No clue whether he actually had this scheduled before telling Mom about it.) She tried to get in on the meeting but Dr. Dad talked her out of it. I'm glad since there'll be less yelling this way. Dad says we're here to *formulate a game plan*. Whatever. I'm supposed to be on vacay.

Dr. Dad's in his scrubs. It's his lunch hour now, which he's *sacrificed* for me (his word, not mine) and which he hopes I appreciate (his hope, not mine). He insisted I wear the ugly wrist braces, so I have on long sleeves and my hands are shoved in my pockets.

The grown-ups are talking about me like I'm not here again, just like at my doctor's appointments. Business as usual.

Principal Piranha goes on about how any further foul language or unexcused absences will absolutely not be tolerated. (She seems to love the word "absolutely.") Then she says I'll have to speak with my teachers about getting a list of assignments I missed—that will be a long list—and maybe some stuff to do for extra credit since everything will be so late.

"I see" and "Yes, of course," Dr. Dad keeps interjecting. They're both being so fake-polite, it's comical.

Then it's Dr. Dad's turn to state his case. "I took a look at Erica's schedule," he says, "and her classes are pretty spread out. Room 220 for first period, then homeroom in 101 and second period in 312. That's a lot of stairs."

"Dr. Bloom, while I'm sympathetic to Erica's needs," Principal Piranha says, sounding anything but sympathetic, "we're really not able to move her classes closer together. We've made an elevator key available to her, if she wants it."

I let out a giant *huff* before I can stop myself.

"Jump right in anytime, Ricky," Dr. Dad says to me.

The two of them stare at me. Waiting.

"It's just . . . the elevator's by the front entrance. That's all the way down the hall from here. So, when I get to school, I have to walk all the way to the office to get the key and then all the way back to the elevator and then do the whole thing over at the end of the day to return the stupid key." *Stupid* wasn't the first word I thought of, but I'm trying to be reasonable.

"Well, that's simple," Dr. Dad says. "The school will provide you with your own key to keep for the rest of the year."

"No they won't!" I say, loud and quick. Dr. Dad thinks everything's so damn simple when it's not. "I asked and they said no."

He gives the principal a look like he's got every lawyer in the state of Pennsylvania in his contacts and says, "Well, *I'm* asking now."

Principal Piranha shifts in her chair, a sour look on her face. "I'll have to contact the elevator company for an extra copy, but I imagine that can be arranged."

Two points for Dr. Dad!

"What else can we do to make things a little easier on you?" Dr. Dad asks.

Put Julio in all my classes.

Suddenly, he's Super-Sensitive-Wonder-Parent to the rescue. It's all just to show up Principal Piranha, but there may be something in this for me.

"Even when I take the elevator, I'm still late for class sometimes. I mean, I can't really walk that fast." Visions of a permanent, unrestricted Hall Pass dance in my head.

"Okay," Dr. Dad says. "A little extra time in-between classes, a little leeway there. What else, Ricky? I'm new at figuring this stuff out, so you have to help me. What else can the school do to accommodate you?"

He shoots a smile Principal Piranha's way. She looks about ready to kill him. I can't help but grin. This is *fun*!

Dr. Dad takes out his cell and opens an app. "I'm going to jot down the list of accommodations we come up with and email them to all parties," he says. "For reference."

Oh yeah. Major fun. With a cherry on top.

10

today is the crappy first day of
the crappy rest of my crappy life

It's my first day back, and one of Dr. Dad's "accommodations" is
that I get to sit in the nurse's office until the first period bell rings
instead of standing around outside before my stupid body's even
half-functional. Plus, Executive Car—aka X-Car—is now my official
mode of transpo. It's like a much fancier Uber, with nicer cars and
more rigorously vetted drivers. Dr. Dad insisted on the upgrade.
Anything to one-up Mom, but since he's paying, she agreed. He
keeps close tabs on my rides to make sure I'm going to school
but, luckily, he'll never know that I stash the wrist braces in my
backpack before I get there.

The door to the nurse's office is only cracked open. Before I can
knock, a guy appears and opens the door all the way. He's kind of
young looking, with dirty-blond hair and wearing hipster glasses,
khaki pants, and a polo shirt. No way he's a teacher.

"Can I help you?" he says.

"Is the nurse here?" I ask, wondering if I got the wrong room.

"You're looking at him," the guy says. He's got a smile on his face, like he gets that all the time.

"Oh, sorry."

He smiles again. "You can call me Nurse Jeff." He waves me into the room, picking up a clipboard from his desk at the same time. "You must be Erica."

I nod, taking in the long, rectangular room. Right by the door, there's his desk with a chair beside it. Next to that, along one wall, is what must be an exam table. It's padded and covered with burgundy pleather. Under the exam table, there's a big bin marked "lost and found." Against the other wall are two cots, like the kind nursery schools have for naptime but a little bigger. And then, down at the end of the room by the window, there's a small table with a chair on either end.

Sitting in one of the chairs is that kid Oliver. Even though I'd only met him once before, his long, stringy hair and Captain America jacket are unmistakable. It's definitely him. He's reading a book, seems lost in it actually.

I must be staring or looking like I've slipped into a coma or something, because Nurse Jeff says, "Do you know Oliver?"

Oliver looks up and smiles. "We have public speaking together," he says.

"Right," I say.

"Make yourself comfortable," Nurse Jeff tells me. "You can go over your homework or read. Even lie down if you're tired. Whatever you like."

I eye the cots. I would *love* to lie down, but it would feel weird to lie down here, in front of Oliver and Nurse Jeff.

I make my way to the table by the window and sit opposite Oliver. I give him a tiny smile, which I hope says *it's none of your business why I'm here* and *I don't care why you're here* and *I don't want to talk about it, so don't bother asking* and *while we're at it, how about we don't talk at all because this is all horribly awkward.*

I stare down at the tabletop in case he wasn't able to get all that. After a moment, I steal a peek at him and see that he's gone back to his book.

Worked like a charm.

Thanks to Dr. Dad, I am the proud owner of my very own elevator key, which I get to keep until the end of the school year. I plug the key in, turn it, and call the elevator. The doors rumble open and before they can rumble shut, a boy rushes in, nearly knocking me over. He's on crutches with his leg in a cast. His height and pug nose make him recognizable immediately. Dread washes over me.

"Ronnie Drake," he says, holding out his hand for me to shake.

I seriously *do not* want to shake hands with him but I figure leaving him hanging might spell worse trouble. I reach out my hand and he yanks it toward his body, specifically toward his *junk.*

I snap my hand away from him—which hurts. "What the fuck?!"

"I don't want your cooties anyway, retard," he says.

The elevator doors open on the second floor and he gets out, *guffawing.*

I'm so stunned, I nearly miss getting out of the elevator before the doors close again. I make my way slowly down the hall thinking, *will I have to ride the elevator with that troglodyte every day?* and *if he touches me again, I'll report him to the principal and maybe even the cops* and *seriously, could Glorious Grant Middle School possibly suck any harder?* Then I remember where I'm headed.

I walk into Jenkins's room, relieved that jerk Ronnie Drake isn't in this class. A quick glance at the back row and I'm certain now that the guy back there is Ronnie's buddy though. I slump into the same desk/chair I sat in before, right across from Oliver. Big surprise, he beat me up here. I still haven't found my public speaking book, so I'm hoping he won't mind sharing again.

I've barely caught my breath before Jenkins says, "Ms. Bloom, you've returned." He gives me a smug look.

Screw you, I think, but I keep it to myself. After class, I need to ask him for extra credit assignments. No need to make him hate me any more than he already does.

A few more people rush in as the second bell starts to wail, their butts hitting plastic before the bell's done ringing.

Class starts with Supermodel Barbie, who I vaguely remember is in my homeroom too, giving a report of some kind—something about how HMOs suck—but the blouse she's wearing today makes it impossible not to notice how big her boobs are. I wouldn't mind having a little more up top myself, but dang—hers are way more than anyone needs.

I wonder if her back hurts? I find myself thinking, and I'm struck by the irony that this ridiculously gorgeous girl and I might have something in common. Glancing around the classroom, I see that most of the boys are transfixed by her appearance, too. Not Oliver, though. He listens intently like he's legitimately interested.

About ten minutes into Supermodel Barbie's speech, someone from the office comes to the classroom door. Jenkins says "Continue. I'll just be a moment" to the girl before he steps outside.

As soon as Jenkins clears the doorway, a voice comes from the back of the room. "Hey. I got a question." I don't need to turn around to know who it is.

Supermodel Barbie stops in the middle of making a point about the high cost of health care deductibles. "Uh, yes?"

The creep says, "Did an HMO pay for your new nose? Because, seriously, great job. Much better than your old honker."

Laughter erupts. The girl freezes, looking half furious, half mortified.

Jenkins comes back in and gives the class the evil eye. "I didn't realize HMOs were such a funny subject."

"Hilarious," Guess Who chimes in.

"Ms. Adams, please continue."

She swallows and says, "I was done, actually," even though she clearly wasn't finished. She was rudely interrupted.

Jenkins seems surprised. "You're certain?" She nods and he says to the class, "Any questions?"

Laughter erupts again and the girl—*Ms. Adams*—returns to her seat in the row behind me, looking shaken up, like she might even cry. I stare down at my desk. Even if she is friends with that bitchy Redhead Barbie, I feel bad for her.

"Okay then," Jenkins says, "there's just enough time left for a pop quiz."

Seriously? He's not going to ask her what's wrong or try to figure out what was so hilarious about her speech? That pompous ass is probably more upset about his darling class not being taken seriously than he is about a girl nearly being reduced to tears by it.

Or maybe not. Instead of handing out a random worksheet with multiple-choice questions, he writes on the whiteboard: *Discuss strategies for staying on message when speaking before an unreceptive audience.*

"Minimum three paragraphs," he tells the class.

Supermodel Barbie starts scribbling furiously. *Good for her.* I tear off a piece of loose-leaf paper and do some scribbling of my own:
Screw those jerks! I thought your speech was good.

I wad up the paper and toss it on her desk when Jenkins isn't looking. She looks at me, her face suspicious, but I nod my head toward the note and try to look sincere.

Then I hear—"Eyes front, Ms. Bloom!"

I do my best to come up with something to write to answer his pop quiz question, but clearly saying *I'd tell them to go screw themselves* is not an option.

I have no idea whether Supermodel Barbie read my note or not.

When class ends, Jenkins says to read pages *blah, blah, blah* for tomorrow. The students are all packing up their books, and I realize—*crap*. I should have listened to the page numbers because I'm supposed to be doing homework now. People file out quickly. I turn in my seat and push myself up. My feet aren't too bad, which is a nice surprise. I make my way up to Jenkins's desk and get in line. Yes, there's a *line* to talk to this snotty-ass teacher.

Oliver passes by and says, "When do you have to do your speech?"

Panic. *Does everyone have to do a speech? Will I have to stand there in front of the class like that poor Barbie?*

"I'm not sure," I say. And then I add, "Hey . . . what pages were we supposed to read again?" thrilled that I thought of asking Oliver so I didn't have to ask Jenkins, who undoubtedly would have given me shit about not writing it down before.

I write down the pages this time and then it's my turn with Jenkins.

"Can I help you?" Jenkins says like helping me is the last thing he'd like to do.

This is gonna suck no matter what, so just get to it.

"I need to get the assignments I missed—"

"Well," he says, cutting me off, flipping open his grade book, shaking his head. "You've missed . . . nearly ten homework assignments, at first glance."

"Guess I'm going to be busy then."

"Then there's the midterm, some quizzes . . ." He flips his book shut. "Honestly, I'm not sure I see the point."

"I need to make it all up. And maybe do some extra credit, since it's all late." He gives me a blank stare, so I add, "So I can graduate."

He shakes his head dismissively. "I seriously doubt that's possible. Not without summer school. Not anymore."

My head feels like it's going to explode. Students from Jenkins's homeroom are shuffling in. It's getting late and I have to take the elevator to get to my homeroom class, which is on the first floor.

I take a deep breath and say, "Why don't you give me the assignments anyway? Maybe I'll surprise you."

A look comes over his face, something I can't quite read. But it's almost like maybe I've surprised him already. "I'll have a list of assignments typed up for you tomorrow. You do plan on attending?"

It's almost funny. "I'll be here."

the vampires' den is full of surprises today

After a grueling school day, I stand on the sidewalk outside Glorious Grant Middle School, waiting for my X-Car. I watch as other Grant students hop on buses or just start walking home. Is it weird for a fourteen-year-old to get picked up by a fancy car service at school? Definitely.

A shiny Audi comes to a stop right in front of me. The driver, an older guy with graying hair, gets out. "Erica Bloom?"

When I nod he comes around to my side and opens the back door for me. I glance around, hoping anyone who's left to witness this will just assume my family's super rich. Getting my knees to bend enough to get in the back seat is a struggle.

"Need some help?" the driver is nice enough to ask.

"I got it," I say, aware that we're blocking a lane of traffic.

As if on cue, the driver behind us leans on his horn. I drag my right leg in and slam the door shut, but not quickly enough for the asshole behind us, who honks *again*.

"Someone got a new horn for Christmas," the driver says as he slides into the driver's seat *effortlessly*.

We start moving. Then stop. The light's red. That's Center City Philly for you. Everything's *right around the corner*, but it can take you an hour to get there.

That's why most people just walk. Normal people, anyway.

"Children's Hospital, huh?" he says, giving me *the look*.

I want to say *mind your own business*, but he's been nice. So I just say, "Yep."

We make it a block before hitting another red light.

Eventually, I get to CHOP. No appointment with Dr. Blech-stein to suffer through today. Something seemed off in my blood work from the last appointment, so he wanted to get it retested. Mom started to freak out over it, but when I admitted I hadn't eaten lunch, Blech-stein said that was probably all it was. Still, here I am getting stabbed again just in case I'm dying from something completely new.

Mom apologized a million times for not being able to meet me here, but it's just a stupid blood test. As tempted as I was to milk her guilt to my advantage, I was feeling generous and let her off the hook. Or maybe it's that I still feel like a jerk for blowing her off before.

I take the elevator to the third floor and head for the Vampires' Den (aka the blood lab). The corridor's busy with kids squealing and pouting, clinging to their parents' hands, begging to stop at the food court on the way out. Why a hospital even has a food court I don't know. I mean, it's not a *mall*.

The door to the Vampires' Den springs open with the slightest tug, which I appreciate. I go in and do a head count, trying to estimate how long I'll have to wait.

That's when I spot him. Oliver.

"Ricky!" His face lights up—like isn't it just so *neat* to see someone you know in such a crappy-ass place. Naturally, he's rocking his Captain America hoodie. "We have to stop meeting like this," he says with an easy laugh. It's official: Oliver is a Class A Goof. (A nice one though.)

I want to bolt for the door (like I could even do that anymore) but instead I say, "Ha. Yeah."

He moves his backpack off the seat beside him, so I guess he wants me to sit next to him. I write my name on the sign-in sheet and sit down. He offers me a squirt of his hand sanitizer and I don't want to seem rude, so I accept.

I want to know what he's doing here, but if I ask, then I'd have to answer the question myself. It's the specifics I'm curious about (but don't want him to know), because we're probably here for the same reason the rest of the people in this waiting room are here—the teenaged girl with mousy brown hair and a portable oxygen tank, the young mom and her sleeping toddler. We're here to get blood tests. We're here because something's wrong with us.

What's wrong with Oliver?

"So. Getting a blood test, huh?" he asks.

"Yup."

"I usually get blood drawn at my doctor's office, but when they're backed up, they send me over here," he says super casually. "I don't mind. They're great at finding veins. I hate getting stuck more than once."

"Tell me about it!" I say without thinking. Oliver sounds like some kind of old pro. "You get a lot of blood tests, huh?" I ask, hoping I can get away with being nosy without having to pay for it by divulging my personal info.

"Yeah. I mean, not as much as I used to," he says, his face showing a hint of what a drag it is to be our age and overly familiar with getting blood tests. Then he adds, plainly, "I had cancer."

Fuck. Me. I have no idea how to respond. I can hardly breathe. I know I should say something . . . *anything* . . . but what the hell do you say when a guy you barely know drops a bomb like that?

"Sorry," he says. "I'm so used to saying it, I forget that it weirds people out." The boy had cancer and he's apologizing to *me*!

"Is it gone?" I ask.

"Yeah. I've been N.E.D. for over five years, which is really good."

"N.E.D.?" I ask.

"No evidence of disease." The little bear clipped to his backpack catches my eye at just that moment.

"Ned," I say, pointing at the tattered bear, putting two and two together.

Oliver smiles sheepishly at the little bear. "Yeah. My mom got this for me after my first clean PET scan." I give him a blank look, so he explains, "It stands for Positron Emission Tomography. It just means they scan for cancerous tissue. Since I got Ned here the first time I was declared officially cancer-free, I'm kind of superstitious about it now. So I keep him clipped to my backpack."

A nurse steps into the waiting room, smiles at Oliver, and says, "You're up."

Oliver pops to his feet, *effortlessly.* "See ya later," he says. Then he trots over to where the nurse is waiting, holding open the door to the back of the lab. "After you, Marnie," he says with a smile, following her in.

Christ. He's on a first name basis with the Vampires.

When I get back to the Batch Pad, it's sweltering. The heat must have been cranking all day. Putting on the AC in mid-February *just seems wrong*, so I change into some sweat shorts and a tank top and collapse onto the Sofa-Bed-From-Hell (sofa mode). That's when I see it—a white drape or sheet or something, covering some kind of large object in the very small corner of the very small room. *Seriously, how'd I miss that until now?* Must have been the heat.

There's a note taped to the drape/sheet that says, *Surprise for you. No peeking! I'll be home at 6:30.* I groan. That's over two hours away and I'm supposed to just ignore something big enough to be a small elephant in the room?

I wake up my computer, feeling more irritated than I should, since whatever the elephant turns out to be, it's for me. I have homework I could be doing but instead—and for some inexplicable reason—I google "childhood cancer." It's pretty stupid since I have no idea what kind of cancer Oliver had and it's one hundred percent none of my business (even though he sort of made it my business by blurting out *I had cancer* like it was No Big Deal). I get a page full of medical sites, cancer fundraising organizations, and treatment centers. I click on "videos" and scroll through page after page of kids' cancer stories, wondering if I'd find one about Oliver if I went far enough back. I go to the bottom of the page and click on the link for page 10, and then for 47, and then for 106.

That deep into my Google search, the offerings have changed from short, homemade cancer story videos to longer videos and old TV shows. I click on a show from the eighties—an Afterschool Special about a teenage girl whose mother is dying of cancer. I make it about five minutes in before I decide I'm not going to learn crap about Oliver from this schmaltzy show. I scan the similar videos that YouTube always lists. It seems like hundreds of these Afterschool Specials with the same overcoming-tragedy theme were made, beginning in the seventies. I see one about a high school track star who was "crippled in a near-fatal accident." The description literally uses the world *crippled*. I guess using words like that back in the seventies was normal. I click on the video like it's some horribly gross insect I don't want to look at but somehow can't resist, and I manage to watch the whole thing, even though it's schmaltzier than the mother-with-cancer one.

I really should get to some homework, so I close my computer, frustrated that I only managed to kill an hour. And then it's just me and the little elephant under the drape with its "no peeking" note mocking me.

I whip the cover off. It takes a moment to register what I'm looking at. It's a desk, total old-school. *Scroll top*, I think they call it, with a wooden cover that rolls down. The dark wood is nicked in places, but it's been refinished and shines even in the dim lighting of the Batch Pad. I slide the wooden cover up, surprised at how smoothly it rolls. I thought it'd be stiff and misaligned, but it's not. Inside are a bunch of cubbyholes for pens and paper clips and stuff and a nice, large surface for my laptop and books. I stand there staring at the desk—at *my desk*—dumbfounded. It's really . . . *really* . . . *cool*!

A pang of guilt hits me then. Dr. Dad wanted me to wait. He wanted to see this first-reaction dopey smile, wanted to be here when I saw the desk for the first time.

I close the top and snag the cover off the floor, trying to remember how it was hanging there before I'd taken it off. I'll have to act surprised when he does his big reveal, but I'm a pro at lying and faking my way through things.

I'll give him an Oscar-worthy performance. Dr. Dad's earned that.

at the very top of my "shit i don't want to do" list

That's why I'm doing it *first thing*. I don't even bother waiting in Nurse Jeff's office before first period. I head straight for public speaking, hoping Jenkins will be there early so I can talk to him before the rest of the class arrives. I actually did the homework he assigned yesterday—reading an opinion piece in the *Inquirer*—and it was, dare I say it, interesting. It's amazing the mundane stuff people get super passionate about.

I arrive at the door to Jenkins's classroom. He's there at his desk, reading something. Somehow I knew he would be. I clear my throat.

"Ms. Bloom," Jenkins says ominously. "I wasn't sure if I'd be seeing you today."

"I said I'd be here." I try to keep my tone even, not nasty.

"I decided that if you showed up, I'd allow you to attempt to pass my class."

Gee, thanks.

"Here's another book, since it appears you've lost the one given to you when class started." He hands me one of his makeshift "books," and then says, "Keep in mind, the goal here is a D. It's the best you can hope for. At least it'll allow you to graduate."

I bite my tongue *hard*. "Did you bring the list of makeup assignments?" I ask.

"That's not how this is going to work," he says. "You're going to meet with me after school for a half hour—Tuesdays, Thursdays, and Fridays—starting today. I've estimated that's approximately the amount of time it will take me to cover the material from the classes you've missed. There will be homework most days—extra homework—but not every day. Your opinion speech will make up a large percentage of your grade, so if you don't excel on that, the homework won't matter. I've scheduled your speech for the very last spot at the end of the year to give you as much time as possible to prepare."

My mouth must be hanging open—either that or I look like I may be about to lunge for his throat or something—because Jenkins pauses.

"I want you to think about my proposal. Make sure you're willing to commit to the requirements. Summer school may be the better option for you, but it's your choice." He opens his briefcase with a loud *snap* and starts rooting around in it. "If you decide to accept my proposal, Ms. Bloom, I expect to see you this afternoon at 3:15 sharp."

Is he fucking kidding me?

I want to storm out of this room but, let's face it, my days of storming out of anywhere are basically over. Plus, if I go all the way back down to Nurse Jeff's office, I'll just have to turn around and come all the way back up here. And I might have to ride the elevator with that buttwipe Ronnie Drake. So instead, I stand there like an idiot.

"You might as well have a seat, Ms. Bloom," Jenkins says irritably, like I'm invading his precious pre-class privacy. "Class starts in fourteen minutes anyway."

He literally did not round that shit up.

I nod and wait for him to go back to whatever he was reading when I so *rudely* interrupted. Then I unlock my knees (yes, after only standing still for like two minutes) and shuffle to my assigned seat.

Slumped there, I stew over having to meet with him after school. I'd gotten a simple list of extra credit and makeup assignments from every other teacher in school. Some were so sympathetic about "my condition" and "how hard it must be for me" that they hardly gave me any makeup work. I hate that pity bullshit, but I'm happy to accept the light workload that came with it.

I can still hear Jenkins's snooty voice in my head.

The goal here is a D. It's the best you can hope for.

As much as I loathe the idea of being Jenkins's new afterschool buddy, the opportunity to put him in his place would be priceless. I don't need all night to *consider his proposal.*

It's. Fucking. On.

After my last class, I decide I need something nice to cling to before I face Jenkins again. So I'm in the hall outside the music room, getting ready to walk by the open door where I might, by some complete coincidence, spot Julio. Even seeing Lex would be okay if I could ask him where the hell Julio's been. He wasn't in English the past two days. For all I know, he could have been signed to play drums for some new boy band and is currently prepping for their European tour. I don't have any classes with Lex, so I don't know if they've both been ditching or what.

I take in a deep breath to settle my nerves. (*Ugh, he's just a stupid boy!*) Then I stretch up on my tippy-toes to try to get the bones in my feet to align right or at the very least to let them know that limping will not be tolerated for the next fifty seconds. Then off I go on my completely coincidental stroll past the music room and—

"Yo, Ricky!"

It's Julio! And he knows my name!

"Oh, hey, Julio," I say just as nonchalantly as I intended. He's sitting behind a drum kit and looking beyond cool. Sitting beside him is Lex, who's strapping into an electric guitar and barely acknowledges my presence.

I waltz into the music room, ignoring the jabbing pain in my left ankle.

"Haven't seen you around," I say to Julio, keeping up my act. "Did you decide just to come for music and the hell with English?"

"Nah. They put me in second period English with the dumbshits."

"Oh," I say, trying not to look devastated.

"Hang out," he says to me, and I go from trying not to look devastated to trying not to *die right there*. But then I glance at the clock. Ten minutes until my first meeting with Jenkins, and there's no way I'm gonna be late for it. No. Way.

"I have to be somewhere," I tell Julio, trying to sound mysterious.

"Come on," he play-pleads. "Stay for one song."

How am I supposed to resist? "Okay, one song." I flop into a folding chair beside them, wishing I hadn't flopped quite so floppily, and plant my feet nice and straight. "Do you guys get to come in here whenever you want?"

"The music teacher, Mrs. Mirkin, would probably let Lex sleep here if he wanted to," Julio says with a snort. "She said he's got a standard invitation."

"Standing," Lex says as he plucks his guitar strings, doing some final tuning. "A *standing* invitation. Which means, yeah, I can be in here whenever."

"I know what 'standing invitation' means," I say to Lex.

"Mirkin's all swoony over his perfect pitch," Julio adds.

"Shut it," Lex barks, turning a little red. "So one song. Any requests?"

Before I can answer, the muffled sound of "Give Me Novacaine"—my ringtone—comes from the front pocket of my backpack. I check my phone and see that it's Mom calling, maybe checking to see why Dad moved my X-Car ride to 4:20. I hit ignore because I can tell her about my delightful meeting with Mr. Jenkins later.

"Was that 'Novacaine' from *American Idiot?*" Lex asks.

"'Give Me Novacaine,'" I say, correcting him. But then I add, "technically," because I don't want to seem like a snobby jerk.

"Such a classic album," Lex says, reverently.

"Dude," Julio says. "'Boulevard of Broken Dreams' is like the saddest song ever."

"Not in my book," I say. I hate to disagree with Julio but he's dead wrong on this one. "In 'Boulevard,' he's alone, but he's still moving forward. He still has dreams. But in 'Wake Me Up When September Ends', it's like he's in a horrible situation with no escape. No hope. That shit's devastating. And the point is—September's never going to end. It's definitely a much sadder song."

"This girl really knows her Green Day!" Julio says and I try not to blush.

Lex nods in agreement and starts playing the opening chords to 'Wake Me Up When September Ends.' Julio joins in on drums at just the right part. No sheet music necessary for these two, I guess. When the lyrics come in, Lex tries too hard to imitate Billie Joe but basically sounds pretty good.

But then he misses a cue and says, "Fuck. What's the next line?"

Without thinking, I sing the next line.

And then the three of us continue singing the rest of the song together.

By the time we finish, my heart's beating like I've run a marathon. All I did was sing a song I'd know in my sleep, but I sang with *them*.

Lex gives me a perplexed look and says, "You can sing."

I look down at my feet because there's no stopping the blush now.

But then he adds, "I mean, you're not a *great singer*, but you can carry a tune."

I roll my eyes. Spell officially broken. "It's not like I'm gonna go audition for *The Voice*," I shoot back at him. "I just sing for fun, like at karaoke and shit."

"Word," Julio says, whacking Lex with a drumstick. "She just sings for fun!" He winks at me and I laugh. Lex just shrugs.

I glance at the clock again, and—*crap and a half*—I really have to go now. I want to go anyway. These last few minutes have been too perfect, and I don't want to ruin them. I shoot up to my feet, hoping all the adrenaline pumping through me will help steady me, and it works. I'm up. Not *effortlessly* by any stretch, but I'm on my feet.

"That's it for me," I announce, feeling a bit cocky now. "I've got this thing . . . with Mr. Jenkins. Please don't make me explain. It's too horrible."

As I head for the door, Julio says, "You should come by again."

"Sure!" I say, forgetting to be nonchalant this time.

I hit the hallway, practically floating, but crash back down to Planet Misery once the horrible truth of where I'm headed hits me. There's no one around, so I let myself limp, which means I can move faster. I drag myself toward the stairwell. There's no time to go all the way to the elevator and back.

As I start up the flight of stairs, my knees straining with each step, that floating-on-a-cloud sensation I had mere moments ago becomes a distant memory. I use the handrail so my knees don't have to do all the work. I can still make it to Jenkins on time if I hurry.

Three minutes later I'm there, standing in the doorway of Jenkins's classroom. He's at his desk writing in a notebook and doesn't see me.

"Mr. Jenkins? I'm here," I say, pretty damn proud of myself. He looks up and then glances at his watch. He does it real quick and covert so maybe I won't see it. But I do. "I'm on time," I tell him.

"So you are," he says, his voice a little less snippy than usual. He's got one of the desk/chair things positioned beside his desk and he motions to it. "Have a seat," he says.

I take a step into the classroom. At least I start to. When I go to move my right leg, to bend my right knee and take a step, a normal little step anyone would take to walk into a room, I realize I'm in deep shit.

One lousy flight of stairs and my whole body suddenly feels like it's on fire. Even my arm hurts from grabbing the handrail. I should have left the music room earlier so I could have taken the elevator. Or just taken the stupid elevator and been late. I shift my weight onto my left side and try to get my right knee unlocked, which hurts like hell. And it takes everything in me to keep from screaming because . . . *he's fucking staring at me.*

If he says *anything*, I'll scream. I'll curse him out way worse than before. Forget graduating ninth grade. One snotty word out of him and I'm done with all of it.

I keep my eyes focused on the floor as I shift my weight to the right and make sure my left knee hasn't locked up. They're both bending okay now, enough to take a few steps forward and get to the stupid desk/chair thing.

I look up, expecting to find Jenkins's face twisted in impatience and disgust and pity, but it's not. He's not even looking at me.

I inch into the classroom. My legs are moving now but everything's still burning, so it's super slow going.

I keep my eye on Jenkins as I creep closer, waiting for him to look up again and sneer at me, but he's stone-cold focused on his desk for some reason. The only thing is—there isn't anything there. The notebook he was writing in before is closed. There's a newspaper off to the side, neatly folded. He's just staring at an empty spot of wood, like he's meditating or something.

And finally I realize what he's looking at . . . or what he's not looking at—*me*.

I reach the desk/chair and lower myself into it, slowly, controlled. And then Jenkins sort of snaps to, as if it hadn't taken me an hour to get into the room, as if absolutely nothing out of the ordinary had just happened.

I can't decide whether I hate him even more now or whether the fact that he kept his mouth shut and didn't stare at my mini-meltdown made me actually, almost, kind of like him the teeniest, tiniest bit.

"Let's get started," he says.

nosy-ass questions i don't want to answer

I'm back in Nurse Jeff's office and so is Oliver. I say hi as I lower my aching body into the seat across from him.

"How'd your blood test go the other day?" he asks.

I shoot a look at Nurse Jeff, not wanting him to know my business, but he's busy folding clothes from the lost and found bin. Besides, being the school nurse, he probably has access to my medical history and knows all about my business.

"Everything *come out* okay?" Oliver horse-laughs at his own dumb joke. "It helps if you drink water first. I mean, if they have trouble getting a vein. My veins are a total bitch. They're scarred up from getting poked so much and, you know, they roll."

No, I don't know . . . and I don't want to know.

"Can we not talk about it?" I say, just shy of exasperated.

"Oh, sure." He makes a face, like he has no idea why I wouldn't want to talk about getting blood tests. "You working on your speech for public speaking?"

"Ugh, don't remind me!" I say, remembering that Jenkins was at least nice enough to give me the final slot for my speech. "I don't go till the last week of school."

"Cool. Then you've got all the time in the world. Should be a piece of cake."

"Yeah, except for the 'standing up in front of the class and making a speech' part."

Oliver laughs. "It won't be that bad."

"If you say so." I shudder just thinking about it.

"I'm having trouble deciding on a topic," he says. "I keep working on one and then deciding I want to do something else. Recycling's sort of a no-brainer, but it's kind of boring. There's the politics of fundraising, which has a lot to it."

"Really?" I have zero idea what he's talking about.

"But I keep coming back to nutrition. I know people think eating right is a drag but junk food and soda and processed stuff is *toxic*."

I don't know which topic he should choose, but no one wants to hear about how they should give up junk food. He's already got people giving him shit in that class. Gushing on about fruits and vegetables is *not* going to help.

"What was the fundraising one?" I ask him.

"Oh—it's cool," he says. "With diseases and medical conditions, there's this thing called a dazzle factor. It's based on number of people affected, cost of treatment, and how much awareness and interest there is." He counts these points off on his fingers, one, two, three. "Diseases with low dazzle factors hardly get any money."

I scrunch up my face, trying to take that in. "That's kind of interesting . . . in a sad, horrifying way. I mean, even diseases struggle to be popular."

He nods. "Lucky for me, the dazzle factor for pediatric cancer is off the charts."

Then he gets a look on his face that sends instant panic through me. He's going to ask. I know it. He's going to ask me about my disease, about my *dazzle factor*.

But the bell rings—sweet, sweet music to my ears.

"Gotta make a stop before class. See you," I say, since I definitely don't want him following me and trying to continue this conversation.

Then I get my dazzle factor–free self the hell out of there.

14

i settle into a sucky routine

Here's how it goes:

I drag my aching butt out of bed—early, because Dr. Dad now
insists I leave with him in the morning, which I can't really blame
him for. Usually the X-Car he ordered for me is waiting at the curb
when we get downstairs. Even if it's not, the service works just like
Uber, through an app, so Dad can look up the ride to make sure I got
dropped off at school. He put the account in his name so he could
track my every move and made it so I can see where my car is on
my phone but can't change, order, or delete rides. Suddenly, he's
some kind of maniac/control freak parent. But again, All My Fault.

At school I wait in Nurse Jeff's office (usually with Oliver, but
not always) and then I have to endure public speaking—*ugh*—followed by homeroom. Next is algebra (math with letters, who thinks
up this crap?). Then I have English, which I like okay, though it
still sucks that they moved Julio to another class. Fourth period is
world history with Ms. Taylor, who does a decent job of making

things interesting, though the text book is huge and weighs about ten pounds.

At fifth period lunch I sit alone, usually with a textbook open in front of me so it looks like I'm choosing to sit by myself so I can study (somehow I doubt I'm fooling anyone). Julio, Lex, and Oliver all have fourth period lunch—which *sucks*. I think they have gym fifth period, which I'm exempt from—not because I'm a freak with a broken body but because I played (badly) on a neighborhood soccer team last summer. The only person I know (and vaguely at that) who has fifth period lunch is Supermodel Barbie, whose name is Kendall (which I learned in homeroom), but she always sits with her Barbie friends. I'm not going to hold my breath waiting for an invitation to their table.

First up after lunch is Spanish, which is *muy fácil* (that's *super easy* for non-Spanish speakers), and then geoscience, where I do my best to be invisible because that buttwipe Ronnie Drake is in that class. Then there's a brief slice of heaven while I hang out with Julio and Lex in the music room, followed by a half hour of HELL on the days I meet with Mr. Jenkins for our Afterschool Specials (as I've decided to call them). Actually, that's not exactly fair. He's not that bad, once you get past the snootiness and his highfalutin vocabulary (which includes words like *highfalutin*) and his odd little huffs and sighs. Sometimes we just read editorials in the *Inquirer* and *Daily News* and talk about them. I like those days. He makes me really think about my words. Like, if I say, "I don't agree with this lady," he'll say, "Why's that?" and I'd better have a good answer.

I take heavenly/hot baths as soon as I get home from school (usually still the highlight of my day), before my dad gets home and we have dinner, which I have to admit he's getting much better at providing.

I spend the rest of the night trying to study.

Sometimes I fall asleep at my desk, partly because I'm so tired and partly because I'm way out of practice with the whole schoolwork thing. When I can stay awake, I split my time between current homework and making up all the stuff I missed. The-Disaster-Formerly-Known-As-My-Parents enacted a bipartisan ruling of no TV and only homework-related internet at least until the first follow-up with Principal Piranha a few weeks from now. They want to make sure I'm on track to graduate before they let me have any fun again. Dr. Dad's always asking me about my homework, like he's interested in what I'm studying, but I'm pretty sure it's because Mom insisted he report back to her.

All the studying's actually not the end of the world. When I'm at my desk and able to stay awake, focusing on the work is a good distraction. It almost makes it seem like my body hurts less. I even feel a tiny bit like my old self sometimes—the one who got good grades and actually liked school most of the time. That fantasy turns back into the Nightmare-That-Is-My-Current-Life when I have to get up to pee and my body reminds me that the ten-foot walk into the bathroom is going to hurt like hell. But the fantasy's nice in the moment.

Once a week, Dr. Dad gives me a shot of medicine that gives me mouth sores, makes me nauseous, will likely make my hair thin out, and might just damage my liver. I take folic acid to help with the mouth sores and I have no idea if they'd be worse without it. Every week Dad asks if I'm ready to try giving myself the shot, and every week I tell him no. I'm still waiting for the medicine to start working, like Dr. Blech-stein keeps promising it will.

I wait and I wait.

That's my routine. It's been a little over two weeks of this Big Fun in Rickyville. I still have no idea if I'm going to pass ninth grade.

"quality time" with jenkins

"Have you given some thought to your opinion piece topic?" Jenkins asks me as soon as I sit down for today's Afterschool Special.

Just like the first time, he always makes a point of not watching me walk in, especially if I'm dragging, and then he snaps to attention once my butt hits the chair.

I've decided that's pretty okay of him.

"Nothing's coming to me," I mumble, which is half-true. The other half is that speaking in front of the whole class, on any topic, makes me so sick to my stomach I refuse to think about it at all.

"Time's a-wasting," he says. "You should already be working on a rough draft of your speech. It's worth twenty-five percent of your grade. As I said before, the work we're doing after school's not going to matter if you don't do well on the speech."

When he finishes his lecture, he looks at me, like he's waiting for me to respond, to say *something*.

What I want to say is: *No kidding. You've only pointed that out twenty times.*

Instead, I take a deep breath and tell him, "I'll come up with something."

He tells me to open up my book, and we go over the two speeches he told me to read at our last session. I was pretty awake when I read them last night, so I can answer most of his questions in detail. He keeps nodding his head and saying things like "good point" and "yes, exactly."

I didn't realize it at first, but this dude seems to really like his job, which is weird because we're all such jerks to him. What I've figured out is this: if I really pay attention so I can ask legitimate questions about the lesson, he drops the snooty attitude and acts like a human being.

When that happens, these Afterschool Specials aren't the worst way to spend time. They can even be the tiniest bit . . . *fun.*

As we discuss last night's reading, he mentions something in a sidebar to one of the speeches that I barely noticed. I'd closed my book, so I reach for it to open it back up and absolutely clobber my macadamia nut pinkie on the edge of Jenkins's desk.

"Ah, fuuu—" I catch myself and say "fudge" instead, giving him a sheepish look. "Sorry," I add, rubbing my pinkie to try to dissipate the pain.

"Are you okay?" Jenkins asks, definitely looking more concerned than angry about my almost-slip.

"Yeah, that just . . . really . . ."

"Hurt?" he suggests.

"Yeah." I look down. It feels weird talking about it so plainly with him. With anyone really, though I don't know why exactly.

"I'm curious," he says. "Why do you think your first instinct was to curse?"

"But I didn't though!" I say, suddenly panicked.

He nods reassuringly. "Yes. And I thank you for that."

"You're welcome," I say, relieved that I'm not on my way to Principal Piranha's office right now. I realize that I'm also glad I wasn't accidentally disrespectful to him.

"So, back to my question, Ms. Bloom, which wasn't rhetorical. Why not just yell 'ow!' or something to that effect?"

"I don't know. My parents curse. Everyone in my old neighborhood curses."

He sighs, like he's disappointed. Like maybe he thinks there's more to it and if I'd given it more thought, I might have come up with a better answer.

"They're just words," I say. "I get that I can't say them in school. But otherwise, what's the big deal?" I give him a wry smile. "That isn't a rhetorical question either, Mr. Jenkins."

"Well," he says, "besides the fact that commonly used curse words are rather boring and unimaginative, I believe that the language we choose is meaningful on many levels. There's the speaker's intent but also the listener's reaction, which don't always match. As your public speaking teacher, that sort of disconnect matters to me. Cursing generally comes across as aggressive, a verbal assault on those to whom you're speaking, not to mention bystanders within earshot."

Wow. All that? Seriously?

He softens a little and adds, "I know you didn't intend to be aggressive when you hurt your hand—"

"Maybe I did," I blurt out. "I mean, not aggressive to *you*. It's just . . . why does it have to hurt so much? Why does it have to hurt at all? Why do I have to deal with this . . . *stuff?* The whole stupid situation just makes me so . . ."

When I don't fill in the blank, he guesses, "Angry?"

"Yes," I say.

"Exasperated?"

"Yes!"

"Furious?" He elongates the word, his eyebrows dancing like a cartoon villain's.

"YES!" I practically shout. Then I laugh, like a weight has somehow been lifted off my aching shoulders.

"See the power that language can wield? How we can get at a deeper meaning if we're a bit more creative with our word choices?" Jenkins says.

I nod.

"Cool, isn't it?"

I laugh again and am about to say *yeah* but instead I say, "Indeed!"

i loooove my desk . . .
but i still don't love surprises

Dr. Dad has another surprise. That's what today's note says. I'm doing homework at my funky old desk, the last thing he surprised me with. I breeze through the Spanish stuff, and then try to tackle the algebra.

The longer I wait for Dr. Dad to get home, the more impatient I get and my impatience makes my mind drift to another surprise of his—the big, horrible one.

I'm thirteen. It's a crisp February day, and it snowed the night before. Dani and I are all bundled up, about to go sledding on the huge hill three blocks away. Everyone in the neighborhood will be there. Dad comes into the hall and "confesses" to us that he's realized that he's "no longer in love with Mom" and that "staying in the marriage would be inauthentic." We are too stunned to say anything, so he adds, "I'm moving out tonight."

Surprise.

By the time I've erased so many incorrect attempts at solving problem number three on my algebra worksheet that the paper begins to tear, I hear keys jangling in the door.

Dr. Dad strolls in, still in the scrubs he usually changes out of for the walk home from his office. I spot a tiny fleck of blood on the front of his scrub top, somebody's dirty mouth paying the price for dental well-being.

"Hi, Dad. Were you in a rush to leave the office?" I say, still wary about his latest surprise and wondering whether he's going to drag things out or just spring it on me.

"Ricky Raccoon," he says, his face all lit up, like he's got a real-live pony hidden up his sleeve. (For the record—I'm *still* not two years old.) He sits on the edge of the Sofa-Bed-From-Hell (sofa mode), super close to me, his long legs squeezed into the space between the sofa and my desk. He looks like he's about to burst.

Fine. I'll bite. "So, what's the surprise?" I ask.

"Well. . . ." he says, taking both of my hands in his, "We're moving."

A million thoughts hit me all at once as I try to process what he's just said. What does he mean *we're moving*? Like, to another city? And do I get any say in it? What if I don't want to move? What if I want to go back and live with Mom? (What if Mom doesn't want me back?)

"Moving where?" I choke out, choosing the question that makes the most sense out of the millions that just popped into my head.

"You'll see," he says.

Ugh. I officially want to kill him.

He's having none of my anger though, as he practically skips into the bedroom to change out of his scrubs. "Hope you're hungry," he calls in from behind the closed door. "We're going out for dinner to celebrate!"

"Dad, come on! Where are we moving to?" I call after him. He doesn't answer, of course.

My stomach grumbles and I decide going out to eat wouldn't necessarily suck. Despite Dr. Dad's recent improvement in providing nutritional sustenance, I'm just not feeling what's currently in the fridge. Visions of a big crunchy chef's salad from Cush's Deli dance in my head.

He reemerges wearing dorky dad jeans and a polo shirt and tells me to "get myself together." I make a pit stop in the bathroom and grab my coat.

As we hit the hallway and head for the elevator, he's all chit-chatty about the home-baked cookies some patient brought in for his office staff. At this point I'm pretty much dying to know where we're moving to but clearly he's not going to spill his beans until he's ready.

When we get to the elevator, he presses the up button.

"Uh, Dad . . . don't you want down?" But he just smiles his corny smile.

An elevator comes and he waltzes aboard. I follow him with a sigh. Inside, he presses the button marked 16 and slowly it dawns on me that he hasn't suddenly gone senile. I get it. We're moving to a different apartment in this building.

Dr. Dad steers me to the left when we get off on the 16th floor, to a door just a few feet from the elevator bank instead of half a mile, like the Batch Pad is. He takes a set of keys out of his pocket—*he's already got keys?*—and unlocks the door to apartment 1601. He opens it with a big flourish, presenting it to me.

Inside, it looks like the Batch Pad's larger, cleaner, altogether nicer cousin. The paint's fresh and the carpet's a pretty light gray instead of diarrhea brown. There's an area beside the galley kitchen that's big enough for a small table (translation: no more uncomfortable stools at the "breakfast bar") and a sliding glass door that leads to a balcony.

"Take a look at the view," he says, pointing out the sliding glass doors. We step onto the small balcony and look out at the twinkling lights of the city. "There's a window in your bedroom, too," he says, stepping back inside the apartment. "Come on."

It takes me a minute to register what he said:

Your bedroom.

As in, *my* bedroom.

As in, my days of less-than-zero privacy are over.

The window in the bedroom . . . in *my* bedroom . . . offers a great view of downtown Philly and the One Liberty building, with its lit-up triangular top floor seemingly floating in the night sky.

I glance around the room and I feel one little burst of excitement after another. A closet! A built-in bookshelf! Enough room for the pullout to stay pulled out and my way-cool desk! And . . . *oh-my-God-what's-that?* I head over to a door at the back of the bedroom, almost afraid to get my hopes up. Could it be . . . is it possible . . . ?

"A bathroom!" I shriek. It's a bit dingy, with off-white linoleum, but it might be the most beautiful bathroom I've ever seen. "Please tell me there's more than one bathroom," I say to Dr. Dad, suddenly imagining the nightmare of him going through my room every time he has to pee.

Dr. Dad laughs. "There's another full bath," he assures me. "Dani's gonna stop by this weekend and help us get settled."

"We're moving this weekend?" I say, shrieking again.

He nods, pleased with himself. "The furniture I ordered will be here on Saturday. I figured you could use a real bed with a good mattress."

I'm not sure how it happens, but an instant later, I have my arms wrapped around him, hugging him as tightly as I can, wanting to laugh and cry at the same time.

It dawns on me that this is probably the first time I've hugged my dad since he moved out, which just makes me hug harder, and suddenly there's so much I want to ask him—like: Wasn't there some way he and Mom could have worked it out and did he miss me before I came to live with him and does he still love me even though he hates Mom now? But I don't ask him any of that because if I did, then I'd definitely start crying and I may not be able to stop—ever.

So I just keep on hugging.

17

i looove my sister . . .
just not first thing in the morning

Dani shows up at the crack of dawn on Saturday. (Okay, 8 a.m.)

I pretend to be asleep while she bangs around in the kitchen and gets the coffee maker started. Soon I hear its *gurgle, gurgle, gurgle.*

Then, without warning, she launches herself onto the foot of the Sofa-Bed-From-Hell (bed mode), probably to create some sort of motivational bounce, but instead she lands like a sack of rocks. The pathetic excuse for a mattress barely moves.

"Rise and shine! Up and at 'em! Come on, come on, come on!" she says, apparently having appointed herself the coach of Team Moving Day.

I groan and bury my face under the covers, so Dani crawls up to the head of the bed and spoons me obtrusively.

"Just think, Roo," she says. "This is the last time you'll ever have to sleep on this monstrosity."

I groan again but it's more *okay, fine* than *leave me alone or I'm going to kill you*. The muffled sound of Dr. Dad's shower stops and something pops up in the toaster across the room in the kitchenette.

"I brought bagels," Dani whispers in my ear. She knows she's getting to me. "Sesame seed . . . and there's peanut butter!" She pulls the sheet away from my face.

"Morning people suck!" I say. "And it better be chunky peanut butter!"

Dani lets out an insulted huff. "Like I would bring you creamy."

Now that she's got my mouth watering for my Favorite Breakfast Ever, getting up doesn't seem like the worst thing in the world, except that first I somehow have to get my body to move. I try to lift up the sheet, but a stab in my right shoulder makes me wince. I glance up at Dani, who ironically at that moment happens to be stretching her shoulder muscles, lacing her fingers behind her back and arching her arms out behind her. The mere sight of it makes me groan again.

"Let me," Dani says. Then she whips away the sheet dramatically, making a whip-crack sound effect.

I giggle as Dani slowly spins my body sideways, so that my legs can bend at the knee over the side of the bed, and then raises my upper body into a sitting position—all accompanied by robotic sound effects.

"You are seriously goofy," I tell her.

"Thanks!" she says. Then she heads toward the kitchenette. "Stay there. One sesame bagel with chunky peanut butter coming up!"

Dr. Dad emerges from the bedroom, dressed in sweats and a Temple Owls T-shirt. Dani gives him a *hoot, hoot* as she serves up our bagels.

"I'm headed downstairs to borrow a hand truck from maintenance," she informs us. "You have till I get back to finish eating."

The girl runs a tight ship.

For a few minutes, there's nothing but bagel munching and sleepy yawns. Dad doesn't seem like he's in much better shape than I am, sleep-wise, but I'm guessing he's not dealing with a throbbing left ankle and a right pinkie that forgot how to bend.

He gulps down about a half a cup of coffee in one swallow and says, "Your duties today are mostly going to be directing traffic and cheering us on. Leave the heavy lifting to me and Dani."

"I can unpack stuff," I grumble. "I'm not completely useless."

He's about to protest, probably planning on saying something like he didn't mean it that way and of course I'm not completely useless, but his cell rings and he answers it instead. It's one of the places delivering furniture later calling, and Dr. Dad takes his time going over the specifics of his order, where it should be delivered, and when.

I go back to munching on my yummy bagel, wishing my pinkie would regain its bendability so I didn't have to worry about dropping the bagel on the carpet, peanut butter–side down.

But wishing that is *completely useless.*

The new apartment seems even more fabulous in the daylight and is so clean it literally *smells* fresh. With both the apartment door and the sliding glass door to the balcony open, there's a nice breeze blowing through the living room. That's where I'm sitting, on the one lonely chair Dani brought up from the Batch Pad, supervising as the lady from the cable company hooks us up.

My request for a TV and cable box in my bedroom was quickly denied by Dr. Dad, which seems totally unfair because he's getting a hookup in his bedroom.

Of course, the fact that I have a bedroom to start with is a huge improvement. I figure if I keep working on the cable-in-the-bedroom thing, I can probably get him to cave by the end of the school year, earlier if I work hard.

I hear Dani out in the hallway, saying to someone, "It's this door here," just before she appears pushing a hand truck piled high with boxes.

Right behind her are the dudes from the furniture place. Their first delivery? A couch! Like a real, honest-to-God couch, with no lumpy sofa-bed mattress squeezed into its innards.

I get up and drag my chair out of their way, ignoring my barking left ankle. They put the couch along the back wall of the living room and then head out.

"Go on. Try it," Dani says.

I plop on the couch and sigh as my butt sinks into a cloud of comfort. "Nice! But what's he doing with the Sofa-Bed-From-Hell?"

"Goodwill's picking it up," Dani says.

"Is he sure Goodwill even wants it?" I scoff.

Dani laughs and then crouches down on the side of the couch near where I'm sitting. "Check this out," she says, pulling on a lever. The couch's footstool pops up and the back of the seat reclines. *Major bliss!*

"You're all set," the cable lady says, handing Dani a remote, which she then hands to me. The TV's already on with the sound down, so I switch to one of the music channels and crank up the volume. Usher's voice fills the room with R&B jubilation.

"Let me know when it's time for lunch," I tell Dani from my totally chill position on my new Favorite Couch Ever.

"Yeah, right," she says, "Dad said you wanted to be in charge of the unpacking, which is a good thing, trust me. If you let Dad decide where things go, you'll never be able to find anything."

Crap. I asked for that one.

We break for a lunch of hoagies and soft pretzels somewhere around noon and then Dani orders me to start unpacking stuff in my room.

My room. I still love the sound of that.

Dr. Dad let me pick out a dresser from a furniture company's website. I went with a big wide one, made of a nice dark wood that matches my desk, with two half drawers on the top and then two full-length ones underneath. The best part is that it comes with a large mirror. No straining to see myself in Dr. Dad's gaudy monstrosity (which, thankfully, went to Goodwill too).

Dani made up my new/real bed as soon as the delivery guys set it up, and I briefly consider testing it out. Just to make sure the mattress is comfortable and all. But if I lie down, I may fall asleep for a decade or two.

I open up the largest of the boxes labeled "clothes." I suddenly feel like I'm eighty when I bend over to pull out the drawer at the very bottom, so I think that one might stay empty. Luckily I'm not some kind of fashionista with a gigantic wardrobe. I empty the four boxes of clothing. Between the upper drawers of the dresser and the closet, I have room for everything.

I'm unpacking my desk stuff when Dani comes in. "So, how's the bed?" she asks. "Did you try it out?"

"I was afraid to," I tell her. "Thought you'd yell at me if you came in here and caught me napping on the job."

"Come on. Let's try it," she says, simultaneously climbing onto the bed and kicking off her sneakers.

She doesn't have to ask me twice. I climb in beside her and we both lie on our backs, our heads sharing the same pillow. The bed seems to cradle my body in a strange mix of soft and firm.

"Well?" Dani asks.

"It's spongy-good," I purr.

"I put a foam egg crate under the fitted sheet. Our point guard, Larissa, had one when she broke her leg and spent a couple nights in the hospital. She said the orthopedic guys swear by them."

I curl up to Dani and rest my head on her shoulder. "You're the most badass big sis on the planet. You know that, right?"

"I know, Roo," she says.

18

I'm at Oliver's house, studying. He invited me to come over after school when we were in Nurse Jeff's office this morning. I said "maybe" because I wasn't sure how shitty I'd feel by the end of the day. But then, all day, he kept sending me strings of random emojis, each one more ridiculous than the last, pleading for me to help him study. I finally texted him back and said I'd come if he'd *just please stop!* I got only his address and a single smiley face after that, so it was a done deal.

We ended up riding together to his place in my rerouted X-Car (luckily Dr. Dad responded to my text and changed the ride for me). It seemed stupid for him to walk and get there after I did. So we piled into the back seat of the sleek silver Lexus waiting for me outside Glorious Grant. It was kind of fun having him with me, like we were celebrity kids being chauffeured around. He kept pointing out different shops and restaurants, telling me funny stories about them, and we laughed the whole way to his house. We'd never really hung out outside of school (except for that time at the Vampires' Den, which I refuse to count), and I was worried it might be awkward, but it wasn't weird at all.

He lives in a townhouse on Pine Street, not too far from Dr. Dad's building. It's nice—with a small kitchen when you first come in, a dining area beyond that, and a living room in the back. We've been camped at his dining room table for a few hours, with nearly every textbook we own spread out before us. We started with public speaking, taking turns reading a speech by Frederick Douglass to each other, which turned out to be super interesting. After that, I tried to help him with Spanish (talk about *no comprende*—he's hopeless) and then we slogged through two boring chapters in our world history book.

We circled back to public speaking about a half hour ago. Oliver's researching his speech topic on his laptop and I'm staring down at a blank sheet of paper in my notebook, trying—and failing—to come up with ideas for my speech. My mind remains completely empty. The metal clank of the mail slot opening breaks the silence. Oliver hops up *effortlessly* to retrieve the mail and it's only then that I realize how stiff my whole body feels. On the bright side, I also notice a delicious scent coming from the kitchen.

When Oliver comes back with a small stack of mail, I ask, "What do I smell?"

He grins. "My mom's the Crock-Pot queen. It'll probably taste even better than it smells." I watch as he flips through the mail, wondering if it'd be totally rude to invite myself to dinner. He sets aside a few pieces of mail, stuff addressed to him. In his short stack is a folded newsletter thing from CHOP (ugh) but a tiny logo on the front page catches my eye.

"Can I see this?" I ask, reaching for it. He nods his approval, so I snag the newsletter. There's a "save the date" announcement for some sort of annual summer party in June, featuring "karaoke hosted by Lovely Rita's"—an awesome karaoke restaurant near Penn's Landing.

"I love this place!" I tell Oliver, pointing out the Lovely Rita's logo. "My whole family used to go there."

A sad/mad/sad feeling instantly bubbles up and I just-as-quickly swallow it down.

He checks out the announcement. "Huh. Cool. They've never done karaoke before." Then he rubs his eyes and says, "I think we're about as smart as we're gonna get tonight. You want to stay for dinner?"

Score! "Thanks. I'm kind of dying to taste what's in that Crock-Pot," I say.

He promises me I won't be disappointed and then says we should clear off the table before his mom gets home. I start stuffing books into my backpack but *World History*, huge as it is, will only go halfway in no matter how hard I shove. I decide to take everything out and repack, but now stupid *World History* doesn't want to come out. Oliver reaches over to help, and yanks out the book, which ends up smacking into my elbow in *just* the wrong way.

The pain is blinding. Like he hit my funny bone. With a sledge-hammer.

"Crap . . . " he stammers. "I'm sorry!"

I cradle my arm against my side and rock back and forth as waves of agony ripple through my body. "It's okay," I say through gritted teeth.

"It doesn't look okay."

"Just give me a minute." The waves begin to subside. I can almost breathe again. Almost. My little rollercoaster ride of pain takes less than a minute, even though it seems like twenty. Finally, it ends.

What are the chances Oliver will just pretend that didn't happen?

One look at his face and I know the chances are no chance whatsoever.

He sighs, like he's exasperated, like he's waited all this time for me to bring it up, but I haven't and now he's just annoyed. "Ricky . . ."

I stare at the table, wanting to disappear. But I remain tragically visible.

"At first I thought it was just your feet or your knee or something. But it's everywhere. It's all over your body. And you seem to be in pain all the time." He puts my stupid history book in my backpack and zips it up *effortlessly*. "You can't blame me for wondering what's going on with you."

I'm in pain all the time. Everywhere. That's what's going on with me.

When I still don't respond, he says, "I have a theory . . ."

"I'm not a vampire," I say back, making a lame *Twilight* joke. He laughs, and I even laugh a little. "Believe me, you'd never guess."

"So just tell me then."

The last time I told my friends, they all abandoned me. I can't risk that again.

But I do risk it: "I have arthritis. And no, I'm not joking. It's called juvenile arthritis. Even babies can get it. And four months ago, I got it. So, now you know."

I wait for him to laugh anyway, like Crush Boy did, or to be grossed out or disappointed at how mundane the truth is.

But he doesn't do any of that. Instead he says, "That's actually what I thought it was. Polyarticular, right? Since it affects five or more joints?"

And I just want to kill him. I'm not even sure why.

I grab my backpack and get to my feet. They burn like hell, but I don't care. "What did you do with my coat?" I snap at him.

"What? I thought you were staying for dinner."

"Just tell me where my fucking coat is!"

He heads to a row of hooks by his front door and brings my coat back, looking confused and maybe a little irritated. "Why are you pissed off? What happened?"

"You think you know everything!" I say, struggling with my coat, which isn't exactly fun with the pain still radiating through my elbow. "You're all—*'That's what I thought it was.'* You don't know shit about my disease."

"Overreact why don't you?" He grabs one end of my coat and threads my sore arm through the sleeve. "I have a friend Mary who's got arthritis. It's no big deal—"

"*FUCK YOU. It's a big fucking deal to me!*" I scream, taking off for the front door.

"Ugh! I didn't mean it like that," he says, following close behind me. "Look, I know arthritis is much worse than people think. I just meant . . ."

I wait for his explanation, wondering how much more it's going to make me want to kill him.

He thinks for a moment before he speaks again. "I meant that you can talk to me about stuff like this because we're friends. Plus I get what it's like to be sick and in pain."

I lean against the wall, angry that what he just said makes sense, angry that I'm already feeling less angry at him when what I really want to be is angry at everything.

"I get it, Ricky," he says. "Really."

He hands me my backpack and I slide it onto my shoulder with the arm that isn't killing me. "You can't tell anyone at school. You may get it but they sure as shit won't."

"Of course."

"I mean it, Oliver. No one."

"I wouldn't."

We hover there for a moment, not quite knowing what to do.

"Come on. Stay for dinner," he says to break the awkward silence.

"Well, now I have my coat on," I say, and he laughs, which is fine because I'm back to joking again. He reaches out and gently takes my coat off, just like Dani might do, and hangs it on a hook beside his Captain America hoodie.

"Since we're confessing our weird shit," I say, "why Captain America?"

"Well, do you know the Captain's backstory?" he asks, leading the way back to the dining room.

I have to admit I don't.

"He was this skinny weakling who wanted to be strong but wasn't. Physically, anyway. But he really wanted to help people and never gave up trying. The government picked him for a special top-secret program because of those qualities and transformed him into a superhero. I like the fact that what was in his heart mattered more than his body's limitations. Plus, science gave him a new life, so there's that."

"Ah," I say, sitting back down at the dining room table.

"My oncologist—that's a cancer doctor—he knew I was into Captain America, so he gave me the jacket." He says this as he heads back to the kitchen and I try to fathom Dr. Blech-stein giving me anything.

Oliver comes back with a set of plates, utensils, and napkins and sits at the table with me. "I'm sorry for . . ."

"Being Mr. Know-It-All-Cancer-Boy?"

He laughs. "Yeah, that. But I'm glad we finally talked about this."

What comes out of my mouth surprises me. "I'm glad too."

19

oliver can be super annoying
when he puts his mind to it

Oliver was AWOL from Nurse Jeff's office this morning, so I didn't get to tell him I have a meeting with Piranha at noon—my progress report. The second I take my seat next to him in public speaking, he says, "Listen, I've been doing some research." If that isn't enough to make me panic, I don't know what is. "You know, about your JA."

He's already abbreviating, like using slang for my misery. "It's not *my* JA," I whisper-hiss, glancing around, hoping nobody's listening. "It's not *my* anything."

"Did you know that 300,000 kids in the United States have some kind of arthritis?" he says, thankfully keeping his voice down.

"Thanks for the public service announcement."

He ignores my sarcasm. "There's all different kinds. Some are seriously nasty."

"The kind I have is pretty nasty." I stare daggers at him. In a second, he's going to start talking about how lucky I am. I just know it.

"Have you ever been to a Phillies game?" he asks instead, out of absolutely nowhere.

I scrunch up my face in confusion. "Uh . . . Dani dragged me to one once. Why?"

"Their stadium holds about 50,000 people, with the ushers and vendors and other staff."

"So?"

"So, if you picture that stadium, with every single seat filled, times six, that's about how many other kids in the country have arthritis."

I stare at him, blink, and try to process that. Before I can respond, the bell rings and Mr. Jenkins clears his throat from the front of the classroom.

Oliver leans toward me, into the aisle between our seats, and whispers, "It's important that you know you're not alone."

Jenkins stashes his roll book in his desk drawer. "Mr. Horn. Is there something you'd care to share with the class?"

God, no.

"Sorry, Mr. Jenkins," Oliver says quickly.

"Very well. Who's come prepared to discuss yesterday's op-ed columns?"

My hand goes up without my really giving it much thought. I cringe a moment later when I realize I'm the only one.

"Ms. Bloom. Did any of the pieces strike a chord with you?" His voice still has that snooty sound but I can tell, underneath that, he's pleased. I've learned to read between his lines.

"Actually, the one about garbage collectors," I say.

"Corruption at city hall, alleged racial inequities at Penn State, a scathing condemnation of Amtrak's safety standards, and you're going to go with the garbage collectors?" he says, raising a skeptical eyebrow. "Why is that?"

I think for a minute. "Well, it was funny, which made it more interesting to read. And I liked what it was saying."

"Which was?"

"That everyone has value."

I'm sitting outside Principal Piranha's office on one of those super-hard chairs that make my hips ache if I sit in them too long, hoping she's going to tell me I'm well on my way to passing ninth grade. Dr. Dad's due any minute.

I've been working my ass off on Operation Catch-Up-So-I-Can-Get-The-Hell-Out-Of-This-Crap-Ass-School for over a month now. To be fair, though, Grant isn't quite the nightmare it was at first, since Dad got them to make accommodations for me (luckily I only had to time my elevator rides to avoid that buttwipe Ronnie Drake for about a week, because his leg healed—lucky him). So I guess I could call it Operation Catch-Up-So-I-Don't-Have-To-Repeat-Ninth-Grade-Because-That-Would-Be-A-Colossal-Drag.

Whatever I call it, I just hope it's working.

I see Mr. Jenkins come in the office, and he glances over at me.

"I'm not in trouble," I say to him.

Jenkins goes to the copier and puts a stack of papers into the feeder tray. "I'm aware of your scheduled meeting with Principal Perdanta this afternoon, Ms. Bloom."

"For a progress report," I say.

"Yes, I'm aware of that, too," he says, giving me that exasperated look of his. "As one of your instructors, I was asked to provide information for said progress report."

Said progress report. Seriously, who talks like that? Although, I guess it was kind of dumb for me not to realize he'd know about the meeting.

"I didn't want you to think I was in trouble," I tell him.

He gathers up his copies and his originals, turns toward me and, oh my God, is that a smile? Is Jenkins actually *smiling* at me? "I didn't, Ms. Bloom," he says, and then he walks out.

Until that moment, I wasn't sure he was capable of smiling. Smirking, sure, but an actual, genuine smile with warmth and all? I thought maybe he was born without those facial muscles.

Dr. Dad walks in a moment later. He barely has a chance to sit down next to me before Principal Piranha comes out of her inner office. She glances at her watch—as if she'd been waiting for him instead of finishing up a phone call like the secretary told me when I got here *on time*.

Her glance is not lost on Dr. Dad. "My last procedure ran a bit long," he tells her.

"That's okay, Dad," I quickly interject, "Principal . . . Perdanta . . ." (always a struggle to remember that) ". . . was running a little late, too. Isn't that right?"

She gets a constipated look on her face and says, "Yes. That's right."

Dr. Dad and I both smile at her innocently. She glare-smiles back.

"Why don't you both come in?" Principal Piranha says, waving us into her office.

We sit there, waiting, as she thumbs through some file folders on her desk. I glance at Dr. Dad, who looks as impatient as I feel.

Eventually, she finds the right folder, opens it, and says, "Let's see . . . Ms. Roman says Erica's completely caught up in Spanish and currently has an A average. She doesn't anticipate that changing."

If only everything were as easy as Spanish.

Principal Piranha scans another page in the folder and then another. "She's made progress in algebra 1 and geoscience, but she still has a makeup exam to take in both classes, so we'll know more when those grades come in."

Dr. Dad nods and then reaches over and takes my hand as Principal Piranha reports on my other classes. I start to fidget and I'm not sure why at first. But then I realize I just want her to get to public speaking already. I want to know what Mr. Jenkins said about me.

Finally, she says, "And for public speaking . . ." She picks up the report from Jenkins and skims it. There's enough light in her office to see that there are big blocks of type on the page. The others all looked like a few sentences. Why am I not surprised?

She keeps skimming and I can't stand waiting anymore, so I ask, "So, what did Mr. Jenkins say?" I realize I've moved to the edge of my seat and I'm biting my lip. "I've been doing everything he asked, so he probably said I'm doing okay." *And she's still skimming!* "He *did* say I'm doing okay, right?"

"Is that the teacher who makes you stay after school three days a week?" Dr. Dad asks me. "I really don't see why that's necessary."

"It's okay, Dad," I say, "he's . . ." Shockingly, the word "nice" almost comes out of my mouth. *Nice? Mr. Jenkins?* "He's fair," is what I say instead.

Dr. Dad folds his arms and says to Principal Piranha, "None of Ricky's other teachers required afterschool sessions."

"Mr. Jenkins holds his students to a very high standard," she says, not bothering to look up from Mr. Jenkins's seemingly endless assessment of me.

I nod in agreement. It's true. Jenkins does have high standards. "So . . . ?"

Principal Piranha puts the report back in the file folder. "He says your work has been satisfactory."

A full page of type and that's all I get? Satisfactory?

"May I have copies of those reports, please?" Dr. Dad asks her. "If you'd like," she says.

"I would like," he says, and then he adds, under his breath, "That's why I asked."

Somehow I manage to keep myself from laughing.

"I suppose that's it," she says, closing the file folder. "I'll have Mrs. Bernardi print out copies for you. You can wait outside. They'll just take a minute."

And we're dismissed, except . . .

"One last thing," Dr. Dad says.

Principal Piranha forces a smile onto her face, clearly annoyed.

"Ricky, how's the school doing in terms of the accommodations we arranged? Everything going okay?"

I think for a moment, trying to remember any promises the school hasn't kept, but there aren't any.

I say, "The accommodations have been satisfactory."

I step off the elevator at the end of the school day, and there's Oliver. He's been everywhere today. He even tracked me down in-between classes to ask how the progress report went. I can't shake him any more than I can shake the stabbing pain in my left knee. He matches my pace, walking more slowly than normal beside me as I head for the exit.

"Where are we going?" he asks.

"*I'm* headed to CHOP," I say. "I have to see the dreaded Dr. Blech-stein."

"I'll assume that's not really your doctor's name," Oliver says. When we reach the door, he offers me a shot of hand sanitizer "for the road." Since no one's around, I humor him. "Do you not like him or something?"

"I can't stand him."

Oliver gives me a sad little look. "I love my doctor."

Of course you do.

"If you hate him so much, why don't you see someone else?" Oliver asks, clueless as ever, like I have a say in anything having to do with my own life.

"What difference does it make?"

"It makes all the difference in the world!" he says, staring at me like I'd spontaneously grown an extra eyeball. "Your doctor's like a teammate or a coach. You have to work together, trust each other. . . ."

"Whatever," I mutter, as I shove open the heavy door using all my body weight. "Have you ever considered that maybe you don't know everything about everything?"

"I know about doctors," he says quietly.

I let the door close again. "I'm sorry," I whisper. "But my thing's different, you know? With cancer, they have things they can try, horrible stuff that makes you even sicker at first but maybe you get lucky and it goes away."

"Or you don't get lucky and you die," he counters.

"Right," I say. "My thing won't kill me. But it'll never go away either."

"Which makes being with the right doctor even more important, right?"

Crap-o-rama. Walked right into that one.

20

dr. blech-stein is extra blechy today

The wait for Dr. Blech-stein is endless. Mom met me at the entrance to CHOP, as usual, and it's been Nonstop Mom ever since. She's asked maybe a million questions about how school's going. I'd say her third degree is mostly to verify that I really am going to school this time (even though Dad dutifully reports in to her now, which he just *loves* doing), but she seems genuinely interested.

Finally, she changes the subject. "So, how did the move go? Do you like your dad's new place?"

"It's awesome," I answer honestly.

Mom's lips tighten into a forced smile. Not the answer she was hoping for, I guess. "That's great, honey," she says unconvincingly.

A nurse, one I don't recognize, calls my name and I'm saved from having to deal with Mom's disappointment that Dr. Dad actually did something right for a change. Not sure why I care that she's disappointed but for some reason I do.

The new nurse leads us down the corridor to an exam room. I always seem to get an exam room three miles away from the waiting room. I hear my mom ask where the other nurse is, the last one. "Working with another doctor" is the explanation New Nurse gives, making me think that even the nurses don't like Blech-stein.

After only a few minutes, I hear Dr. Blech-stein barking orders to someone out in the hall before he comes in. He nods *to my mom* and logs into the exam room computer to check his notes from the last visit.

"How is everything?" he asks *my mom*.

Mom opens her mouth, like she's about to respond, but then she seems to draw a blank. "Ricky?" she says, looking my way.

Fury burns at my insides. "Why didn't he ask me in the first place?" I grumble.

"How *are* you feeling, honey?" Mom asks me, giving me a look like maybe she realizes I have a point.

I swallow down my irritation and say, "My feet are still really bad. Everything else hurts, too, but I can deal with that. Isn't there some way to make my feet better?"

Dr. Blech-stein browses my file on the computer screen. "Your lab work shows improvement in inflammation levels," he says without looking at me. "Sometimes your body takes a while to catch up."

"And there's nothing else—?" Mom interjects.

But Dr. Blech-stein interrupts her with, "She's just going to have to be patient."

"Why bother asking how I am if there's nothing you can do to help?" I ask, somehow managing not to scream it at him.

"To document your condition." He waves at the computer to emphasize his point, like this whole stupid conversation makes perfect sense.

That's pretty much it for conversations. Dr. Blech-stein does his doctor thing, listening to my heart and lungs with his stethoscope, bending the different joints and feeling my skin to see if the joints are hot (they almost always are). Last but not least, he examines the macadamia nut pinkie.

"Does this hurt?" he asks, squeezing the knuckle.

"Only when I knock it against something," I tell him. It's mostly gross (but I don't tell him that).

Moments later, Mom and I are riding the elevator down, when she says quietly, "I know he doesn't have the best bedside manner."

"That's putting it mildly," I huff.

"He's the top pediatric rheumatologist in the city and he came highly recommended," Mom insists.

"By *who*?" I ask.

"One of your uncle Evan's colleagues."

Uncle Evan is what my Bubbie jokingly calls a doctor-doctor, unlike Dr. Dad, who's just a dentist-doctor. She always says it with a super-heavy East Coast Jewish accent that makes the joke even more hilarious—especially when she says it in front of Dr. Dad. She's his mother, so I guess she's allowed.

The elevator door opens at the lobby level, so I don't bother continuing the discussion. It's not like anything I have to say about it matters anyway. We go outside and I wait, while Mom heads off to get her car.

When she picks me up, she says, "Well, are you tired and hoping to go straight home again? Or would you like to stop somewhere?"

I'm about to tell her to take me straight home, to punish her again, but suddenly a feeling washes over me. It's sadness and loneliness with maybe some regret or guilt in there too. "I could eat," I say.

Mom's face bursts into a smile but she quickly reels it in, pretending it's no big deal that her selfish, bratty daughter has agreed to spend time with her. "All right then," she says. "Where to?"

"How about Lovely Rita's?" I ask, surprising myself.

Mom seems surprised too and basically abandons any effort to keep her excitement in check. "That's a little out of the way, but sure!" she says, a twinkle in her eye. "It's been forever since we've done karaoke!"

Lovely Rita's hasn't changed much since the last time I was here. It still has the cheery red chairs and tabletops, the hand-printed menu board, and an insane dessert case with decadent pastries and a giant penny jar full of individual Peanut Chews candies. Of course there's also the stage in the back right corner and the costuming area beside it. The idea is that you can dress up as a character while you sing if you want, so they have all kind of wacky capes, feather boas, weird wigs and hats, funky jewelry, and other props.

I ask Mom to order me some cheese fries—a Lovely Rita's specialty, made with layers of real sharp cheddar and baked in the oven, not microwaved—and then I go grab a table toward the back. There are only a few other people in the restaurant and no one's singing at the moment. I'm perusing the thick songbook when Mom arrives. It's a little limited since Lovely Rita's is a family place (minimal hip-hop beyond Will Smith), but they still have a decent selection. Mom grabs her own songbook and seems to be looking for something specific.

"Ah," she says, obviously finding her desired jam. "Shall I start us off?"

I nod my approval and watch as she heads for the karaoke area, wondering whether she'll go for a crazy costume like she always used to. She's been different since Dad split, though, tentative instead of confident and carefree, so I'm not sure. When I see her grab a wacky hat and some oversized sunglasses before punching her song number into the keypad, I suddenly have a thick lump clogging my throat.

Her song starts with a dramatic instrumental flourish, drawing the attention of a few diners, who clap. I join them because I can't help but encourage this retro version of my mom and honestly, I'm jazzed to be here. It takes me a minute to recognize the song—an old disco hit by Gloria Gaynor that Mom loves called "I Will Survive" that I've heard her play in the car. It's about a jilted woman professing her ability to survive without her deadbeat lover (three guesses where she gets the motivation for that). Mom sings it like she's performing at a sold-out arena and soon everyone in Lovely Rita's is paying attention. She slays it the whole way and arrives back at our table breathless and giggling.

"Oh my God, Mom . . . that was freaking awesome!" I really wanted to say *fucking awesome* because it *was* fucking awesome but, like I said, it's a family place.

"Why, thank you," she says, like she's acknowledging an adoring fan. "Your turn." When I hesitate, she adds, "Go on before our food gets here."

I struggle up to my feet, already a bit stiff from sitting. Everyone's sort of gone back to paying attention to their food and the people they came with, which suits me. Within a few painful steps, I can walk okay again. I picked out the only Green Day song Lovely Rita's has—"Good Riddance (Time Of Your Life)," which I love anyway. I glance at the wigs in the costume area to see if they have a green punky one so I'd look like Billie Joe. They don't, so I don't bother dressing up. I punch in my song number and stand before the mike, waiting.

But it hits me that, even though Lovely Rita's seems to have worked some kind of magic on Mom, transporting her back to a better time, *I still feel hopelessly damaged and different.* I'll never be the same person I was the last time I was here, when the whole family was here and I sang like a dozen songs and didn't care if I got every note right because messing up was part of the fun. Now everything feels too messed up, too wrong, too different.

"Ricky?" It's Mom. She's standing beside me, with her hand on my shoulder. I've missed several lines of the lyrics already. "Would you like me to sing with you?"

I nod and she goes over to the keypad to restart the song, returning to my side as Billie Joe's guitar notes ring out.

I watch the white dots on the screen count down to the song's opening line and, somehow, having Mom here with me keeps my head from spinning. We jump in at the appointed time and mostly just sing to each other. I gain confidence as I go and remember how great the song is and how happy singing makes me feel. When we finish the little crowd gives us a round of applause.

Mom hugs me tightly and then says, "Look. Our food came."

I inhale my cheese fries (which are just as amazing as I remember them) while Mom eats her salad and we chat about why I prefer Billie Joe with green hair over blond or his natural black and how she's starting to see daffodils peek out of the ground in her garden. And it's almost like Lovely Rita's is working some magic on me too. Almost.

When Mom's done with her salad, she asks, "Feel like a Peanut Chew?"

I grin. Anyone who sings the Beatles' song "Lovely Rita" gets a free Peanut Chew from the penny jar. We go back up and Mom finds some round John Lennon–type glasses to wear and even manages to convince me to wear a silly hat, which is vaguely reminiscent of something an old-timey meter maid might wear.

The opening chords of "Lovely Rita" elicit hoots and hollers from everyone in the place. At Lovely Rita's, it's *everyone's* favorite.

21

someone let the cat out of the bag and
i need to figure out who to kill

This will be just another normal, pain-in-the-ass, tiring, possibly
mildly enjoyable, but more likely dull-as-dirt school day. That's
what I was thinking on the ride to school, while I was waiting
in Nurse Jeff's office (no Oliver today), and when I got on the
elevator a moment ago. But then the elevator doors open on the
second floor and I find myself face-to-face with that buttwipe
Ronnie Drake and his best bud, Matt (who's in my homeroom too,
though I mostly know him as Mr. Booker from public speaking).
It's like they were waiting for me.

Ronnie pounces. "Are you gonna start going to the senior
center and shit?"

"What?" I ask, instantly on edge. Whatever Ronnie Drake is
getting at, it's not good. Matt stifles a snort, definitely in on the joke.

"My grandma goes every day," Ronnie continues. "She really
likes it. I bet you would too."

Matt doesn't even bother stifling his laughter this time.

I pretend like I still don't have the slightest clue what Ronnie's talking about, but a hole opens up in the pit of my stomach, so huge it could swallow a piano.

Somehow they know. They know about me.

Ronnie gives me a shit-eating grin. "The big van with the wheel-chair ramp comes and gets her every day, so, like, if you need a ride, I could get the number from my grandma."

The two of them burst out laughing, drawing attention from . . . *everybody.* I got on the elevator later than usual today, so now the hall-way's crowded with people—not only a throng of Barbies but practically every other member of the student body too.

Were they all waiting for me today?

I head for public speaking, my heart racing. Ronnie and Matt walk alongside me with exaggerated limps.

"Don't go so fast, Ricky," Matt says in some sort of shaky old-man voice—but LOUD. "My *arthur-itis* is acting up!"

"Mine, too," Ronnie shrieks back. "Shoulda brought my walker!"

I consider heading back to the elevator, taking it back down to the first floor, and getting as far away from this place as possible. But fuck if I'm going to miss public speaking or any of my other classes. *Fuck them.*

I keep walking, trying not to look at all the students around me. And it's not my imagination this time. Everyone *is* staring at me. They're in small groups, staring and whispering.

And laughing.

I can't breathe. I can't do this.

I go faster, even though it makes me limp worse. At least I'll get to Jenkins's classroom more quickly. And who cares anymore anyway, because now they know.

They all know.

I take one lurching, quick step after another . . . almost there.

"Damn!" I hear some guy say. "She is *messed up*." It sounds almost sympathetic, except then he and his buddy crack up.

I block them out but my head is still spinning. It seems inconceivable that Oliver would blab my secret, but he was the only one who knew. So who else could it have been? I'm suddenly so furious I worry the smoke coming out of my ears might set off the fire alarms.

I finally make it to Jenkins's classroom, contemplating whether I should go kill Oliver immediately or maybe wait until after class—except his desk is empty. When he's not in Nurse Jeff's office, that usually just means he's running late and came straight up here. Frustration and anger tear through me—and then relief, because killing him would have meant a mess of blood and guts all over the classroom floor (and yelling at him, which is what I would have done in reality, certainly would have involved *grounds-for-expulsion* language).

I slump into my desk/chair and rest my head in my hands, waiting for the late bell. I can hear the whispers but I'm not going to look. *Screw those assholes.*

The bell rings and Jenkins calls the class to order. I'm home free for the next forty-five minutes, because no one would dare say a word while Jenkins is holding court unless they want to be verbally eviscerated.

I listen as he talks about what we're going to be studying next during the Supreme Court unit. Then a piece of folded paper lands on my desk. It's glossy, like a page from a magazine. I pick it up and it takes a minute for the information to register in my brain.

It's an ad for adult diapers from some magazine called *Senior Living*.

The snickers start, and I can't breathe all over again.

"Something you care to share with the class, Ms. Bloom?" Jenkins snaps. He's standing right beside my desk, having used his ninja teacher skills to sneak up on me. He snatches the magazine ad from my hand.

"NO!" I shout, knowing what comes next. He'll read it aloud to the whole class. That's what he always does.

But he doesn't read it. Not aloud, anyway. I watch as he takes in the magazine ad, rage rippling across his face. Without a word, he crumples it up, spins on his heels, and heads back to the front of the classroom.

"Perhaps a pop quiz will help you all to improve your focus," Jenkins snaps. "Textbooks under your seats." He starts writing an essay question on the whiteboard using an extra-squeaky marker.

Everyone does the usual moan and groan and I wonder, *Is that it? Is that all he's going to do?* But what else *can* he do? Conduct a witch hunt to find out which one of these jerks tossed that magazine page on my desk? Give the class a lecture about tolerance and how everyone should be nice to me? Either would just make my life more miserable. To his credit, he probably gets that.

He steps aside, revealing the quiz topic:

Discuss the impact Brown v. Board of Education *had on the U.S. beyond desegregating public schools.*

"One full page, front and back, minimum," he says, setting off another round of protests. "Anyone failing to answer the question satisfactorily has obviously not been doing the assigned reading and will have to write an additional paper."

Jenkins and I spent our whole Afterschool Special talking about *Brown v. Board of Education* last week. I could write a thousand words on it and he knows it.

He looks right at me, still too angry to allow a smile to grace his lips. But it's there, in his eyes.

I eye-smile back—and start writing.

Fifth period, I wait in the cafeteria line, my eyes glued to the unappetizing food. If I can't be invisible, at least I can pretend everyone else is. The Macaroni/Meat Loaf Surprise on today's menu surprises no one. (And seriously, who puts macaroni in meat loaf?) They serve it every Monday, so they could easily call it *Macaroni-Meat-Loaf-Like-Last-Week*. I usually pass on this monstrosity, but my stomach's been upset all day, probably from last night's shot, and I need to put something solid in it. So I take some.

No big surprise that everyone's staring at me either. It's been going on all day. My body calmed down some midway through second period, so I'm currently almost walking like a normal person. But people are staring anyway.

Even with my slight limp, the greasy gravy on my Macaroni/Meat Loaf Surprise sloshes around as I carry my lunch tray to a table. Ronnie Drake's buddy Matt sticks his leg out to trip me, but I see it a mile away and walk around him.

"Careful," he says. "You don't want to break a hip!" The jerks around him laugh.

An hour later (okay, two minutes), I reach a table, just wanting to sit down and see if the food's in any way edible, but before I can put my tray down an arm blocks my way.

"This seat's saved," says Redhead Barbie, who seems to be the bitchiest of the group. She smiles at her cluster of Barbie friends, the beautiful Kendall among them.

I'd accidentally picked their table. There are plenty of empty seats at other tables but *screw them.* "Who's it saved for?" I ask.

"Uh, not you."

They all titter—except Kendall, who bites her bottom lip to keep from tittering, like that makes her a better person or something.

I shove off to the next closest table and sit, just happy to be off my feet, and contemplate the dreaded Macaroni/Meat Loaf Surprise on my tray. If only I weren't so hungry. But I am, so I take a tiny forkful. *Surprise*—it's actually good!

Back at home, that cheesy "I Will Survive" song Mom sang at Lovely Rita's keeps running through my head while I slog through my homework. I even looked it up on YouTube and found an ancient performance from some TV show in the late seventies. Gloria Gaynor's gold lamé jumpsuit and two-foot hairdo were a little over the top but she was amazing anyway. I *did* survive. I'm going to keep on surviving, pass ninth grade, and get the hell out of Grant for good.

That's the plan.

My English homework requires typing answers to study guide questions about a short story we read and my wrists start to throb. I actually put on the hideous wrist braces so I can keep going. I hate to admit it, but they do help. I try to focus on my homework but it's still hard to shove what happened at school today out of my brain.

I wish Dr. Dad would get home already. I'm kind of dying to talk to him. I don't plan to go into specific detail because he'd probably rant and rave and threaten Principal Piranha with a lawsuit. I just want to tell him I had an awful day and have him make some dorky dad jokes to cheer me up.

I finish all of my homework and Dr. Dad still isn't home. So I google "Afterschool Special episodes" and actually watch another one—*a teen struggles to come to terms with her parents' divorce* is the subject this time. It's awful but strangely comforting, too.

An hour later, still no Dad. But then he calls and I'm pretty sure that means he's not coming straight home from work.

"Hey, Dad," I say when I pick up, choking down my disappointment.

As expected, he says he won't be home for a while, maybe not even before I go to bed, and that I should "do whatever I want" for dinner (*I* want *to have dinner with* you).

"Yeah, okay," I grumble.

"You all right?" he asks. He gets two points for realizing I'm not all right but negative five points for his impatient I'm-asking-because-you're-obviously-not-OK-but-really-I-don't-have-time-to-listen-to-you-whine tone. He's at negative three, in case math isn't your best subject.

"I'm great," I tell him in my best you-know-damn-well-I'm-not voice.

"Okay then. See you later!" *Click.*

I assign him negative ten points for clearly not giving a crap.

I toss my phone across the room, tears streaming down my face.

I didn't cry all day. Not with everyone staring and laughing. And now I'm crying over Dr. Dad disappointing me when that's what he does and I should be used to it already! I try to shut off the waterworks and get back to my homework. But . . . I can't.

Instead I get on my bed, crawl under the covers, and cry my fucking eyes out.

the real culprit . . .
and it's not even someone i can punch

I peer into my homeroom, dread filling my entire being.

The whispering and snickering that's been going on all week starts as soon as I limp in. I never ended up telling Dr. Dad anything, because I'm still too angry that he wasn't there for me the first night, when I really needed him. The shock of my secret being out has worn off some too. I haven't cried over it since that first day.

I focus on the floor and nothing else as I head into the classroom. Today's problem joints are: left ankle, right elbow, both knees. The pain is both dull and sharp. (Not sure how that's even scientifically possible.) It takes me a full hour (okay, a full minute) to get to my assigned seat. Kendall, who sits across the row from me, averts her eyes as I slouch into my desk/chair.

"Freak," Matt Booker says, pretending to cough out the word.

Naturally, my ancient homeroom teacher, Mrs. Hunter, who's also my ancient geoscience teacher, doesn't seem to have heard him.

I've been waiting all week to confront Oliver—and once he confessed to the crime, my plan was rip his head off, scoop out his brain, and plant weeds in his skull (aka end our friendship officially). But he was a no-show at Nurse Jeff's office and public speaking again today, like he has been all week. Suddenly a wave of nausea hits me.

What if he's sick, like—really sick?

I whip out my phone and text him in a panic, feeling bad that I hadn't tried to reach him before and hoping to hear back before homeroom starts, hoping the late bell's somehow late today. Although the sooner it rings, the sooner Mrs. Hunter will take attendance, the sooner homeroom will be over, the sooner all my other classes and yet another sucky day—and the whole school year—will be over.

Then what? Won't it be the same whatever school I go to? My "friends" at West Mount Airy High knew me my whole life and they still wanted nothing to do with me once I got sick. I'll still be me. I'll still be sick. I'll always be sick.

The shrill sound of the bell pierces the air and I put my phone away (no response from Oliver yet). Mrs. Hunter fishes around in her blue-gray poof of hair to retrieve the reading glasses she'd stashed on top of her head and starts calling out names on her attendance list. I brace myself for when my name's called, even though I doubt my classmates will hassle me while Mrs. Hunter is paying full attention. Being at the beginning of the alphabet at least gets it over with quicker.

"Erica Bloom?" she calls out moments later.

"Here," I say loudly, the strength of my voice startling me. For the first time since I entered the classroom, I look up, look around. *That's right. I'm here. Deal with it.*

Mrs. Hunter ticks through the rest of the names and then makes a couple announcements I don't really listen to. She ends by suggesting we spend the rest of our homeroom time reviewing homework from last night. I take out my algebra worksheet and double-check my answers, grateful for the distraction.

Ten minutes later, we're set free. I let the rest of the class pour out ahead of me. When the coast is clear, I swing my legs to the side, brace myself, and hoist my ruined body up.

I stand for a minute, testing my feet. Not too bad. My left ankle's still burning some, but much less than when I first got to school. My knees and right elbow all still kind of suck. There's a stab in the arch of my right foot when I first take a step, but it's gone by step three.

I'm almost out of there when—

"Erica, dear," Mrs. Hunter says, delaying my escape. "How are you feeling?" She says it in an oh-so-concerned tone that makes me want to strangle her.

"Okay," I say, not wanting to let her suck me into a conversation and make me late for algebra.

"I think it's important that everyone give you as much support as possible," she continues. "That's what I told the class last Friday, when you were absent. I didn't want your classmates to worry."

My heart starts racing. "What did you tell them exactly?" I ask.

"I just let them know how painful arthritis can be," she says. "I have some myself. It's just awful."

I want to scream. I want to curse her out, to pound her frail little body with my stiff, burning fists, to *hurt* her. But she's probably somebody's grandmother, so all I say, through gritted teeth, is, "Great."

I ignore the memo from my body about how a girls' room pit stop wouldn't be a bad idea, because I only have a few minutes to get from algebra to English before the hallways are crammed with bodies. Mr. Senkowsky was nice enough to let me out early, giving me a head start. I'm blissfully alone on the third floor, moving as fast as my legs will take me, limping full out because there's no one around to see and gawk.

I'm almost home free when I spot them, down at the end of the hall.

Julio and Lex.

The LAST people I want to see.

I've managed to avoid them all week and I'm in *no way* ready to face them yet. Especially Julio. I duck into a doorway and flatten my body against it, staying out of sight. I can hear them talking but can't make out what they're saying. I hear them laugh and, in a fit of paranoia, I worry that they're laughing about me. They must know by now. *Everyone* knows.

A door creaks, and their voices fade away. I peek out into the hallway and find it empty. But when I step out of my hiding spot, the bell rings and I quickly take cover in the doorway again. It's only then that I realize the doorway leads to the girls' room. Guess I'll make that pit stop after all. My English teacher, Mr. Cohen, is pretty cool and respects the leeway granting me extra time between classes that Dr. Dad arranged with Principal Piranha.

From inside my stall, I hear other girls come in. They hover at the sinks, probably reapplying makeup and brushing their hair and doing things girls do when their biggest worry is looking their best all day. I know I should walk out of this stinky bathroom stall with my head held high and get to class. But I just can't.

The girls talk and laugh, taking their time. I'll wait them out.

At the end of the day, I lower my aching body into the desk/chair Jenkins has put into position beside his desk. He's not here for our Afterschool Special yet, but I'm early since I sure as hell haven't been stopping by the music room this week. He'll be here before our appointed start time unless the world ends. Reliable with a capital R, that's Jenkins. It's kind of nice, actually.

The window closest to Jenkins's desk is cracked open, letting in a sharp/chilly breeze, which at least helps wake me up a little.

I glance over at Oliver's assigned seat. Empty—normal at this hour—but seeing it makes me worried all over again. I texted him again after homeroom and even tried calling. Still no response.

When I look forward again, Jenkins has entered the room in that quiet ninja teacher-mode of his. He peers over his glasses at me.

"Everything all right, Ms. Bloom?" he asks, and there's something about the way he asks that makes it okay.

"Just tired," I tell him, code for *we both know I've had a shitty week.* I glance at Oliver's empty desk/chair again and add, "I was wondering about Oliver."

"What about Mr. Horn?" Jenkins asks.

"He's been out for a while. I was wondering . . . if he's sick."

"His absences have been excused, but I'm not officially allowed to pass on a student's private information."

Tell that to Mrs. Hunter, I think, but what I say is, "It's just, when he was a kid, he was . . . really sick."

A look crosses Jenkins's face and I know he knows that Oliver had cancer. "I haven't heard anything to that effect, unofficially," he says. I know he means, *I haven't heard anything about Oliver's cancer being back.*

"He's probably fine," I say, and Jenkins gives a little nod, like, *yes, you're probably right. Let's hope so anyway.*

It's spooky how well we communicate with our nods and looks and code language.

"Have you tried calling him?" Jenkins asks, like now I've got him worried too.

"He isn't picking up his phone or responding to texts. I'll keep trying."

"Please do let me know how he is once you've reached him."

I nod. "Sure."

After that, Jenkins and I do our thing, and our time together is pretty useful and interesting, as it usually is now. I'm convinced I learn more in the thirty minutes I spend here at my Afterschool Specials than I do all week at "regular school."

When he announces we're done for the day, I pack up my stuff and carefully get to my feet. He doesn't bother looking away while I get my body up to speed anymore. At some point, I stopped minding if he happened to witness the process. "See you tomorrow," I tell him, slinging my backpack on my right shoulder despite my elbow's protests.

I check my cell after I get off the elevator . . . and there's a text from Oliver!

Sick. Ugh!

I'm worried to death and all I get is a two-word text?

I call his number as I head outside to look for my X-Car. It takes several rings, but he eventually picks up sounding half-asleep.

"Oliver," I whisper. "Are you okay?"

"Ricky. Hey. How are you?"

"Never mind me. How are you?" I say impatiently.

"Didn't you get my text?" he says. "I'm sick."

I grip my phone tightly. "*How* sick?"

It takes him a beat to catch on. "Oh, no!" he says, laughing at me but in a nice way. "It's just bronchitis. I get it a lot. It's not related to the cancer but my mom always freaks out. Pulls me out of school for weeks sometimes. Guess I can't really blame her."

Now I'm laughing, too. Laughing at myself for getting so worried. Laughing because *I'm so freakin' relieved.*

"Okay, so your turn," he says. "How are you? How's your week been?"

I think about the week I've had. About the teasing, the snickering, the staring. About Dr. Dad being AWOL when I really needed him.

"My week sucked with a cherry on top."

And now we're laughing together.

23

matzo ball soup is a proven
cure-all . . . really

The X-Car driver holds my bag with soup from Cush's Deli while I climb out of the back seat. "Thanks again," I tell him before he leaves. When he picked me up at school, I tried to reach Dr. Dad to get the route changed but never got a reply. I managed to convince him to change the route without authorization by playing the Sick Kid Card times two. (Seriously, when is Dad going to trust me with the log-in info so I can change routes myself?) The guy was really cool and even waited while I went in to buy the soup, so I texted Dr. Dad and said to up his tip big time.

I take the steps of Oliver's townhouse one-legged and ring the bell. He's expecting me but the soup's a surprise.

He answers pretty quickly for a sick person. He's wearing his Captain America hoodie, blue sweatpants, and a plain white T-shirt. He yawns, like maybe he caught a quick nap in the twenty minutes since our phone call and just woke up.

I hold up the soup. "Special delivery from Cush's Deli."

Oliver's eyes light up. "Matzo ball?"

I roll my eyes. "What else?"

He leads the way inside, stopping by the kitchen.

"You hungry?" he asks. "Should I grab a bowl for you?"

"For Cush's matzo ball? Um . . . *always.*"

I give up on trying to be ladylike pretty quickly, and we end up having a contest to see who can slurp the loudest. The whole time I keep thinking about what a relief it is to be able to relax and be dorky if I feel like it, because Oliver's likely to out-dork me at some point anyway. It's so different from being around Julio and Lex, when I'm always on edge and desperate to avoid embarrassing myself.

When we're done eating, we head to the living room and Oliver unmutes the TV. As if to prove my Oliver-out-dorking-me point, the TV's tuned to a YouTube channel called Soap's Up.

"Soap operas?" I ask. "Seriously?"

"Not just soap operas," he says, "*classic* soap operas. Trust me. They're hysterical."

I watch as a lady who looks like a football player because of the huge shoulder pads in her dress and her giant helmet of hair tries to convince her lover to abandon his evil plan to freeze the planet, like *literally.*

"Oh, my God. Did people really watch this stuff?" I ask, laughing.

"They *lived* for it," Oliver says.

He fills me in on the different characters and what crazy things they've done, one thing more insane than the next. When a commercial comes on, he asks if I want a bottle of lemonade.

"Sure," I say, and he heads for the kitchen.

While I wait, I spy a framed photo on the coffee table and pick it up. It's Oliver, younger and with a buzz cut.

He actually looks super cute.

I'm still staring at it when Oliver comes back with our lemonade. He opens my bottle before handing it to me.

"Wouldn't have picked you for a buzz-cut type," I say.

"My hair was just growing back," he tells me.

"Oh." *Could I be a bigger idiot?* "Sorry."

He shakes his head like, *no worries.*

I look at another photo of Oliver, a little older, with a woman. "That your mom?" I ask. Oliver nods yes. "What about your dad?"

"He's not in the picture."

"I can see that, doofus."

"I mean, he's not around," Oliver says.

Apparently yes, I could be a bigger idiot. "Sorry," I say again.

Oliver shrugs. "Not everyone's up for dealing with a four-year-old with cancer."

"God. You were four? What was that even like?" I ask because I can't begin to imagine.

Oliver thinks for a minute before he answers. "I don't remember that much. What I do remember is that I always got a milkshake after chemo, like a treat to make up for how awful it was. And there was this one time, I was trying to drink my milkshake, and I totally knew I was going to puke. But I drank it anyway. Then I puked all over."

"Gross! And like—that's horrible. All of it."

"It wasn't *that* bad—"

I laugh. "Come on. That completely sucks!"

He laughs too and says, "You're right. It was completely horrible. But you just deal with it. You do the next thing on the list of horrible things you have to do. And keep doing that, and hope you get cured. And I did, so . . ."

I'm not sure how to respond. I think about how annoying it is when people tell me I'm brave but right now, I want to say the same dumb thing to Oliver, to say how brave he must have been to get through that, how brave he still must be. "Do you worry about it coming back?"

"Sometimes," he says, "but I tell my mind to change the channel. Worrying is counterproductive. I try to stay in the present. But being proactive is important, too, so I try to take care of myself. Survivors of ALL—that's short for the kind of leukemia I had—can get overweight if they're not careful, so I eat right. I get enough rest, try to avoid exposure to germs, that kind of thing. There's a whole list of possible late effects."

"Wait. Late effects?" I ask.

"Kind of like side effects," he clarifies. "But they happen after treatment ends, so they call them late effects."

"Late, not side. Got it," I say, nodding. It dawns on me that Oliver has done a bunch of research on my thing, while I haven't done much beyond watching a bunch of cancer-related Afterschool Specials to learn more about his. "So what late effects do you have?"

"Not too many," he says. "I get these weird panic attacks every once in a while. Like, if a bunch of people crowd around me, I feel like I can't breathe. It's freaky. That's why I hang out in Nurse Jeff's office before first period. That and because I'm tired sometimes." He takes a gulp of his lemonade. "Chemo can cause other problems down the road, too. Serious stuff, like organs failing or whatever. If any of that happens, I guess I'll just deal with it one horrible thing at a time like I did before."

I sigh. "Do you ever feel like you're cursed? Like maybe you did something horrible in a past life? Or the universe just randomly picked you out and said, "Bam—cancer!" or "Oh, you feel sorry for yourself because your daddy left? Here's something to really feel sorry about—arthritis!"

I'm joking but he doesn't laugh.

"I guess I don't really think of it like that," he says. "I'd say it's more like I feel *lucky* because I was cured, but that would probably make you want to strangle me."

"Correct," I tell him. I realize I'm still holding the buzz-cut photo, so I put it back on the coffee table, stealing another glance. "For the record . . . the buzz cut's really cute on you. I mean, if it weren't for the whole lost-your-hair-because-you-had-cancer part."

Oliver blushes a little, which is kind of sweet.

"Wait," he says, like he *just-this-moment* remembered something. "You said your week sucked before."

"Yeah, like an hour ago," I say, teasing him. "But thanks for asking."

He shrugs. "Blame it on chemo brain."

"Is that really a thing?"

"Diminished short-term memory and difficulty with focused thinking," he recites, like he's reading a dictionary definition for comic effect. "It's totally a thing."

"Okay."

"So . . . why'd your week suck?"

I groan. *Do I really want to dredge it all back up? Can't we just go back to laughing at the stupid eighties soap operas?*

But I cough up the deets. "You know Mrs. Hunter? Do you have her for science?"

"Had her last year," he says.

"Well . . . she thought it was *super* important to tell everyone that I have arthritis and that they should be nice to me because it's *super* painful, which she knows firsthand because, being ancient, she has arthritis too!"

"Oh man!"

"At first I thought it was you who told everyone," I confess.

"I would never do that," he insists. "I mean, I'm totally out of the closet about my cancer, but that's my choice."

"I got shit all week. Whispering, staring. Hilarious jokes from that buttwipe Ronnie Drake—"

"Ugh! He is literally evil!" Oliver says. "The people at Grant are kind of tools. They weren't as bad when we were all at Oak Lane Elementary together. Ronnie was even kind of a friend back then."

"Seriously?"

Oliver shrugs. "Around seventh grade people split up into cliques and everyone kind of turned into the worst version of themselves. That's why most of my friends are from CHOP now. They have this great support group. You should—"

"Pass," I say quickly. I lay my head back on the couch and close my eyes.

He's quiet for a moment and then he says, "They'll get over it. They'll move on to tormenting someone else."

"But I'll never be just me anymore. I'll always be . . . *that girl.*" My eyes are still shut but that doesn't prevent a tear from slipping out. "That girl with arthritis."

He takes my hand, his skin soft against mine. I'm not even sure why but tears start streaming down my face. At least someone knows my awful truth and isn't freaked out or disgusted by it. I'm afraid he'll try to talk me out of feeling the way I feel or say that I shouldn't care that the whole school made fun of me for a solid week. But he doesn't.

He just holds my hand.

I'm drained by the time I get back home. I find a couple pieces of mail sitting on my desk. Dr. Dad must have come home at lunch and brought it up. There's an actual snail-mail card from Dani—another one of my sister's odd-yet-delightful quirks—

which I slice open with the *Dr. Peter Bloom, DDS,* promotional letter opener Dad gave me. The card inside will for sure feature a kangaroo. How she finds so many cards with kangaroos, I'll never know. Sometimes she just puts kangaroo stickers on random cards. Sometimes she crosses out whatever's printed in the card and writes in her own message—like I'll get a kids' get-well card with a kangaroo nurse that says "Hopping you're feeling better soon!" but Dani will cross out "feeling better soon" and write in "having a great day." They're cheesy but I love them.

Today's card is a bland "thinking of you" card with kangaroo stickers "hopping" along the edges of the mushy greeting. She's added a note saying she's sorry we haven't seen much of each other lately, and that she's swamped with schoolwork but she loves me and promises to come hang out soon. I stick the card in the frame of the mirror on my dresser, adding it to two other cards Dani sent recently. (Never mind that the other ones promise we'll get to hang out soon too.)

The other piece of mail is a large postcard—from CHOP. I'm about to toss it in the trash can but the Lovely Rita's logo catches my eye. The postcard has details about CHOP's annual summer party, which I remember from the newsletter I saw at Oliver's house. It'll feature pizza (*whatever*), a sundae bar (*well, that actually sounds kinda promising*), face painting (*back to ugh*), and karaoke, compliments of Lovely Rita's.

Fine. Maybe I'll go. It's not like my schedule's full of hot dates with Julio.

I take out my cell and open the calendar app, typing in **CHOP party?** on June 8th. The only entry in the app other than national holidays and family birthdays is an appointment to get my teeth cleaned at the end of April.

I really should start in on my homework but my eyelids are drooping. So I stretch out on the bed instead. Even lying down, as tired as I am, it's hard to stop my brain from spinning at full speed, racing through the events of the last week.

Stupid Ronnie Drake and Matt Booker. Mrs. Hunter and her big fat mouth. Ditching Julio and Lex like a coward (but knowing I'll have to face them at some point). Dr. Dad being AWOL, yet again.

And Oliver. Finding out he wasn't that sick but that his organs could fail at some point and that there's a thing called chemo brain. Slurping soup with Oliver, holding hands with Oliver.

I'm suddenly warm and tingling. *What if it had been Julio holding my hand?*

My mind stops spinning and starts drifting, starts filling in a blank. Starring Julio.

24

time to face the music (room)

I'm biding my time until the end of school because I've decided today is the day I end my Julio drought. When public speaking lets out, I stop by Mr. Jenkins's desk.

"Can I help you, Ms. Bloom?" he says.

No Afterschool Special today, so this is my chance to fill him in on Oliver. "I wanted to tell you I saw Oliver. He just had bronchitis. He's almost better now."

"That's good to know. Thank you for passing that on." Jenkins gives me a nod. "You two are good friends then?"

For some inconceivable reason, my face flushes hot pink. "Kind of."

"He's a nice young man," Jenkins says, an amused smile on his face.

Oh, great . . . he probably thinks Oliver's my boyfriend!

I split before things get any more awkward, knowing I can at least trust Jenkins to keep his mouth shut about his wrong ideas.

I sit through the rest of my classes, trying to focus on the teachers and block out everything else. Mr. Cohen asks me how I'm feeling after English class, but at least he does it quietly, when all the other students have already left the room. Ms. Taylor is less subtle when I get to world history. I limp in as the late bell's ringing, and she loudly instructs a dude sitting in the first row to switch seats with me (my regular seat's toward the back). All morning, there's been some of the same whispering and stares but it does seem like there's maybe less of it. Maybe Oliver's right and the target on my back is fading, getting ready to reappear on some other poor kid.

At lunch, the closest seat is on the far end of the Barbies' table. I take it and they don't protest. No one messes with me in Spanish, but of course that buttwipe Ronnie Drake starts in on me as soon as I get to geoscience. Every time Mrs. Hunter turns her back, he tosses folded magazine ads onto my desk (more senior citizen products, I assume). I crumple them up without reading them and do my best to pay attention to the lesson.

When class ends, I get up right away (despite my feet and left knee burning), scoop up the pile of crumpled paper, walk two rows back to where Ronnie sits, and dump the pile onto his desk.

"I think you lost these," I tell Ronnie triumphantly, and then I turn to leave. I hear kids snickering in my wake, but I think some of them are laughing at *him* this time.

When I step off the elevator on the first floor, I seriously consider abandoning the mission but I head for the music room anyway.

My head seems okay about where I'm going, but my heart is panicking. As I get closer, my head starts having its doubts, too. Somehow I keep moving forward.

You can't avoid them for the rest of the school year. And unless you want Oliver to be your only friend, you'd better just get it over with.

If you say so, head.

I'll know soon enough if they don't want anything to do with me anymore. The awkward, freeze-out silences my friends back home gave me once they found out I was sick were easy enough to pick up on.

I march (okay, Ricky-march) into the music room.

"Ricky, where you been?" Julio says, and my stupid heart starts to flutter because it means he *noticed*. Plus, there's definitely no freeze-out vibe.

"Around," I say.

Lex pulls out a chair and pats the seat. "Here, sit," he says. He's kind of nice about it, not weird or anything. I sit slowly, making sure I don't plop.

So far, so good.

"I can only stay five minutes," I say, glancing at the clock.

"Meeting with that moron Jenkins?" Lex snorts.

I flush with anger and want to say *you're the moron*. But instead I say, "No. I have to be outside for my ride. And Jenkins is actually pretty okay."

Lex ignores my Jenkins comment, which just irritates me more. But I refocus on my mission. The longer I avoid the topic of Me-And-My-Ruined-Body, the weirder it's going to be.

I take a deep breath and jump in: "So I guess you guys heard last week's breaking news about me."

Julio laughs. "Yeah, we heard something."

"The whole school's been having an awesome time giving me shit about it."

"Who's giving you shit?" Lex asks.

"Uh . . . *everybody*."

"Fuck those assholes," Lex says with a shrug. Julio nods his agreement.

And that's it.

They change the subject, start talking about some new song Lex is trying to write and how he can't quite figure out the bridge and how it's pissing him off.

I try to follow along, nodding when I'm supposed to nod. But inside I'm so surprised and thrilled and relieved I can barely sit still. It's like they couldn't care less—but in a good way, in the best possible way.

The five minutes pass and I tell them I have to go.

I test my feet and can tell immediately it's not going to be a graceful takeoff. For a second, I panic, but then it dawns on me—they know, everyone knows, so what difference does it make? I try to get my weight evenly distributed, with my right foot under my chair, knee bent as much as it'll bend, and my left leg out to the side for balance. Then I give my body the old heave-ho, swinging my arms for momentum.

Right away, I know I'm doomed. I don't have my balance. The arm-swing momentum wasn't timed right. My "heave" didn't "ho." My butt only rises a few inches before I plop back down to the chair. It's officially my worst nightmare.

But then I look up and realize they're both focused on Lex's song in his composition book and not even paying attention to me. I position myself to try again, course-correct from my previous attempt, and get to my feet.

I guess it's no big deal to them. It's obviously not suddenly going to be the main topic of conversation, like it is with Oliver. *Thank God.* But at the same time, I feel a tinge of disappointment, like maybe I want them to care a little. But do I?

"Catch you later, guys," I say.

And Julio says, "Don't be a stranger!"

And my stomach feels better after that.

25

fireworks . . . the bad kind

I wake up on fire.

Everything hurts . . . every*where* hurts. I try to raise my arm and that sends a jolt of intense pain ripping through my shoulder and neck.

I'm stuck here. I'm on my back, and I can't move.

I can't move.

I start to cry, big heaving sobs that make my ribs feel like they're exploding. I cry harder. It hurts worse.

I feel warmth on my forehead. It's Dr. Dad kneeling beside the bed, checking me for fever. "What is it, Ricky?" He's still half-asleep, his hair mashed about.

"It hurts!" I can't tell him more because I don't know what's happening.

He rushes off toward the bathroom.

"Daddy, don't go . . ." It's a whimper, but he hears me and hurries back.

"I'm running you a bath," he says, stroking my hair. "We'll get you in the hot water, and you'll feel better.

I can hear the water running in the bathroom, thundering at full blast.

"I can't make it in there," I tell him. "I can't move."

"I'll carry you," he says.

The thought of him carrying me is only mortifying for a second, because I know he's right—the hot water will help. It has to.

He throws off my covers and slides his arms underneath me, one below my knees, the other behind my shoulders. He lifts me gently, but I still scream.

"I'm sorry," he says, his voice breaking, "I'll go slow."

And he does go slow, taking tiny steps, trying hard not to jostle me. I gulp in air and try hard, too, really hard, not to cry, to contain my pain, to bear it.

When we finally reach the bathroom, he lowers me into the steamy water, nightgown and all. I keep my muscles tense until I'm submerged, and then I slowly let them go. Slowly.

It's better. Right away, it's at least a little better.

Dr. Dad shuts off the faucet and slumps onto the toilet. He looks down at his feet, looks . . . so down.

And then his eyes fill with tears.

"It's okay, Dad," I say, but I'm crying again too. For a moment that's all there is—just the two of us crying. "The water's good," I add, trying to make us both feel better.

He tries to get it together, but he can't quite manage it. "It's not fucking fair," he says, and then he stalks out of the bathroom.

I slide down deeper into the water, letting it flow around my shoulders and neck. "Tell me about it," I whisper.

I hear him out in my bedroom, talking on his phone. "Yes," he says when someone answers, "I need to get in touch with

Dr. Blickstein. My daughter woke up in terrible pain. I need to know if I should take her to the emergency room."

I try not to panic. How would we get to the emergency room when the trip into the bathroom nearly killed me?

"Well, who's on call? Great. I'll hold. . . . Why not? My service always has my patients hold while they try to reach me," Dr. Dad snaps. He's acting a bit undoctorly, which would normally be a load of laughs. "Fine," he barks into the phone. "Have this Dr. Hunt call me." He must have ended the call after that, because he lets loose with a highly impressive stream of curse words. If only Principal Piranha were around to hear *that*.

It's less than fifteen minutes later when Dr. Hunt calls. I'm still soaking, moving my arms and legs gently, trying to get my joints to loosen up. We've added more hot water to keep my bath nice and heavenly/hot, the way I like it.

"The doctor wants to talk to you," Dr. Dad says, a surprised look on his face. He holds the phone next to my ear.

"Hello?" I say, not sure what to expect.

"I hear you're having a pretty bad flare," this new doctor says. There's a warmth to his voice that puts me at ease.

"A flare? Is that what's happening?" I ask.

"Sounds like it," he says, "and the good news is—it's temporary."

Tears burst out of me again because I'm so relieved. I'm so fucking relieved. Until that moment, I was afraid this might be my new normal.

On fire. Unable to move. Every moment, every day.

But it's not my new normal. It's *temporary*.

"I'm going to call in a steroid prescription for you. It'll just be for a few days. But it should help knock the severe flare out of your system."

"That sounds great," I say.

Dr. Hunt goes on in his comforting tone, telling me the bath was a great idea and that I should eat before I take the medication he's ordering for me. Then he says he wants to see me tomorrow afternoon.

"But tomorrow's Saturday."

"That's okay," Dr. Hunt says, "I'll be in the office doing paperwork."

Dad takes the phone then and writes down the info for the new doctor's office. "He's at Pine Medical Plaza," Dad whispers to me with his hand over the mouthpiece. "That's right down the block." A moment later, he dials another number and I hear him telling the powers that be at Glorious Grant Middle School that I won't be in today because I'm sick. *That's putting it mildly.*

After he hangs up, he asks me, "What do you want to eat?"

"We don't have any food," I tell him. "You were going to shop today on your lunch break, remember?" He keeps the kitchen stocked regularly now. Today was just bad timing.

"Well," Dad says, "how about a nice bowl of soy sauce soup? There's gotta be at least forty soy sauce packets in there."

"Don't make me laugh! It hurts!" But the bath's numbed the pain enough for a little giggling to be a non-issue.

Dad comes back a moment later. "Okay. Ice cream and cookies it is," he says, holding up a big-ass bowl of Coffee Blast ice cream with ginger snaps.

"No whipped cream?" I ask innocently.

If I know him, he'll want to scale my teeth later today.

26

so this is what oliver's talking about

Pine Medical Plaza really *is* right down the block, as I discover when my X-Car only drives a block and a half before pulling over to the curb. Even I could have walked here, it's that close.

Dr. Dad was called into the office for an emergency at the last minute, so he's not with me. He was going to set the patient up with a dentist colleague of his, but I told him not to. If it was my dental emergency, I'd want my dad to handle it, not some random dentist I didn't know. Besides, the medication Dr. Hunt prescribed was kind of amazing. It knocked out the crazy burning pain by the end of the day. The flare thing was temporary, just like Dr. Hunt said it would be.

I press the button for the elevator in the lobby, wondering if I could convince Mom she doesn't really need to tag along on my regular appointments either. I don't need my hand held like I'm some kind of toddler. Fortunately or unfortunately, I'm getting used to this crap.

I find Dr. Hunt's office pretty easily. The waiting room's empty, and when I peer through the window into the space where the office staff usually is, I find that empty, too. "Um . . . hello!" I call out.

A woman comes into view. She's older than the secretaries at Blech-stein's office, has flowing auburn hair, and is wearing jeans and a pretty flowered blouse.

"Dr. Hunt asked me to come in," I say, handing over the insurance card. It's usually the first thing a doctor's office wants.

"Me too." She smiles. "Have you seen Dr. Hunt before?"

"No. I usually see Dr. Blickstein."

"Oh," she says, like she knows him and doesn't think much of him. Or maybe I'm imagining that. "You'll like Dr. Hunt. I'll take you back in a sec."

I eye the chairs in the waiting room. They're nice and high, like maybe the doctor put some thought into it when he picked them out. Before I can even sit, the secretary comes to get me. She leads me to a small room with a round table and chairs, a refrigerator and a counter with a microwave and a coffee maker.

"Am I interrupting his lunch or something?" I ask the secretary.

She laughs. "He likes to meet with new patients in here so you can get to know each other a little before he does the exam. I'm Charlotte, by the way," she says as she heads for the door, "if you need anything, give me a holler."

O-kaaay. That's different. I sit at the table and try to find a position that won't aggravate things, planting both feet evenly on the floor. Even though the flare's over, my feet are still my feet, and I'd like to walk home if possible. The two-second X-Car trip was kind of embarrassing.

About a minute later, I hear a squeaking sound come from out in the hall. The squeaking comes closer and then there's a short rap on the door.

The man standing in the doorway must be Dr. Hunt. (His white lab coat's a dead giveaway, even though he's wearing jeans underneath.)

"Hi," he says, entering the room, his shoes *squeak, squeak, squeaking.* He's on the short side and doesn't look that old despite his salt-and-pepper hair. "Sorry to keep you waiting."

He calls that waiting?

"I'm Dr. Hunt. It's nice to meet you." He reaches out for a handshake and I hold my breath as I oblige, hoping he doesn't squeeze the crap out of my hand like nearly everyone I've shaken hands with lately seems to. But he's super gentle, a firm grasp with a small shake. It doesn't hurt at all.

"How's your pain now?" he asks.

"Much better," I tell him. "That medicine was amazing! Can I stay on it?"

"I'm afraid not," he says. "Long-term use causes more damage than good."

Figures.

"How about in general? Does the medication you're on manage your pain well?"

I pause for a minute, wondering if this doctor really wants an honest answer, unlike Dr. Blech-stein. "Not really. Dr."—I'm careful to use his real name—"Blickstein keeps saying I need to be patient and that my blood work looks better even if my body still sucks."

Dr. Hunt scrolls through something on his phone. "Your CRP and sed rate have been going down."

"And that's good?" I ask.

"Down is good," he says with a nod. "Tell me about when you first started having pain. Where did you feel it first?"

"My feet. I started limping a lot. No one really noticed, except my sister, Dani."

"Not your mom or dad?"

I shake my head.

"They were too busy hating each other." I don't know why I just told him that. It's true but not really part of my medical history.

"So then what happened?"

"Dani threatened to tell Mom if I didn't tell her myself. So I did, and she took me to a doctor who said we needed a pediatric rheumatologist. We got Dr. Blickstein's name from my uncle, who's a *doctor-doctor*, not just a *dentist-doctor* like my dad." I say that last part with a heavy accent just like Bubbie.

Dr. Hunt chuckles softly and then nods, encouraging me to continue.

"Dr. Blickstein's office gave me some pamphlets that had teddy bears with swollen paws and canes and stuff, like I'm a five-year-old. It was ridiculous."

Dr. Hunt grimaces sympathetically. "You're what? Fourteen?"

"Almost fifteen."

"You don't necessarily need a pediatric rheumatologist. CHOP is an outstanding hospital but it isn't always the best fit for teenagers."

"Yeah, well, teenagers *are* mega-scary," I say with a snort.

He laughs with me and I realize this is probably the best doctor's appointment I've ever had.

"Would you say there's one area that bothers you more than others?" he asks, getting back to business.

"Definitely still my feet," I tell him, bracing myself for another non-answer.

He nods. "That's pretty normal. Combined, your foot and ankle have thirty-three joints, which bear all your weight. They're bound to hurt. Are you using ankle braces?"

I shake my head no, imagining a foot version of the hideous wrist braces. "Are they ugly like the wrist braces I'm supposed to wear but don't?"

"Just a thin, neoprene sleeve you wear under your socks," he says, reassuringly.

"And they really help?"

"My patients swear by them. Most wear them every day."

I should be excited. After months of agony, finally someone says there's *something* that can help. So why am I suddenly tearing up?

Dr. Hunt offers me a box of tissues. I take one, drying my eyes.

"Your other patients, do they feel like they're cursed?" I ask him.

"Don't know if they'd use that word exactly," he says quietly.

"I *hate* having arthritis," I say, making more tears spill down my face. "You know, for the record."

He smiles sympathetically. "The only people who think of arthritis as minor aches and pains are people who don't have it."

I nod, blow my nose, collect myself.

"Has Dr. Blickstein ever discussed adding one of the newer medications with you, the biologics? People are getting a lot of relief with them."

"Dr. Blickstein doesn't really *discuss* things, especially not with me," I say.

He straightens up in his chair and his face gets serious. "You know, your arthritis is something you're probably going to be dealing with for the rest of your life. I wish I could tell you different and I know it's not particularly fair. But that's the reality."

Finally, someone's speaking the truth, minus the sugarcoating. I'd be even happier about that if the truth didn't suck so much.

"Ever hear the Serenity Prayer?" Dr. Hunt asks, "'God, grant me the serenity to accept the things I cannot change'?"

"My family's not very religious," I tell him.

"Even so, there's common sense to it. Some things aren't in our control, but we do have some control over how we respond to our circumstances. For you, that means how you decide to approach your treatment."

"So you're saying I need to be all positive attitude and glass half-full?" I ask, feeling a bit frustrated with him for the first time.

"No. Not at all," he says reassuringly. "What I mean is that having open lines of communication with your doctor is essential. It's your body, your life. You absolutely have a right to be involved in the decisions made about your treatment."

Ha! Tell that to the Disaster-Formerly-Known-As-My-Parents.

"How about I ask Charlotte to give you an information packet on the biologics before you leave. No teddy bears. I promise. She can give you a set of ankle braces too."

I smile. "Dr. Hunt? I've made my first medical decision."

"What's that?" he asks.

"I want you to be my doctor."

27

i know better than to get my hopes
up but up they go anyway

Charlotte has a bunch of brochures and a couple small boxes waiting for me once Dr. Hunt's finished with the actual exam. "What size shoes do you wear?" she asks me.

"Seven and a half," I tell her, a bit irritated. I could probably wear a seven if my ankles didn't swell so much.

"Hmmm," she says, "I'll give you mediums. If we go bigger, they might not give you enough support." She hands me a box with a not-too-creepy-looking picture of the brace on it. It basically looks like a sock, minus the heel and toe sections.

I thank her and head out. It only takes a few steps down the corridor for my feet to start complaining. I spot a restroom near the elevator lobby and go in, figuring I'll try the ankle brace. It can't make things worse. Luckily it's a toilet with a full lid to put down. I sit and slip the shoe and sock off my right foot, which is currently barking louder than my left. The brace looks pretty much like the photo on the box, except it's white in the picture and an ugly tan color in real life. At least it'll blend in with my skin better.

I try to get it onto my foot but with sore, swollen fingers, it's slow going. I have to wriggle it on little by little. After an hour of that (okay, five minutes), part of me wants to just throw out the piece-of-crap brace, but another part of me is determined to conquer the damn thing. *Finally* I get it on and position it correctly. (I have to twist it a little to get the heel opening in the right place.) It's super tight and my flesh kind of bulges out a little over the top of the brace (not exactly an attractive look). Maybe Charlotte was wrong about the mediums?

I don't have it in me to wrestle with the left one too, so I put my right sock and shoe back on and figure, here goes nothing. I stand and . . .

I can feel it. I can feel a difference. It's like I have two shoes on, or one super-supportive mega-shoe that squeezes my foot, holding all the bones in alignment so the joints don't shift and rub and sting.

I sit back down and start in on my other foot. This one takes me less time because I've figured out what kind of tugging and pulling and twisting works best. I don't even have to readjust the heel this time.

Minutes later when I hit Pine Street, it's not like my feet don't hurt at all. It's just that the pain feels contained. Like a dull ache instead of *stab, stab, sting!* No wonder Dr. Hunt's patients swear by these braces.

As I walk toward home, I find myself feeling . . . I'm not sure. *What is this I'm feeling? How do I describe it?*
And then I realize: it's hope.

28

next step: break the news to dr. dad

Back home I'm at my desk looking over the pamphlets from Dr. Hunt's office and trying to figure out how to tell Dr. Dad that I am never seeing Dr. Blech-stein again. I love how none of the pamphlets use the word *needle*. Instead it's "injection" or "infusion" (meaning the medicine's delivered through an IV, which is—you guessed it—a needle). Each pamphlet lists a website for further information. All of the biologics claim to offer a real "breakthrough" that can "greatly diminish the long-term effects of arthritis" and potentially bring about "drug-induced remission," meaning it could be like I didn't even have arthritis as long as I stayed on the medicine. Sounds amazing—like the next best thing to a complete cure. (If there was a pamphlet for a medicine that totally cures you without having to stay on it, I must have left it behind.)

There's one drug where you only get an infusion once every six to eight weeks at a doctor's office. With the others you have to inject yourself (*with a needle*), usually once a week, but there's one where you have to do it daily. *Um, hell no.*

I'm kinda liking the infusion one, since I seriously don't want to add a second weekly shot to my routine. I go to that website and the first thing I notice is that it can take "two to twelve weeks" to start feeling the benefits of the medicine. *Sheesh.* I look at the site for one of the weekly shots medicines and the timeframes are basically the same. So I go back to the infusion one, brace myself and click on the (dreaded) possible side effects. The list starts out with minor stuff like body aches, runny/stuffy nose, and fatigue (I'm already two-for-three on those). Then they hit you with the Major Suckage stuff, everything from serious infections to cancer to death. I look up one of the weekly shots ones and it's the same.

Infection.

Cancer.

Death.

Crap on a stick.

I hear Dr. Dad's keys in the door and quickly straighten up the pamphlets. I want him to know I'm being very thorough and scientific about this. That said ten seconds ago I was sure I wanted to try one of these new drugs and wondered how hard it was going to be to convince him. Now I'm not so sure. Maybe suffering horribly isn't so bad if the alternative is getting an infection my body is helpless to fight off.

"Hey, Ricky Raccoon," Dr. Dad calls out as he comes in.

"Seriously over the Ricky Raccoon thing, Dad," I call back.

He pops his head into my room and holds up a takeout bag from Cush's. "Well, I have a chef's salad. But it's for Ricky Raccoon, so if she's not here . . . ?"

Oh, for God's sake! I'm hungry, so I follow him back out to the dining room, the pamphlets hot in my hand.

"How'd your emergency go?" I ask.

"Good," he says from the kitchen as he pours us drinks. "Sorry again about not going with you. I want to hear all about your appointment."

"I liked the doctor a lot," I say as I unpack my chef's salad and what I'm guessing is a Reuben for Dr. Dad (the smell of sauerkraut is pretty hard to miss).

I give Dad a full report while we eat and show him the infusion drug pamphlet.

"Some of the side effects are pretty horrible," I say.

Dad nods and squints to read the tiny print on the back of the pamphlet. "*Possible* side effects," he says. "All medications come with some risks."

He reaches into his pants pocket, pulls out one of those single-dose pill packets and hands it to me. It's Advil. I check out the list of Bad News (in teeny-tiny print since it's such a small packet): Seizures, chest pain, confusion, depression.

I toss the packet back to him, irritated. "Terrific. So the next time I get a headache, I could end up with seizures and chest pains!"

Dr. Dad rolls his eyes. "My point is that potential side effects always sound ominous. Legally, the pharmaceutical companies have to divulge any potential risks."

He starts reading the other parts of the pamphlet while I pick at my salad. Maybe he's right. The stupid medication I'm on now has side effects and it's not even working. Maybe these new drugs will have an upside to go along with the scary side.

"Maybe you and Mom can discuss the biologics with Dr. Blickstein at your next appointment," Dr. Dad says, interrupting my self-pep talk.

"About that . . ." I say, "I want to see Dr. Hunt from now on."

Dr. Dad looks up from the pamphlet. "You liked him that much?"

I nod. "It's okay, isn't it?"

"It's okay with *me*." He lets out a snort. "We'll just have to figure out a way to sell your mom on the idea."

29

next-next step: we break the news to mom

I arranged to meet Mom at Coffeeland on 16th Street. The place is pretty small, which is part of the reason I chose it. Fewer innocent bystanders if she blows her top. She's *not* expecting Dr. Dad to be here with me, but I needed him here to make sure she listens. I glance around, noting with relief that there are just enough people here to make a screaming match unlikely (though not out of the question, since a crowded Temple Owls game was apparently "okay").

I nurse a hot chocolate, rehearsing what I plan to say to Mom in my head, while Dr. Dad empties three Splenda packets into his cappuccino. He suggested that I do most of the talking to make it clear that it was my idea, which it was. Not to mention my idea has to do with which doctor *I* want to take care of *my* body.

Mom arrives moments later, looking almost stunning in a pretty yellow sweater and jeans, her hair grown in just right. I wave at her and watch as her face registers Dr. Dad's presence—the initial happy smile at seeing me is replaced by a tight pursing of the lips, then replaced again with a slightly less authentic smile. I try to hang on to how the first smile made me feel as she glides to our table in the back corner of the room.

"Hi, sweetie, you feeling better?" she says, sitting beside me on the plum-colored sofa and giving me a peck-on-the-cheek/sideways-hug combo. "You had me worried."

"I'm good," I tell her. "It was just a one-day thing."

She acknowledges Dr. Dad with a curt nod. "Peter. Wasn't expecting to see you."

"I asked him to come," I say quickly, hoping to put Mom at ease, but there's no way she doesn't think we're about to gang up on her. In a way, I guess we are.

"Joyce, you're looking terrific," Dr. Dad says.

"Thank you. I feel terrific," she replies, her tone light, but I can tell she's bracing for the potential ambush. "So, what's all this about?"

Dad nods at me, encouraging me to start.

"I've decided I want to switch doctors."

Mom's face registers surprise. "Oh. I thought maybe you'd gotten us together to campaign for a new phone for your birthday next month."

"I do desperately need a better phone!" I say.

"Yeah, your dad and I already discussed it and decided a kid who cuts six weeks of school, regardless of the reason, doesn't exactly deserve a shiny new phone."

I shoot an annoyed look at Dr. Dad. *Traitor*. He shrugs. Then I remember what we're all here for. "But about switching doctors—"

"I know Dr. Blickstein is prickly but I don't think making a change so early on is a good idea."

I want to snap at her, but I bite my tongue. I need to come off like I've thought this through (which I have) and like I'm mature enough to make this decision for myself (which I am).

"Mom," I say firmly, "prickly is an understatement. You know I can't stand Dr. Blech-stein . . . Blickstein!"

Whoops.

Dad chokes back a laugh. Mom stares daggers at him. "You find that amusing, Peter? How would you like it if one of your patients created a nasty nickname for you?"

"I'd wonder what I might have done to make my patient dislike me so much," he says back, amused rather than angry.

"Mom . . . *please* let me talk."

Mom folds her arms. I figure I have about fifteen seconds to turn this around.

"I have this friend from school. Oliver." Mom eyes me skeptically, so I talk faster. "He had cancer." (That gets Mom's attention.) "He's better now, but he was telling me how important it is to have a doctor you like, someone you can talk to, someone who *listens.*" I can see a little crevice of consideration opening up on her face and I jump on it. "I saw Dr. Hunt yesterday. He saw me on a Saturday because I had the flare. And he's awesome! He talked to me for, like, an hour, asking me questions—how it all started, which joints hurt the worst. He said I should have a say in how my doctor approaches my treatment, like a partner, you know? Oh, and he gave me these . . ."

I hoist my foot up onto the chair opposite my mom and me and slide down my sock to show her the ankle brace.

"Remember how Dr."—(*concentrate, concentrate*)—"*Blickstein* said there was nothing I could do about my feet?"

Mom nods, looking over the ankle brace with interest. "Do they help?"

"They totally help!" I put my foot back on the floor. "I mean, my feet still suck, but they suck much less."

I shut up after that because I have her. I know I have her.

She looks over at Dr. Dad. "What's your feeling on this Dr. Hunt?"

"Well, I only spoke to him on the phone briefly—"

"Because Dr. Hunt asked to talk to me right away," I interject, "like I'm an actual human being!"

Mom gives me a smirk. "I'd like to meet him," she says.

I'm prepared for that and hand her Dr. Hunt's business card with his phone number on it. "Here's his info. Make an appointment and we'll go."

"If you give me some advance notice, maybe the three of us can go together," Dr. Dad says, not to be outdone.

Ooof. Just when things were going so well . . .

But Mom surprises me. She doesn't snap back at him with some "oh, suddenly you want to be a parent" remark. Instead she nods and says, "I'll call your office to coordinate a date that works."

Who are these people and what have they done with the Disaster-Formerly-Known-As-My-Parents?

i rescue a barbie
(like any decent human being would)

I duck into the girls' room after my last class. It was either swing by the music room or pee, and pee won. I get my business done quickly and go to wash my hands. I'm due at my Afterschool Special with Jenkins in ten minutes.

My phone pings with a text from Oliver asking if I can quiz him on Spanish vocab tonight. I text him back a thumbs-up. I filled him in on everything Sunday night and he was, like, *giddy*. Not about the flare, obviously, but he was thrilled about Dr. Hunt. He let me know I missed Matt Booker's speech in Jenkins's class, which was basically Matt rambling on about fantasy football for ten minutes. We had a good laugh about it, but at the same time a queasiness bordering on dread washed over me because it reminded me that I still have no clue what topic I'm going to do my own speech on.

I'm about to head out when I hear an angry string of curse words coming from inside a stall. The initial curses are followed by some muffled sniffling. I saw Kendall scoot in here before me, so it's obviously her in there and she's obviously experiencing one of those *I-have-completely-had-it* situations I know too well.

I inch toward the stall and ask, "You okay?"

"I'm fine," Kendall sort of snaps.

I almost laugh at how familiar that is—insisting you're fine when you're *anything but.* "You're obviously not fine," I say. "What's going on?"

She sighs. "It's nothing. I got my period."

"What? Like for the first time?"

"No," she says flatly. "I've had my period since I was eleven."

"Shit, that sucks." And I mean it. Eleven? That legitimately must have sucked.

"It's just . . . I'm not *prepared.* I changed purses this weekend and somehow I forgot to transfer the tampons. You'd think, after four years, I'd be better at this." She pauses to blow her nose. "Why does everything have to be so fucking complicated?!"

"Hell if I know," I snort. *Look at me. Bonding with a Barbie.*

It all dawns on me at that moment. This whole body-changing-whether-you-want-it-to-or-not crap—it wasn't invented solely to make my life a living hell. It sucks for everybody. Particularly everybody *female.*

"I have tampons," I tell Kendall, riffling through my bag for my little purple tampon case. When I can't get my fingers to work the clasp, I pop it open with my teeth. (Sorry, Dr. Dad.) And even though I'm basically handing a canteen full of water to a dying (wo)man, I'm still glad Kendall didn't see me gnaw the case open.

I hand her a tampon under the stall door, and wait. I don't know what I'm waiting for. I've done my good deed, earned my brownie points. It's not like she's gonna hug me and tell me we'll be best friends from now on.

Finally, she comes out of the stall and heads to the sink to wash her face, which is streaked with mascara. "Thanks," she says.

"Sure," I tell her. I still don't know what I'm waiting there for.

"Don't say anything about this to anyone, okay? Please?" Kendall says.

Like I'd casually bring this up in conversation. "Of course not," I tell her.

She leans over the sink to splash water on her face and that's when I see it—a dark spot on the back of her pants. It's not that big but it's there.

If it was me with the spot, would she tell me? Or would she just snap a picture and post it on Instagram for all her friends to laugh at?

Kendall runs a brush through her hair, trying to pull herself together.

"Thanks," she says again, before heading for the door.

I feel sick. "Kendall, wait!"

She stops and looks back at me, not mean or spiteful. Just open.

"There's a spot—"

"Fuuuuck!" Kendall screams. She heads back into the stall and slams the door. I can hear her sniffling again and I get it—like it's all so pointless and why do we even bother to try to *do life* when nothing works out and it's all so colossally tragic anyway.

"Maybe you can . . ." But I don't know what. Then I remember the lost and found bin in Nurse Jeff's office. It's not like there's going to be a pair of pants in there that just happen to be Kendall's size but there's bound to be a jacket she can tie around her waist to hide the spot or something. "Wait here, Kendall. I have an idea."

"You're just going to leave me here?" she says from behind the stall door.

You'd probably leave me here is what I think, but what I say is, "I'll come right back. I promise."

I hustle out of the bathroom. Like *for real* hustle, because some-how being on a mission makes me forget about my aching body. The hall's deserted, so I'm free to limp as much as necessary. I take the elevator down and head for Nurse Jeff's office.

"Hi, Ricky," he says when I walk in. "What's up?"

"I left something in the cafeteria last week. Can I check the lost and found?"

He waves me in and goes back to what he was doing. I rummage through the overflowing crate. Apparently boys lose a lot more stuff than girls do. I dig past a ratty white sweatshirt with a gross greenish stain. Then I hit pay dirt—a pretty, red cardigan. It even looks like something Kendall might wear.

I fly back up to the girls' bathroom. Kendall's out of the stall, leaning on the sink and looking spent.

I hand her the cardigan. "Here, tie this around your waist."

"Is it yours?" she asks, like she's astonished that I'd be willing to lend her my pretty, red cardigan for such an unpleasant job.

I consider lying just for the hell of it, but instead I tell her, "Lost and found."

She ties the sweater on and twists around to check her backside in the mirror. It definitely covers the spot. We're both all smiles, pretty pleased with ourselves.

"God . . . *thank you*," Kendall says. "Really, thanks a lot."

I nod and tell her I have to get going. It's only then that I realize I'm late for Jenkins.

Crap and a half.

Jenkins raises an eyebrow—high—when I come in his room ten minutes late.

"Ms. Bloom," he says, sounding a bit annoyed. "I suppose you have a good excuse for wasting ten minutes of my time?"

"I do," I say, "I was . . . doing something important. Helping someone. Believe me. You don't want to know the details."

"Oh, I don't, do I?"

"You *really* don't." His eyebrow is still way up on his forehead, and he's looking at me expectantly. So I add, "I apologize for being late."

He releases the eyebrow and says, "Very well. Apology accepted."

"Did you see the letter to the editor about the missing stop sign where that kid got hit?" I ask as I scramble through my backpack for my notebook. "That lady was piss—"

Eyebrow reengaged.

"I mean *angry*. She made some good points, but I think she messed up with the approach she took."

"You think she would have drawn more flies with honey?" he asks.

"Yeah, she was too angry and mean, so it was hard to really hear what she had to say." He smiles and I add, "I guess I'm kind of making the same point you made before, about how cursing can cause your message to get lost." I pull the clipping from the *Inquirer* out of my notebook and show him all the notes I made in the margins. I also highlighted and underlined stuff. I had a lot of thoughts about that lady's brief letter.

"May I take this home and return it to you tomorrow?" Jenkins asks. "I have an appointment later, so I'm afraid we won't be able to make up the ten minutes we missed."

"Oh, sure," I say, and something comes over me, a fog-like feeling. I'm astonished when I figure out what it is—disappointment.

i hope they like him, not that it matters (okay, it totally matters!)

I'm fidgeting, because it's weird to be at a doctor's appointment with both Mom and Dad. Hell, it's weird to be with Mom and Dad together, period. Here's hoping it's the Pleasant-And-Cooperative-Coffee-Shop-Version of them.

So far, it seems like maybe I'm in luck on that front. I worried about this all last week, while studying for tests in algebra and geoscience, writing a short paper for world history, and trying to help Oliver pick a topic for his speech. (I'm still pushing for recycling, which is just boring enough for Matt Booker to completely ignore.) Still no progress on figuring out my topic.

I take a deep breath and blow it out, trying to bring my head back into the room.

"Relax, Ricky," Mom says. "If you like this doctor so much, I'm sure we'll like him too."

Anger flashes through me. *I don't care if you don't!*

I take another deep breath, and the feeling goes away. Besides, the truth is I *do* want them to like Dr. Hunt. And I want to like him as much today as I did the last time. What if he's different with my parents in the room, talking to them instead of me, ignoring me like every other doctor always has? Just as my thoughts start to spin with worry, I hear his squeaky shoes coming down the hall.

"That's him. His shoes squeak," I say to my parents with a laugh. I kind of love his squeaky shoes.

When he comes in, he says (to me, not my parents), "Hi there. Good to see you."

"You too," I say.

Dr. Dad's about to introduce himself when Dr. Hunt says, again to *me*, "Why don't you introduce me to your parents?"

All my nervousness melts away after that.

Dr. Hunt examines me, doing all the things Dr. Blech-stein does—the poking, prodding, and squeezing. But he chats with me the whole time, asking me stuff about my body but some other stuff, too, like where I go to school and whether I like it.

"I'm doing a lot of extra credit stuff," I tell him. "To make up for days I missed."

"Ah," he says, nodding as he gently bends my elbow.

"No," I quickly confess. "Not because of my body. I cut school." I steal a glance at Mom and Dad, hoping they're not embarrassed, but they seem focused on the doctor. For some reason, I want to be completely honest with Dr. Hunt.

"Why was that?" he asks, as he flexes my right knee.

It dawns on me that no one's actually asked me that before. Not Mom. Not Dad. Certainly not Principal Piranha. Not even Jenkins.

"Um . . ." Another glance at my parents, and now they're completely focused on me. *Great.* "I guess part of it was my body. I mean, walking to school was really hard, but now I'm taking a car service. But the rest was like . . . I just wanted to stay home and sleep and not think about how awful everything was." I'm not sure how else to explain it.

"Makes sense," Dr. Hunt says.

It does?

He sits on a rolling stool and scoots over to a computer. "Dr. Blickstein had his staff send over your records."

He did?

Dr. Hunt chuckles at my shocked expression. "Patients change doctors all the time. We try not to take it personally."

"That's right," Dr. Dad chimes in. "Of course, I have voodoo dolls made of the patients who leave me, but I hardly ever use them."

"*Shhh,*" Dr. Hunt says. "That's our secret."

Mom rolls her eyes, but she's smiling. I'm pretty sure Dr. Hunt has completely won them over. He clicks out of my file on the computer and turns away from the monitor to face me.

"Okay. Questions?"

Out of the corner of my eye, I see Mom open her mouth, but Dr. Dad places his hand on her forearm and she nods at me, encouraging me to speak for myself.

I am seriously not used to this doctor-patient partnership thing yet but it's definitely cool. "I . . . we wanted to talk to you about the medicines you told me about."

"The biologics," he says.

We all nod.

Dr. Hunt's face lights up. He seems excited for me. "All right then. Let's talk."

"I don't want to have to get another shot every week, so the one you get with infusions seemed the most interesting." I hand him the corresponding pamphlet.

"Okay," he says, nodding for me to go on.

"These biologics are more dangerous than the medication I'm already on though, right?" I ask. "I mean, there must be some reason Dr. Blickstein didn't put me on them."

"Some doctors prefer a more conservative approach at first. Arthritis treatment often requires patients to switch medications from time to time. You can be on one very successfully for years and then have its efficacy wear off. If you start with the more traditional medicines, it leaves all of the biologics as an option in the future."

"But is it riskier?" Mom interjects. I'm not annoyed by her intrusion because I want to know too.

"It is," Dr. Hunt says, directing his response at me even though it was Mom who asked the question. "The biologics are considerably more immunosuppressive than the medication you've been on, so when you get a cold or the flu, it might hit you a little harder and take you a little longer to recover. You'll have to try your best to limit exposure to germs. Wash your hands frequently. Maybe not hang out with your friends if one of them has a cold."

That last part shouldn't be difficult, considering my lack of friends. "The patients on the website talk about it like it's some kind of miracle."

"A lot of patients feel that way."

That dizzying feeling of hope washes over me again. I want to be on this medicine, like—*yesterday*. "Is there any possibility it makes the arthritis go away completely? I mean, even if I eventually stop taking the medicine?"

Dr. Hunt looks me straight in the eye and says, "Full remission, without medicine, is rare. It does happen for some patients, but it's extremely unlikely."

I nod. I knew that but I had to ask him anyway. I had to hear him say it. "So it can take up to twelve weeks to start working, right?"

"Typically you start to feel a difference earlier than that. It can be a bit inconsistent in the beginning. You'll feel better for several days or even weeks but then start having pain again before your next infusion. If the inconsistencies continue after your initial three infusions, we can adjust the schedule or the dosage."

I look at Mom and Dad. "What do you guys think?" I ask.

They look at each other, like they're not sure what to say or who should say it. Finally Dr. Dad says, "What matters is what you think."

32

waiting and wondering and worrying and . . . whatever!

I'm distracting myself with homework, which is easy considering there's always so much of it between the regular assignments and the catch-up stuff. Today at least it's keeping my mind off the call that's probably coming later—with the results of my tuberculosis test (necessary before I can have my first infusion). I'm not concerned about actually having TB (pretty sure I don't). It's the idea of getting cleared for medicine that may turn me into a total germophobe that's making me queasy. (For the record, I refuse to carry around bottles of hand sanitizer.)

It's not normal for a person to hope she has TB, is it?

My cell *ping-ping-pings*, letting me know I got a text. It's from Oliver, naturally.

Test results?

I text back:

Nope. Homework. TTYL.

Really, I don't want to talk to him later because all he'll want to talk about is the stupid new medicine and how great everything's going to be soon. I'm still going to have stupid arthritis. And sometimes I just want a break from talking about health stuff all the time. I text him a smiley face so he won't be pissed.

The not-quite-as-disastrous Disaster-Formerly-Know-As-My-Parents already checked their schedules and coordinated with Dr. Hunt's office to get me an appointment for next Friday. Mom's going to go with me and then Dani's going to hang out with me until Dad gets home, in case I need anything. I have two more infusions scheduled after that, the second infusion two weeks after the first and a third infusion at the six-week mark. The infusions will go to every six weeks after that. And I'll have to continue the stupid weekly shots too.

It dawns on me that if they were still making Afterschool Specials, they could make one about me: "*A teen, crippled with arthritis, freaks out about starting a scary new medicine.*"

For now the TB test is the only thing standing between me and going ahead with Infusion Number One.

My cell plays "Give Me Novacaine," meaning Oliver's *calling* too.

But it's not Oliver. It's Charlotte from Dr. Hunt's office.

I answer, trying not to sound nervous.

"Hi, Ricky," she says. "The test came back fine. You're good to go next Friday. I already let your mom know."

"Great!" I say.

It's not normal for a person to be slightly bummed she doesn't have TB, is it?

33

the day before the big day,
aka big-day eve

I'm finishing up with Jenkins, packing my backpack and thinking about how tonight will be Big-Day Eve and how I'm excited but nervous and honestly a bunch of other emotions I can't quite identify.

"Oh, Mr. Jenkins," I say. "I forgot to tell you. I can't meet tomorrow. I have a medical thing." I look down at the floor. "I can bring you a note if you want."

"That won't be necessary." He gives me a quizzical look. "I trust you."

"You do?" I blurt out. That actually makes him laugh, not a mean, snooty laugh like when I first started coming to school again, but a nice laugh. "It's this infusion thing and it takes, like, two hours. My doctor suggested I schedule it on a Friday. Then if I'm tired or feel off or something, I'll have the weekend to recuperate. It's my first time, so we don't really know how my body will react."

I have NO idea why I'm spilling all this on Jenkins.

He inhales a deep breath. "Sounds a little overwhelming."

"Just another fun day in Rickyville," I say with a smirk. "It might make things a lot better, so . . ."

He nods. "Let's hope it does."

I nod back. "Let's hope."

I head down the hall for the front entrance, kind of happy it's too late for Oliver to still be around. He's so excited for me it's getting a bit nauseating. I get that he's not as freaked out about my getting a dangerous substance pumped into my veins since, when he was in my shoes, it was chemo being pumped into him and it cured him. He's assuming my new medication will have the same *super-awesome* effect on me, even though it's not a cure. I hope he's right, but it's hard to imagine this pain going away. I mean, it's been . . . God, almost six months now, and I can barely remember my life Before Arthritis.

As I pass the office, I hear a *psssst*.

I look in and see Julio riding one of the hard wooden chairs outside Principal Piranha's office.

"Miss you around here," he says.

I lean against the doorjamb, smirking. "You're here late. What unspeakable crime did you commit this time?"

Julio laughs. "Principal Piranha called some meeting with my folks," he explains with a shrug. "Hey, we should hang out this weekend."

My stomach nearly explodes with butterflies. *Julio wants to hang out with me!*

"Sure," I say as casually as possible. Then I remember I have no idea how I'm going to feel after tomorrow. "I may not be available this weekend though."

"Hot date?" he asks. "Give me your digits and we'll figure it out."

He hands me his cell, which is huge and shiny and everything my phone is not. I type in my number, nerves making my fingers jittery, and somehow manage to not drop his phone. Just as I'm handing it back, Principal Piranha steps out of her office.

"Can I help you with something, Erica?" she asks, glaring at me with no intention of helping me with anything.

Beside her, I see Julio mouth the word *piranha* and then bare his teeth. I laugh. Principal Piranha glares back at Julio, who gives her an innocent look.

"I'm good," I tell her and then I take off before I get Julio into more trouble.

Outside, I spot my X-Car and get myself in the back seat. The whole ride home I keep thinking—*Julio wants to hang out! He asked for my number! And he asked if I had a hot date!* I know the last part was a joke, but it's still hysterical and awesome and amazing. It sounds like one of my fill-in-the-blanks:

I could put his mind at ease, tell him there's no hot date on my weekend schedule. But I don't do that. I let him suffer.

The rest of the afternoon and evening drag big time. I get into bed with my geoscience book, hoping it'll put me to sleep. No such luck. All I can think about is tomorrow and how the stupid medicine with all its potential side effects probably isn't going to help anyway. Although maybe it will. Maybe my first infusion will be the start of good things, the beginning of the end of my being in pain all the time, the "first day of the rest of my life" and all that crap.

Maybe.

After lying awake in bed for God-knows-how-long, I check the time on my phone. 1:06 a.m. So much for getting a good night's sleep like Dr. Hunt suggested. Mom's meeting me downstairs at 7:15 sharp tomorrow morning. Getting up is going to be brutal.

I decide trying to sleep is useless, so I crawl out of bed and turn on my computer. Then I google my new medication and 368,000 results come up. There's a YouTube video—"Katie's Infusion Day"—on the first page. I click on it.

The video is of this eight-year-old girl with strawberry-blond pigtails in a hospital setting. I watch as a nurse preps her arm, then pokes her with a needle.

"You're such a brave girl," a woman off-camera says. Again with the "you're so brave" thing. *Ugh.* But this little girl? And Oliver when he was four? Shit, they *are* brave.

"It only hurts a little," Katie says, her bottom lip quivering.

I click out of the video. I'll see it all firsthand tomorrow anyway. Hopefully I can be as *brave* as little Katie (but Mom still better not try that "you're so brave" crap on me).

My phone *ping-ping-pings* back on my bedside table. It can only be Oliver, but what the hell is he doing up at one in the morning?

Can't sleep. Excited 4 u. Sure new meds will b gr8!

I type:

Go 2 sleep stupid!

But then I change "stupid" to "dummy" and add:

I will if u will. Text u tomorrow.

He texts back:

U better. R u nervous?

I text back:

Duh!

It takes Oliver a minute to respond, but then his text comes in:

Don't b. Everything gets better starting 2morrow.

I text back:

Yup.

But what I'm really thinking is: *maybe.*

34

big-day day

As Mom and I walk to Dr. Hunt's office from the elevator, I start wondering if this whole thing is a big mistake.

Maybe switching to Dr. Hunt was a mistake too. What if he's some kind of radical and these biologic medicines he suggested are way too risky?

Ugh, Ricky, suck it up. Dr. Hunt rocks. And the medicine's going to rock too.

When we get to the check-in window, Charlotte greets us with a bright smile. "Your first infusion! Very exciting!"

"If you say so."

"The infusion itself is no big deal. And the medicine usually makes a huge difference." Charlotte types some stuff into her computer and tells us to take a seat, warning us that it may be a while, as they're a bit backed up.

I know Mom sees the dread on my face but instead of saying something stupid, she just smiles reassuringly. She really is getting better at treating me like . . . I don't know . . . like I'm not still seven years old.

"Have to admit," she says as we sit down, "I'm a little nervous."

I fight my initial urge to automatically lash out at her. *What's up with that anyway?* Instead I say, "I am too."

The waiting room is the fullest I've seen it. There's an old couple a few seats away from me. They both look so frail, it's anybody's guess which one's the patient. A skinny guy, probably in his twenties, sits across from me, messing with his drool-worthy iPhone. *Lucky him*, I think. But then I realize—if he's here, in this waiting room, how lucky can he be, really? The last two patients are a woman and a young boy. The boy sits there limply, leaning against the woman, his mother I'm guessing. I glance at her, and I wonder if that's how Oliver's mother looked when he was sick—worried, exhausted.

I catch the mom's eye and give her a smile. She smiles back before turning back to her son to ruffle his hair.

I riffle through the magazine rack beside me. It's all finance, fashion, or sports—not exactly my thing. Would it kill them to have a *Rolling Stone*?

I offer the current issue of *Golf Enthusiast* to Mom as a joke. "Magazine?"

She grimaces, and I laugh.

I decide to hit the bathroom to kill time. I drank a whole bottle of water before coming over here, since I knew I'd be getting *stuck*. (Turns out, Oliver's tip about drinking water to make your veins pop was right on.) I'm just coming back when I hear a woman call my name. She's wearing dark-purple scrubs.

"I'm Martha," she tells us, holding open the door to the back. We shuffle through, and I alternate between feeling doomed, like I'm going to the electric chair, and excited, like I'm starting a tour of Willy Wonka's chocolate factory.

We stop at a scale in the hallway, and Martha tells me to get on. My weight's about the same as the last time I was weighed, pretty average.

Martha jots down the number, explaining that my weight determines the amount of medicine I'll get. Then she leads us down the hall.

"How are you feeling today?" Martha asks.

"Okay, I guess," I tell her.

She ushers us into a room. It has a comfy recliner chair, instead of an exam table. Martha tells me to have a seat and make myself comfortable.

For a second I consider running out while I still can (okay, Ricky-running) but instead, I do as I'm told. I sit. "I have my ankle braces on. Is that okay?" I ask.

"Totally fine," Martha says. She positions a regular chair beside my recliner. "Mom, you can sit right here." Mom sits, letting out a big sigh.

"It's your first time. Are you nervous?" Martha asks—both of us, which doesn't annoy me this time.

"A little," I admit again. "We both are. How big is the needle?"

"Not big," she answers. "Plus, I'm pretty good at stabbing people."

I chuckle. But Mom grimaces at Martha's joke. So I say, "A nurse who's skilled at stabbing people is a *good* thing, Mom."

She nods but still looks uneasy, so I squeeze her hand. She squeezes back, a little too hard, but I ignore the jabbing pain because it seems like she needed that squeeze.

Martha readies some supplies—alcohol swabs, cotton balls, a roll of tape, and some other stuff I don't recognize. She pre-tears a couple small strips of the tape and sticks them to the edge of the recliner.

"Be right back," she says, giving me a pat on the back of my hand, which normally I find soooo irritating, but today nothing's normal.

"Dr. Hunt said it takes about two hours, right?" Mom asks.

"Yeah," I say, wondering if his estimate included the waiting and set up or if he meant it takes two whole hours just for the medicine to go into my veins. I hope not.

Martha's back, carrying a plump IV bag filled with clear liquid.

"Is that the medicine?" I ask her.

"Saline," she tells me. "We'll get the IV in and start running in the saline. Then we add the medicine and they go in together." She hangs the bag to an IV pole and then starts pressing buttons on a little rectangular machine about the size of a large shoebox bolted to the pole below where she hung the bag.

"What does that do?" I ask, genuinely interested. Oliver's always telling me I should ask questions.

"It monitors the medicine as it goes in. We can set the delivery speed and it shows how much you have left to go."

"The quicker, the better," I say. Maybe I won't have to be here for more than two hours after all.

"We start slow, to make sure you don't have any adverse reactions," Martha says.

I nod, like I understand completely, even though I completely don't. What kind of *adverse reactions*? Is my arm going to swell up like a balloon? Or turn green and fall off?

"Dr. Hunt ordered Benadryl, which should keep you from getting too itchy. It'll probably make you sleepy though," Martha continues.

I shrug. Napping through the two hours doesn't sound like a bad deal to me.

"If you feel anything unusual once we start the infusion—dizzy, sick to your stomach, anything—let me know."

"Got it," I say. She's holding a needle, looking at me in that vampire kind of way, so I offer her both arms, opening them out as straight as possible (which isn't completely straight anymore because my elbows are too stiff). "Which arm do you want?" I ask.

"We're going to try for the hand first," she says.

My hand? With its teeny, tiny little veins?

"Are you right handed or left?" Martha asks.

"Right."

"Okay. We'll go for left." She ties the tourniquet around my forearm and gives me the squishy ball to squeeze.

I squeeze, hoping this isn't the one time Oliver's water trick doesn't work.

"Look at that beautiful vein!" Martha says. "You're making my job too easy."

Sure enough, just above my fingers, there's a plump, purplish vein. Martha swabs the area with alcohol, waving her hand over it to dry the alcohol so it doesn't sting when she puts in the needle. She tears open the needle's sterile packaging, ready to rock.

"Do you look—or look away?" Martha asks me.

"I look," I tell her.

She winks at me. "I knew you were a looker."

I watch as the needle pierces my skin, feel the prick, see the red flash of blood in the tubing below the needle, which means she got it on the first try.

"You *are* good at stabbing people," I tell Martha.

She smiles as she lays a sticky, clear plastic sheet over where the needle is to keep it in place. There's a long tube connected to the needle that has a few stopper/plug thingies on it. Martha uses the strips of tape to secure the tube to my arm and then connects it to the bag of saline.

"Is the saline going in?" I ask. I don't feel anything.

Martha nods and puts a blood pressure cuff on my right arm. After she takes my blood pressure, she takes my pulse and temperature. Then she picks up a syringe and draws medication out of a vial. "The Benadryl," she explains.

"I have to get stuck again?" I groan.

She shakes her head. "It goes right into the IV." Sure enough, she sticks the needle into one of those stopper/plug thingies in the IV tube.

"I'm going to go prep the medicine and then we'll get started, okay?"

She leaves again, and then it's just me and Mom and all our nervous-hopeful feelings crowding the room. Mom roots through her giant purse, pulling out a book.

"Did you bring the op-ed section from the paper for me?" I ask.

She pulls that out of her purse too and then we're back to the silence and waiting and the feelings.

We both smile when Dr. Hunt pokes his head in the room. I was so distracted I didn't even hear his squeaky shoes.

"Hi," he says. "I'll be back at the end of your infusion but thought I'd pop my head in now just to . . ."

"Say hi?" I suggest.

He chuckles. "Any questions?"

"You really think this is going to work, right?" I blurt out. That's the most burning question I have, the only one that really matters.

"I do," he says nodding, looking very certain. "I really do."

Martha's back after that. She hangs what I assume is the bag with the medicine on the IV pole near the saline and fiddles with some tubing, presses buttons on the little machine, and eventually says, "That's it. You're all set. Just relax and I'll be checking back in with you every twenty minutes or so. If you feel anything unusual, have Mom come get me."

I lie there waiting to feel sick or weird or *something*. All I feel is sleepy, like Martha warned me I would, but also because I hardly slept at all after Oliver's last text message. The next thing I know, I'm waking up from a nap.

Martha's got the blood pressure cuff around my arm and she's pumping it up. "Sorry to wake you," she says, holding out a thermometer to put under my tongue.

"How much did I miss?" I mumble around the thermometer.

Martha checks the machine. "You're about a third of the way done."

I nod, still feeling sleepy.

Martha removes the thermometer, types my vitals into the computer, and heads back out.

"What's your book about?" I ask Mom to try to keep myself awake.

She says it's about a guy who joins a circus and falls in love with the lion tamer's wife, which sounds kind of cool. But I fall asleep again before she can tell me more.

well, am i cured or what?

I wake up with a sleepy, dreamy feeling. Sunlight's peeking through the blinds, so it must be morning. After getting home from the infusion yesterday, I spent the rest of the day lounging in bed, with Dani bringing me food and the two of us streaming movies on my laptop. She didn't let me get out of bed for anything other than to go to the bathroom, insisting it was "doctor's orders," which wasn't really true. Today, Dani has practice, so it's Dr. Dad's turn to over-pamper me. It all feels a bit ridiculous, but it's also kind of nice.

I stretch my body, half-expecting it to be gloriously pain free. *Nope.* My neck's a little stiff. My left knee's a little achy. My right elbow is not thrilled with the prospect of moving at all. And, of course, my macadamia nut pinkie is its usually cranky self. But all in all, my aches and pains seem minor. Most mornings, it's a lot worse than this.

I let myself conjure up a post-infusion fill-in-the-blank:

The new medication makes the giant difference everyone thinks it will. I see myself walking without a limp. Running. Climbing up the stairs at school two at a time. Maybe even dancing . . . but who am I kidding? I was never much of a dancer anyway. I could thrash around at a Green Day concert. Yeah, that's better anyway. Dani gets me tickets to see Green Day for my birthday. And we go to the concert and thrash in a mosh pit full of punks while Billie Joe kills it on guitar.

My phone vibrates.

I press the little bubble on my screen to open up Oliver's text.

Do you feel different?

I text back:

You mean since you asked last night?

Well do you?

Actually yeah . . .

Really?

My body feels awesome. Full of energy. I even grew two inches overnight!

I almost add "And my boobs grew three cup sizes," but that would be too weird.

It takes him a minute to answer, and I worry that maybe he doesn't appreciate that I'm joking about something I'm supposed to be taking seriously.

Finally, he writes:

Ha ha. OK . . . so you don't feel different . . . yet!

Sheesh. The boy just can't help himself. His perky, positive attitude has a mind of its own. I text back:

Maybe I do feel a little different.

Because maybe I do, a little. Maybe I have a tiny bit of hope that things will get better, that the medicine will work like it's supposed to.

I hear a soft knock on the door. Dr. Dad calls out my name. I quickly text:

L8r. Gotta go.

I have zero interest in discussing my texting habits with my dad, even if it's just with Oliver.

"Come on in," I say once I stow my phone under the covers.

"I'm going across the street to pick up bagels," he says. "Any special requests?"

"Sesame." Never mind that everyone else in my family knows that sesame bagels are my favorite and basically the only bagels I eat. It's the thought that counts, right?

"Okay. Sesame bagel breakfast in bed, coming right up!"

"No, I'm getting up," I say, suddenly realizing that I'm sick to death of lying in this bed, comfortable as it is.

"You sure?" he asks. "How do you feel?"

"I feel good."

And it hits me—I *do* feel pretty good. Other than the slightly achy body parts, I feel rested and kind of full of energy. I try to remember the last time I felt so awake, and I realize it was way back in the fall, before everything went to shit, Before Arthritis.

Dad opens his mouth to say something but then seems to decide he doesn't want to jinx it. I'm glad. I don't want anything to jinx it either. He tells me he'll be right back and heads out.

I sit up on the side of the bed, and it seems easier somehow, like I'm not dragging my body upright against its will. The real test will be when I stand up—or try to stand up. I test my feet. Left ankle stings a little, but overall, my feet aren't bad.

So I get up and, out of habit, I lean on my dresser for support (the mirror frame now has six kangaroo cards). I'm definitely walking like a human being, rather than staggering into the bathroom. When I turn on the water to brush my teeth, my macadamia nut pinkie sends a brief shooting-pain reminder that I still need to be careful.

Yeah, yeah, Pinkie. Got it.

It may totally be my imagination, but something seems different.

oliver's day to stand naked in front of the class

My X-Car was late, so I went straight to public speaking this morning. I had just enough time to wish Oliver good luck before Jenkins started class. Now I'm fidgeting in my seat and trying to beam supportive vibes at him, like that will somehow make a difference once he has to give his talk in front of these jerks.

We texted a bunch last night, and he seemed to have his speech fully prepped. He's reviewing his stack of 3x5 cards, looking ridiculously calm. I wish he'd turn his Oliver-ness down a notch when a situation calls for it, but that never seems to occur to him. As if to make my point, he pumps a squirt of sanitizer into his hand, rubbing it in vigorously.

"Mr. Horn," Jenkins says. "Ready to give your opinion piece?"

"Totally ready," Oliver says. He gets up and heads for the front of the room.

"*Olivia*," Matt Booker sings from the back of the room.

Snickers follow.

Jenkins scowls at the class. "That's enough."

It barely fazes Oliver. It's like he's made of Teflon. At least he finally looks the tiniest bit nervous now, but it's more like he's afraid he'll forget an important fact or something.

"I'm Oliver Horn and the title of my speech is Better Nutrition, Better Life."

Just his title elicits more snickers, but Oliver forges ahead.

"You can buy a big bacon dog, a large soda, and a bag of chips for under five dollars at any Wawa. That may seem like a bargain, but what you don't realize is how much it's really costing you. Eating an excess of trans fats, high-fructose corn syrup, and heavily processed foods increases your risk of developing many different health conditions, from obesity to diabetes to cancer. I know all about that last one. Trust me. Cancer is no joke."

I glance left and right for a moment, suddenly squeamish when he mentions being sick. Kendall's texting, hiding her cell below her desk. And she's not the only one ignoring Oliver. *Good.* I focus all my attention back on him. If it's just me and Mr. Jenkins listening, maybe he'll make it through this without getting hassled after all.

Suddenly my cell *ping-ping-pings* with a text alert. *Shit! Forgot to turn it off!*

"Phones off in class, Ms. Bloom," Jenkins barks.

"I'm sorry!" I say, fumbling for my phone to turn it off and . . . *OMG! The text is from Julio!!!*

Can u study 2nite @ my place? Need ur help! Desper8! J.

OMG OMG OMG. Another text comes in.

228 w rittenhouse sq. 7pm. There will b pizza. Say yes!

"It's about a change to a doctor's appointment," I bold-face lie to Jenkins. "I just have to send a quick reply and then I'll shut off my phone."

I hit reply on my cell, but then I freeze. How do I reply without sounding like I'm *dying* that he even asked (although I'm totally dying that he even asked!!!). I go with:

C u @ 7 :)

"Please continue, Mr. Horn," Jenkins says coolly. He watches me to make sure I put my phone away, which I do, and then I mouth the word *sorry*, which I am.

Oliver clears his throat and jumps back in. "The good news is healthy food actually tastes a lot better than you might think. Hungry for a snack? Try some raw veggie sticks and hummus or a piece of fresh fruit."

Suddenly, a banana flies toward Oliver. "Here's some fruit for you, you fruit!"

Jenkins leaps to his feet. "Who threw that?" Of course there's no answer, but Mr. Booker is the obvious culprit. Jenkins repositions his chair so that he's looking at the class instead of Oliver.

Two interruptions now, one totally my fault, and Oliver barely misses a beat. If he's upset at all, he's sure hiding it well. The guy is total Teflon City.

37

. . . and now i'm freaking out

No amount of apologizing to Jenkins and Oliver made me feel better about my disruption in public speaking. The disruption itself was bad enough . . . but the lying about it made me feel particularly shitty. But I just couldn't *not* respond to Julio's text.

Crap. Julio. Right.

I'm due at his place in twenty minutes and I still haven't figured out what to wear. Dani's girly-girl jeans were the obvious lower-body choice. Now what? I picked out six different blouses to try on over the plain white tank top I'm wearing, but I'm not feeling any of them. The blue frilly one is too frilly. The green mock turtleneck has a seam that's unraveling up by the collar, right where you can see it. And the beige one is *beige*, for God's sake.

Dr. Dad knocks on my open bedroom door, making me jump. "You sure you don't want some pot roast and potatoes?" he asks. "Should be ready in another ten minutes." He's got on the BBQ King apron that he always wore for family cookouts (back when we were a family). It's super dorky but carries the permanent stains of delicious memories. I'm glad I seem to have motivated him to get back into cooking. I love all the corned-beef sandwiches, but they get *très* boring after a while.

"Julio said there'd be pizza." I tell him.

"Well, if he doesn't feed you enough, the pot roast will be in the fridge."

"Great. Thanks." I turn back toward the mirror, letting Dad know I don't have time to chat. He's been finding excuses to check in with me ever since I cleared going to Julio's with him. I told him Julio's "just a friend" (leaving out that I'm hoping he might be more than that by the end of the night), but I think Dad saw right through me. He's been moony-eyed ever since, like I'm going on my first-ever date or something. I have to bite my tongue to keep from pointing out that he blew his opportunity to be all moony-eyed over my *real* first-ever date last year, since it happened after he left.

I riffle through my dresser skeptically, hoping to find *something* acceptable, and unearth a long-sleeve Temple Owls T-shirt I'd forgotten all about. It's snug and looks great on me. I put it on, my shoulder barking a little when I reach up over my head, and then check myself in the mirror. . . . *I look pretty darn good!*

I smile into the mirror, showing off my perfect teeth.

"Hey, Julio," I practice, "what's up? Ready to get your English on?" I cringe. I try giving the mirror a few sexy smiles, but I just end up laughing at myself.

Focus! Only thing left to do is put on a little makeup, just some lip-gloss and mascara, because I don't want to look like I'm trying too hard.

Then I'm ready to go.

To Julio's house.

And suddenly I'm in *what-the-hell-was-I-thinking?* mode. I look in the mirror again, and I don't look as good as I thought.

What if I do something horribly embarrassing like, I don't know, fart or trip or think he's about to kiss me and try to kiss him back when, really, he was just reaching for his phone. Maybe I shouldn't go, maybe I could get out of it, say I'm not feeling well. . . .

I shake all that off—literally shaking my body to get all those crap thoughts out of my head—and just in time, too, as the X-Car app chimes on my phone, letting me know my car's downstairs.

I head out to the living room. The smell of the pot roast is intoxicating. Maybe I will have a late-night bite when I get home.

"I'm off!" I tell Dr. Dad, grabbing my backpack.

Off to go study with the cutest boy in school!

like, julio's . . . actual house!

I can't believe I'm doing this! I also can't believe I'm letting my head make it into such a big deal. I'm just meeting a classmate to study. And sure: it's Julio, not Oliver, but it's still not a big deal, right?

Keep telling yourself that, Ricky.

I wait in the elevator lobby in Julio's building, after the doorman called up to Julio's place to make sure I'm legit and not some freaky stalker. This building is a lot fancier than Dr. Dad's. The doorman's stationed behind a marble counter, and the lobby is decorated with plush couches and fresh flowers. I'm wondering if Julio's family is rich—and *how* rich—when an elevator comes. I step aboard. Here goes nothing.

On the ninth floor, I walk down the hallway, the carpet cushy under my feet, and find his apartment, number 930. The door-mat—*Julio's doormat*—says "Wipe Your Paws!" I ring the doorbell.

Deep, throaty barking comes from within the apartment.

Definitely not a Chihuahua in there. A moment later, a woman who looks like she could be a model answers the door. She has long blond hair, a flawless face, and a slim build under chic clothes. Even her glasses are cool. I figure she's Julio's mom, and suddenly his light-brown skin and dirty-blond hair make perfect sense.

She's got a firm grip on the collar of a huge beast of a dog, who's panting and slobbering and wagging its tail. "Say hi, Chooch!" she says to the dog, who woofs on command.

"Is he friendly?" I ask, even though it's pretty obvious Chooch is a sweetheart.

"Very," Julio's (probably) mom says.

I pet Chooch's giant head. He plunks down to a seated position and pants some more. Even sitting, his head reaches my waist. "Is he a Great Dane?"

She nods, smiling proudly. "Shake, Chooch."

The beast offers me his gargantuan paw, and we shake.

"Come on in, honey," she says. "I'm Mrs. Santos, but you can call me Jennifer."

She clears Chooch from the doorway. I "wipe my paws" on the doormat, just for fun, and Julio's mom—*Jennifer*—smiles her appreciation at me.

I step into their apartment and am greeted with warm, earthy colors everywhere—the sofa, the walls, the beautiful wood furniture. The décor definitely looks like someone planned out every detail, every throw pillow and candle, with thought and care and lots of money. But it looks lived-in, too. There are toys scattered here and there—stuffed animals, a set of large, colored blocks, and the same Fisher-Price xylophone I remember playing with as a kid.

And in the middle of all of it, there's my new buddy, Chooch, strolling through the room on his long legs like a miniature horse.

"Who are you?" a small voice asks. At first I don't see anyone, but then the blond head of a little girl, maybe four years old, pops out from behind the plush arm of the sofa. She's got beautiful light-brown skin, just like Julio's.

"This is Julio's school friend," Jennifer pipes in, putting a motherly hand on my shoulder. "What's your name again, honey? Julio told me but I forgot."

Julio told his mother my name!

"Ricky," I tell her, smiling ear to ear.

"That's a boy's name!" another small voice insists. This one comes from under the coffee table. A little boy crawls out and stares me up and down. He's blond too, and looks about the same age as the girl.

"It's short for Erica," I tell him, and he seems to ponder my explanation thoughtfully.

"These are the twins, Lily and Luke," Jennifer says. "Lily, how about you take Ricky to Julio's room?"

I'm going to Julio's room!

Lily blushes shyly, but then she comes over to me and takes my hand, tugging me in the right direction. I follow her down a long hall with several doors. The door at the very end opens and Julio comes out.

"Ricky!" he says. He meets me halfway . . . and hugs me!

I'm glad Lily's still holding my hand because, if not, I might have floated up to the ceiling.

"Scoot, Lilykins," Julio says, waving his hand at her playfully. Her peals of laughter echo in the hallway as she dashes off. Julio and I float . . . Actually, he's walking, I'm floating . . . back to his room. I step inside.

The first thing I see brings me crashing back down to Earth.

Lex.

He's sitting in a black beanbag chair, a video game controller in his hand. I hadn't even noticed the sounds of explosions and people's heads being lopped off until this moment, but now there's doom and gloom everywhere.

"Hey, Ricky," Lex says, his attention remaining glued to the mayhem on the large flat-screen TV in the corner. "You play?"

"Not really," I tell him, trying not to sound horribly disappointed (which, for the record, I am).

Julio steers his desk chair, a fancy black-leather model, into the middle of the room. "Here, sit," he says, and then he hops onto his bed and sits cross-legged.

I glance around the room and see that the desk chair and the beanbag are the only seating options other than the bed (yikes) and the floor (ugh), and I realize I dodged a bullet without even knowing it. At least there's *that*. I sink down into the desk chair, feeling miserable, but then it's like I'm transported into cloudland by, quite possibly, the most comfortable chair in the known world. "Wow!"

"I know," Julio says. "That chair is *awesome*! It's one of my dad's castoffs. I fall asleep in it some nights." He grabs another game controller and jumps into Lex's game.

He falls asleep in this chair . . . the chair I'm sitting in right now.

I take another glance around the room. The walls—what can be seen of them behind all the rock posters—are creamy white. A dark-green curtain is drawn over the large window. He's got a desk, nowhere near as cool as mine, that's so covered in sheet music it doesn't look like he studies there much. And in a corner, opposite the TV and some electronics stuff, is a drum kit with sparkly deep-green and chrome drums.

Mental note: Julio likes green.

There's a knock at the door and Jennifer pops her head in. "Pizza in ten, gang."

"Sweet," Julio and Lex say in unison, like they're some kind of synced robots or something.

"We've got plain cheese and pepperoni. Your choice, Ricky," Jennifer says to me before she pops back out.

I realize I'm still holding my backpack, so I let it slide to the floor. The guys are completely engrossed in their game and are kind of ignoring me. As comfortable as the Wonder Chair is, I feel annoyed, disappointed. "We *are* going to study at some point, right?" I ask them. Even doing homework for world history would be more interesting than watching them play video games all night.

"After we eat," Julio says. "You want to play? Come on. I'll show you how."

"Okay," I say. Maybe video games could be fun after all.

"I'll show her," Lex says.

Aaaaaaannndd—we're right back to the night sucking.

But it's actually not so bad. Lex shows me what all the different buttons on the controller do and explains how the game works (basically, kill or be killed). He kneels on the floor beside my chair, coaching me patiently, despite the fact that I keep dying five seconds into a new round. He even puts his fingers over mine at one point, helping me press the buttons, which is a little weird, but at least I manage to kill a bad guy! The whole time I try to focus on not getting killed and remembering which button does what, but my brain keeps drifting to:

Julio's fingers press all these same buttons.

Julio sleeps in this room.

He showers *right down the hall.*

"Watch the cobra!" Lex says. But it's too late. I'm dead again.

The door opens and Lily marches in. "Pizza!" she says, and then she tears back down the hallway for the kitchen.

The guys jump up *effortlessly* to follow her, but when I first stand up, my feet are kind of wonky. They glance at me, and I stretch, like I have a kink in my back or something (never mind that it's probably physically impossible to have any kind of kink after sitting in the Wonder Chair, at least for a normal person).

"I like to stretch when I've been sitting for a while," I lie. Even though my freaky body barely seems to register with them, I still don't necessarily want them watching me go through the process of toughening up my feet. "Be right there."

My have-to-stretch ploy works. They head out. My feet are decent within a step or two, which seems like an improvement. I take it slow anyway, so I don't have to limp. I can smell the pizza once I'm in the hall. In fact, it's like I can smell each individual ingredient. It's maybe the most delicious-smelling pizza *ever*. Up there with Dr. Dad's pot roast for sure.

Figures. Is there anything that isn't completely awesome about Julio's awesome life? Gorgeous apartment. Beautiful, classy mom. Great dog. Adorable siblings. Now add amazing pizza to the list. If Julio wasn't so hot, it'd be annoying (truth be told, it's a little annoying anyway).

"You good?" Lex asks quietly once I get to the kitchen.

I really wish it was Julio who'd asked me, but I nod at Lex and then ask Julio, "Where do you order pizza from? It smells great."

"Oh, my mom makes it herself," he says.

Of course she does.

The twins are already sitting at the table. I glance at the open chairs, wondering, *where does Julio sit?*

"Sit here!" Lily squeals, patting the seat next to her. I sit beside her, and Lex almost immediately sits next to me.

Of course he does.

Jennifer's in the kitchen, using a fancy pizza cutter with a round, rotating blade on her fancy, homemade pizza. There's a man in there with her. He's tall and lean like Julio. His hair's nearly black and short, with tight curls. When he turns away from the refrigerator, where he'd been filling glasses with ice from the in-door ice dispenser, I can see Julio's features in his face—the same nose, same eyes, same strong jawline. He stands behind Jennifer and wraps his arms around her. She smiles over her shoulder at him and lets him taste a dab of pizza sauce on her finger. He makes *yummy* noises and whispers something in her ear.

I hear Lex *harrumph* next to me. "My parents get that close, I might have to call the cops," he whispers. "These two are a little nauseating, huh?"

"I don't think so," I say, pretending that watching two parents fawning over each other doesn't make me so jealous and angry that I want to pretend that they're nauseating because it hurts just to look at them. I want to pretend that I have no idea what Lex is talking about. But of course I know *exactly* what he's talking about.

In the X-Car on the way home, I'm trying to remember the stuff I studied, but mostly what's running through my head is how Lex pretty much ruined everything. Every time I turned around, there he was, butting his nose into everything. Didn't seem to bother Julio at all. The longer I stayed, the more I just wanted to get out of there. I did my geoscience homework while Lex kept drilling Julio on beginning Spanish vocab. (I discovered Julio doesn't speak any Spanish beyond *hasta la vista, baby*.)

I left at about nine o'clock, and Lex left with me, walking me to the elevator. Thank God he was going up to the twelfth floor (where he lives) and I was going down. When the up elevator came first, I was finally rid of him.

Downstairs at their *oh-so-luxurious building*, the doorman didn't automatically open the door for me. It was only after I went to grab the door handle myself that their guy got up, and that was just for show because I went out on my own anyway.

Back at home, Gus has the door open, waiting for me as I get out of my X-Car. We might not have marble and flowers, but our doormen are pros.

"Welcome home, Miss Erica," he says as I pass through the doorway, like I've been away on a long vacation or something. "Where were you off to this fine evening?"

"Studying at a friend's house," I tell him. For some reason, his question doesn't seem nosy today. It just seems nice. "You know what, Gus? You're a great doorman."

He blushes and looks down at his shiny black shoes.

"Really. You always have the door open, waiting for me."

"I just try to make things a little easier on folks," Gus says, still blushing. Then he catches sight of a lady with a bunch of department store shopping bags exiting a cab right out front and he hustles off to make things a little easier on her.

I head for the elevator, grinning, warmed up from the inside.

Upstairs, I find Dr. Dad snoozing on the sofa. I close the door quietly, but it wakes him up anyway.

"You're back," he says before a big yawn takes over his face. "Is your head crammed with knowledge now?"

"Big time." I say, as I plop down on the sofa.

"Did this Julio feed you enough? I could warm up some pot roast."

"Yes, Dad." I say, rolling my eyes. "His other friend was there, too. It was more like a group thing."

"You look awfully nice for a 'group thing,'" he says, giving me a look like he actually *gets it*, like maybe he gets everything—how much I like Julio, how excited I was that he invited me over, maybe even how disappointed I am that the evening didn't turn out like I hoped.

"It's not like he noticed," I say, sighing deeply.

Dr. Dad gives me a grin. "Don't be so sure." Just when I'm feeling all warm and gooey, Dad produces the pack he keeps my weekly shot supplies in and says, "We forgot this earlier."

He forgot. I avoided reminding him.

"How about you give it a try?" he asks.

"*Fine*," I say, surprising both of us.

He reminds me that the alcohol wipe comes first and I should apply it in a circular motion. I choose my abdomen today since I got the shot in my thigh last week. Then he coaches me through the other steps—putting air in the syringe, measuring out the precise amount of medicine, and how I can pinch the skin if I want to.

Then it's just me and the needle.

"Insert the needle at a forty-five degree angle," he says.

I adjust the position—and then go for it. The medicine burns slightly as I push it into my skin, but it's over in a few seconds.

Dad gives me a *bursting-with-pride* look like I've accomplished something momentous, which is ridiculous.

I roll my eyes. *Yay me.*

39

adios, fourteen, don't let the
door hit you on the way out

It's my birthday and my family has the whole day planned for
me. Stop one was McGonigle Hall to attend a rally honoring the
women's Owls basketball team, which got knocked out in the first
round of the playoffs but did better than anticipated overall. Their
coach said the team's unexpected success was "due in no small
part to rookie sensations Bloom, Daye, and McCaffery"—before
giving Dani, Noland, and their teammate Deb McCaffery special
awards. The whole thing was super cool.

Dr. Dad and I are waiting in the lobby for Dani and Noland to
come out. He'll be handing me off to Mom for a special birthday
dinner back at the house in Mount Airy—like it's a birthday relay
race and I'm the baton. But I'm a happy baton because Mom's
serving up her famous strawberry-short birthday cake, made with
shortbread biscuits and fresh strawberries. She even whips the
cream herself. It's seriously delicious.

"Do you need to sit?" Dad asks me.

"I'm good," I say, and it dawns on me that I'm not just saying that because it's what I always say. My feet actually don't hurt at the moment.

Suddenly, Mom appears, all bubbly and proud. "Wasn't that terrific!" she says.

I watch as Mom and Dad exchange nods of greeting, still not used to this Pleasant-And-Cooperative-Coffee-Shop-Version of them. Chances are this current version is like a rainbow—nice while it lasts, but probably brief. The Disaster could resurface at any time.

"Should we find you a seat?" Mom asks me.

"I asked her that too," Dad says, a bit defensively.

As I was saying . . .

But thankfully it doesn't turn into a contest to determine which one of them is the more caring parent. Dani and Noland show up a second later, and after a round of hugs and congratulations and Happy Birthdays, Dr. Dad takes off and Mom tells us to wait outside while she gets the car.

We head out of McGonigle Hall and Dani says, "You're walking good, Roo."

"Yeah. It's weird," I say back. "Good weird, though."

I spy what looks like a wrapped birthday gift in the shopping bag that Noland's carrying, and say, "Oooh. Is that for me?"

Noland moves the shopping bag to her other arm, away from my prying eyes. "Maaaybe."

We pile into Mom's car, with me awarded shotgun, supposedly for my birthday but we all know it's because it's harder for me to climb in the back of a two-door car.

"On to Roo's Birthday Bonanza—stop two of three!" Dani announces.

I look back at Dani and Noland. "There's a third stop?"

Noland smiles and says, "Maaaybe."

Mom, Dani, and Noland sing "Happy Birthday" while I wait, staring down at the plate of pure happiness before me that is Mom's strawberry-short birthday cake.

Finally they get to the "and many more . . ." part and I dive in. The strawberries and whipped cream bulge out from in-between the biscuits but I somehow manage to get a little bit of everything onto my fork, which I happily shovel into my mouth.

"Mmmmm!" I say, licking an escapee smudge of whipped cream from my lip.

"Ma," Dani says in-between inhaled bites, "you've outdone yourself."

"Why thank you," Mom says with a big grin. She scoops up a bite herself but then says, "Time for your present, Ricky."

I have no idea what she might have gotten for me (other than *not the new phone I desperately wanted*), but the strawberry-short birthday cake has me in such a great mood, I decide to shriek and say I love it—whatever it is.

Mom presents me with a box about the size of a brick (but lighter). She grins ear to ear. "It's actually from me and your dad," she says.

Huh. Unexpected. If both Mom and Dad chipped in and wanted their names in the "from" column, it must be kind of a big deal. Dani and Noland both have the same bursting-with-anticipation smiles on their faces, so they must know what's in the box.

My fingers struggle to pry open the wrapping paper, which Mom seems to have used an entire roll of Scotch tape on.

"Try this," Mom says, handing me a *Dr. Peter Bloom, DDS*, promotional letter opener, like the one I have back at Dad's. I guess it was way too handy for Mom to throw away.

It easily breaks the hermetic seal, like some kind of magic tool in a video game. I tear off the rest of the paper, and . . . it's a new iPhone!

"Yes, yes, yes, YES!" I legit–shriek when I get over being speechless. "But you said you and Dad were *in agreement* on the no-new-phone front."

Mom's grin threatens to take over her entire face now. "We also agreed to intentionally throw you off the track. We wanted it to be a surprise."

"Sneaky, Mom," I say, as I wrangle the box open. "Super sneaky." Dani and Noland hover over me as I pop the phone out.

"I already activated it for you. Same number," Dani says.

The phone's up and running in mere seconds and the screen is downright huge! Before I can even begin to explore my big beautiful new phone, it makes a loud, single *ping*.

"You got a text!" Dani says.

Three guesses who the text is from.

He seems to have sent me a picture, which now, thankfully, won't be the size of a postage stamp. I open up his text and a selfie of Oliver holding a handwritten sign that says, "Happy B Day to the coolest girl I know" appears. The sign's sweet and all but it's his new haircut that stands out—an almost buzz cut, like in the post-cancer/hair-just-growing-back picture. The one I thought he looked super cute in.

"Whoa. Who's that?" Dani asks.

I quickly cover the screen. "No one," I blurt out, but I realize answering like that is just asking for trouble. So I add, "Just a friend."

"Mmm hmm," Noland says.

"It's not like that with Oliver. Really."

Noland slings an arm around Dani's shoulder and says, "Sometimes it's like that way before you realize it's like that."

"Can I please just enjoy my new phone in peace?" They back off but I can still *feel* Noland grinning. I want to text Oliver back but then they'll just give me more shit. "So who should I text first from my awesome new phone?" I ask.

"Not gonna holla back at the buzz-cut cutie?" Noland suggests. I smirk at her.

"Nuh, uh," Mom says, "I ought to get the first text. Either me or Dad." She laughs. "No, definitely me."

Mom for sure deserves the first text after that delicious dinner. I cock my thumbs at the ready, wondering what I should type, wanting to come up with something *special*. She deserves that too.

Mom holds her cell phone, waiting.

Inspiration strikes. My thumbs fly.

I wait, nervous for some reason. Mom's phone vibrates and, as she reads my text, she gets an on-the-verge-of-tears smile on her face. I have a feeling I do too.

What I wrote was: **We will survive no matter what! Luv u!**

Just when I think I can't possibly take any more awesome . . . there's more awesome. The third-and-final stop on Roo's Birthday Bonanza turns out to be a house party. A *college* house party, which apparently involves blaring music and about a hundred people crammed into a house built for a family of five. Not that I'm complaining.

I cling to Dani and Noland as they weave me through the throng of people in the living room toward a kitchen in the back of the house. There's a cooler on the kitchen floor, which is packed mostly with beer, but Dani roots around and manages to find me a can of lemonade. She grabs two beers—she and Noland are only nineteen but it's not like I'm going to narc on them—and then leads the way to the back door and out of the house.

It's nicer in the backyard, cooler and quieter.

Flickering light from dozens of candles illuminates a green leafy space where several small groups of people sit and chat.

We head over to one group, which consists of four girls and one guy. I recognize their teammate Deb McCaffery.

"This is my kid sis," Dani announces. "Roo, this is, basically, the people worth hanging out with at this party." Her friends laugh. I'm about to let them know, for the record, that my name's really Erica, or Ricky if they want, but then I decide to just be Roo for tonight.

Dani sits cross-legged on the grass beside a couple of the girls, and that's when it dawns on me—they're all sitting on the grass. Even my new-and-improved body isn't going to be thrilled with that.

Noland saves me, snagging a beach chair from a nearby patio and presenting it to me. "Here you go, birthday girl. You get the place of honor on your special night." She's so slick, she makes the whole *chair-because-it's-my-birthday-and-not-some-other-weird-reason* thing totally believable. She even holds the rickety beach chair steady as I sit.

"Today's your actual birthday?" one of the girls asks.

I nod, and they all sing "Happy Birthday," raising their drinks in my honor.

Dani reaches into her messenger bag (she doesn't do purses) and hands me a small, squishy package. It's the same wrapped present I saw in the bag Noland was carrying earlier.

"It's from both of us," Dani says.

I tear open the (thankfully non-hermetically sealed) wrapping paper and find a Temple Owls jersey! I hold it up for a better look as Dani's friends chant, "*Hoot, hoot!*" It's got Dani's number four on it and ROO on the back.

"You likey?" Dani asks.

"I lovey!" I say, hugging the jersey to my body.

"So, how old are you?" the one guy asks.

"Fifteen," I say, trying to sound . . . I don't know . . . seventeen?

"Wow," he says. "I would have guessed a little older." He winks at me and I blush a little, which is totally dumb because he probably just said that to be nice. For a moment, it's like a sudden wave of self-consciousness nearly drowns me. But then I think about Oliver and can almost hear his voice in my head: *stay in the present.*

The present is: I'm in a pretty backyard lit by candlelight, hanging out with college kids at a *college party*, on my fifteenth birthday. I'm with Dani and Noland, who I love, who love me. And a cute guy—a cute college guy—winked at me. I'm here.

The conversation turns to basketball and classes and campus gossip, and I hang on their every word, even though I don't know much about any of it.

And the whole time, I keep thinking to myself—Best. Birthday. Ever.

fifteen is the new fuck, i still have to go to school

Even though I printed out Oliver's photo this morning and stuck it in my mirror frame with all the kangaroo cards, I'm kind of dying to see his buzz cut IRL, so I hustle (okay, Ricky-hustle) out of my X-Car and into Nurse Jeff's office. Oliver's already there, sitting in his usual spot by the window.

As I slide into the seat across from him, I find myself wondering if he's been dying for me to see his buzz cut IRL too.

"Cool haircut," I say. It even makes his Captain America hoodie look hot.

He grins. "I wanted to get you something special, and I figured sacrificing my hair in your honor would work." He takes an envelope out of his backpack and slides it across the table toward me.

Wait, is he giving me a lock of his hair? Um, way-weird.

But inside the envelope is an acknowledgment from a company called Locks of Love, thanking me for hair donated in my name, which, it goes on to say, will be used to create wigs for low-income kids with hair loss caused by medical conditions.

I stare at the card, at its adorable little logo—two faces, a boy and girl—in a pink heart, and I'm kind of amazed and surprised and gushy all over. I barely know what to say and finally come up with, "This is crazy-awesome-cool!"

Oliver grins again. "So how was your birthday?"

"Pretty crazy-awesome-cool all around." I show him my fabulous new iPhone.

"Nice!" he says.

"And my sister gave me this way-cool jersey," I say, beaming. Naturally I wore it today. I show him the back, adding, "Four is her number."

"Roo? Is that her nickname?" Oliver asks.

"No, I'm Roo." Before I can explain further, I get a text alert on my fabulous new phone. I practically cheer because I *love* my fabulous new phone!

I read the text. "It's just Dr. Hunt's office confirming my second infusion on Friday," I tell Oliver.

"That's right! Your infusion's coming up." He grabs his phone and taps around on the screen.

"Did you just put it in your calendar?" I pretend to be annoyed but I'm laughing.

"Guilty," he says with a shrug.

"You know. When I dreamed about high school boys obsessing over my body, this *wasn't* what I had in mind."

He laughs. "I'm just happy for you."

"What's all this?" I ask, waving at a collection of pamphlets and envelopes spread out in front of him on the table. I hadn't even noticed they were there—blinded by his hot haircut, I guess.

"Some stuff my mom wants me to look at."

I pick up a brochure from the pile he's formed, realizing I'm being nosy, but it's not like Oliver would mind. It's a school brochure of some sort. "God, are you shopping for colleges already?"

"High schools," Oliver says, handing me a different brochure. "This is where I'm going. My parents want me to at least look at some other schools but it's no contest."

I look at the brochure for his no-contest school. It's called Hayre Community Leadership Academy, a school close by in Center City. "Why are you so high on this one?" I ask.

"HCLA is all about getting involved, making a difference. Community service is part of the curriculum," he says. "It just seems like the perfect place for me."

I glance at the brochure again. It does seem right up his alley.

"Do you know where you're going?" he asks.

His question stumps me. I've been so focused on getting all the catch-up work done so I can graduate and get out of this hellhole, I've barely thought about life afterward. "I guess I might go back to West Mount Airy High, where I started back in September. I mean, hopefully. If my body calms down enough." *It would probably mean going back to live with Mom. Do I want that? Does she?*

"Did you like it there?" Oliver asks, in that practical way of his, like my opinion and feelings matter.

"Yeah. I mean, at first I did. Everyone from my neighborhood goes there. We all know each other. I had friends there. It was cool."

"Wait," he says. "Why did you only like it 'at first'?"

All I can think is—*I do* not *want to talk about it.* I've never really told anyone what happened, not even Dani. But Oliver's kind of the perfect person to tell, so I do, I tell him:

"When I got sick, everybody just . . . dropped me. Friends I'd known since grade school flat out stopped talking to me. People didn't give me crap about it, like the shits at this school, but the silent treatment was almost worse. If I tried talking to my friends, they'd be polite but they'd find some excuse to get away from me as quickly as possible. Like I was contagious or something."

I watch as Oliver tries to process what I've just confessed to him. For once, he's speechless. All he can come up with is, "Why?"

"I seriously have no clue," I say. "It's like it was all just too colossally weird for them to deal with."

"Lucky them," Oliver says, sounding somewhat pissed off. "They had a choice."

"*Right?!*" I say.

"Why would you want to go back there?"

"I don't know. If the new medicine really works, maybe I'll be more normal again and . . ." Oliver folds his arms, skeptically. "I don't know, okay? It's just where I always planned to go. It's a good school."

I'm pretty sure he wants to argue further, but to his credit he drops the subject and goes back to collecting his papers.

"Do you know about the party?" he says, fishing the familiar large postcard out of his pile and handing it to me.

"The CHOP party?" I ask, half-relieved there isn't some cool party I wasn't invited to and half-bummed there isn't some cool party I *might* have been invited to. "Yeah, I got the same postcard." Clearly I'm less excited about this than he seems to be.

"You should come!" Oliver says in his clueless/cheerful way. "They're fun. I go every year."

Of course you do. Hot haircut or not, Oliver's gotta Oliver.

surprise número tres . . .
this is getting to be a thing

School had the nerve to *not drag* today. Of course this happens on a day when my post-school plans are getting toxic medicine pumped into my veins for two-plus hours. Worse yet—my X-Car made supernaturally good time getting to Dr. Hunt's office from school.

I thank the driver and extricate myself from the back seat. Mom's waiting for me at the entrance to the building.

"Hi, honey," she says once I reach her. I give her a big hug because I'm still all mushy and warm with post-birthday glow. I've been texting Mom every day just for fun, and I'm even wearing my Temple Owls jersey again so I could show it off to her.

We ride up in the elevator, just the two of us. "The jersey fits great," Mom says. "Dani wasn't sure about the size. Do you like it?"

"I love it," I say. "And look . . ." I turn, showing her the "ROO" on the back.

"Ah, perfect," Mom says. "Dani wasn't sure what to put on the back either."

We get off at the sixth floor and head for Dr. Hunt's office. Everything is pretty much the same as last time: Martha weighs me, gets the IV started, takes my vitals.

"Do we have to do the Benadryl?" I ask her. "It made me tired, like, *forever* last time."

"I'll check with Dr. Hunt, but we can probably hold off," she says. "If you start to feel real itchy during the infusion, we can give it to you then."

When Martha gets back, she lets us know Dr. Hunt was fine with holding off on the Benadryl. She gets the infusion started and now there's just the two-hour wait.

Crap. Maybe sleeping through this wasn't such a bad idea.

"How busy with homework are you this weekend?" Mom asks me.

"Not too busy," I say. "Why?"

"I was hoping maybe Dani could bring you up to Mount Airy on Sunday. There's something I want to show you." She takes her cell out of her purse, brings up a website, and then hands the phone to me. "Here's a preview."

It's a real estate listing of some sort. I flip through photos of a nice-looking place. Wood floors. A fireplace. Large windows. There are some outside shots too. Lots of grass and flowers. Very pretty. "What is this?" I ask, flipping through the photos a second time.

"It's the condo I've made an offer on."

I stop flipping. "You're selling the house?" I feel angry/guilty/sad. "Why? Because of me?"

"Honey, it's more house than I need with Dani gone. And the condo's all on one floor. It'll be much easier for you."

I hand her phone back. I feel sick to my stomach, and it's not the medicine. "You don't have to move for me," I whisper.

"Of course I do," Mom says firmly. "Why wouldn't I move out of a house that's no longer suitable for my daughter? That was the plan all along."

"It was?" I say, genuinely surprised.

"Yes! Sending you down to your dad's was always supposed to be temporary. I told you that, but I don't think you heard me."

I lie back and close my eyes, wishing I'd taken the Benadryl so I'd be sleepy enough to nod off on this conversation. "Now Dad's moved too. Everyone's changing their whole lives just because I got sick."

"Lives change for all sorts of reasons, Ricky," Mom says. "Our lives changed when your dad left. Dani's living with Noland. I'm thinking of going back to school—"

"You are?"

"Yup," Mom says, her face lighting up in that striking way that makes me proud to be her daughter. "So . . . if you come up on Sunday, you can see the condo . . . what do you kids say now? IRL?"

I give her a playful eye roll.

"It's so pretty, honey. I just know you'll love it."

I already love seeing her this happy. "Sure. I'm game," I tell her.

And I start thinking about moving back to Mount Airy, living with Mom again, instead of staying with Dad. Maybe going back to West Mount Airy High and hanging with my old friends again (and forgetting about how they all ghosted me).

The problem is—I'm not sure I want to do any of that . . . *IRL*.

The condo is just as gorgeous as Mom said, possibly even prettier than in the pictures. It's part of a large complex of condos and apartments in Chestnut Hill made up of about a dozen separate buildings surrounded by green as far as the eye can see. The unit she bid on even has a back door, like a real house, with a patio. It's amazing.

So that's what I tell Mom: "This is amazing!"

"Seriously awesome, Ma," Dani chimes in, with Noland nodding in agreement by her side.

"Isn't it?" Mom says. She leads us into what would be my bedroom. It's smaller than my room at Dad's but has nice light and the same beautiful view as the rest of the place. No private bathroom like at Dad's though.

Mom points out a different, smaller bedroom. "I'm thinking I'll use this as an office, but I'll put a sofa bed in here for when you guys visit," she says, smiling at Dani and Noland. The mere mention of the words *sofa bed* makes me recoil, but I'm sure Mom will get some nice, new, Not-From-Hell version.

She leads us back into the main room, stopping briefly to make note of a loose door handle on a linen closet in the hallway.

"We'll be just half a block from the train station, Ricky. And the train will take you practically to West Mount Airy High's front door. Of course, you'll be able to drive in another year. Might be time for me to get some new wheels, give you the Honda?"

I listen to her happily rattle off details of her plans for me—for us—and I can't help thinking about Dr. Dad, about how he moved into the new apartment basically for me. I find myself worrying that he's gotten used to having me around and might be lonely without me. But then a second later, I think: *Did he worry about Mom and Dani and me being lonely when* he *left?* He obviously wasn't worried enough to stay.

We leave the building and the loudest sound is a mower in the distance somewhere. This neighborhood is practically freaking paradise but I've grown used to the obnoxious buzz of Center City. It might be *too* quiet here for my tastes.

I hug Mom goodbye and get into Dani's car. Noland decides to drive, so Dani gets in the back.

"We're gonna stop at the co-op for produce," Dani reminds Noland once we get on the road. A short while later, we park on Germantown Avenue. I get out of the car with them since it's kind of hot out, but I see a low wall along the store entrance where a few people are sitting and decide to wait there.

I sit on the far end of the wall and close my eyes, resting. There's a slight breeze that cuts through the heat of the sun. It's a somewhat ridiculously beautiful afternoon.

"Oh my God . . . Ricky, is that you?"

My eyes shoot open. It's Meghan. My *former* friend. She sits beside me on the wall, all bubbly.

"It's been, like, forever! My mom ran into your mom at the CVS. She said you're living downtown?"

"Yeah. With my dad," I say.

"Oooh, right! I forgot." Meghan grimaces, like the dissolution of my family was an unsightly mole I had removed, better left unmentioned. "You look really good," she goes on. "You were so sick before. I felt so bad for you."

"I'm still sick," I say bluntly.

She ignores what I said and instead lifts up the sleeve of her T-shirt. "Look what Jenna and I did!" There's a tiny tattoo of a bunny on her shoulder. "Jenna got a star. You should get one too! Maybe a little kangaroo? Or a music note? I know you love to sing."

I seriously wish I could punch her in the face but I know it would just hurt my hand. "Yeah, I'm on this big-deal medicine now," I tell her. "I have to be super careful about avoiding infections. So I can't do anything stupid like get a tattoo."

Her face goes from confused to weirded out to pissed off—it's fun to watch.

"Um . . . *whatever*," she says in response.

"Yeah. *Whatever*," I say back.

Meghan up and leaves after that, just as Dani and Noland arrive beside me. I get up and stretch out some kinks in my legs.

"Was that Meghan?" Dani asks.

"Yep," I say.

"Did you want to hang out with her for a bit?"

"Nope."

power to the polka dot

The South Street Goodwill may not be Teen Heaven, but Dani swears it's the best place to get clothes. She asked if I was up for a detour before she dropped me off back at Dad's and I said *sure.*

Dani and Noland are looking at army jackets, since the one Dani practically lives in has gotten so ratty Noland threatened to set it on fire. I checked out the CDs first, like I always do, and picked up *Best Disco Hits, volume 1.* (I blame Gloria Gaynor—and Mom—for my recent interest in disco.) Now I'm searching for hidden treasure among the racks of clothing. I grab a brand-new-looking white, sleeveless top with blue stitching on the neckline and scan it for stains or other blemishes. It checks out, so I add it to the collection of stuff I'm taking to the dressing room.

The next rack is mostly dresses, which I don't wear that much, but some of them are super cute. I grab one that's dark-blue with bright-blue polka dots and hold it up to my body in front of a mirror.

Who knows if I have the chutzpah to rock polka dots in public, but the size seems right and it's only seven dollars. Plus, it buttons down the front, which makes things easier. I add it to the pile, and for the first time all day, there's a twinge in my left elbow, the one that's supporting the mound of try-ons.

It dawns on me: I've been at this—walking, standing, bending, carrying a mound of clothes—for at least forty-five minutes. And that's after the visit to Mount Airy. I'm not exhausted and my feet don't even hurt. There's just been that one twinge in my elbow. I straighten my arm to get the stiffness out and the twinge goes away.

A rush of emotion comes over me. It's been happening all week. It's like all this hope/excitement quickly followed by *don't-get-your-hopes-up* dread/worry.

I hear Oliver in my head again: *stay in the present.* I shut my eyes for a second and take a deep breath, trying to free my mind of all of that stuff.

Okay, I'm here in the South Street Goodwill. My body doesn't hurt and that's a good thing. And I hereby vow to publicly rock those polka dots if that dress fits.

I head into the dressing room and survey my collection of possibilities, even though all I really want to try on is the dumb dress. The hang-up is that it's so *girly*, and for months I've felt like a blob of pain that's not female or male.

But today, in this moment, I feel human, *human-girl* even.

I grab the dress and start undoing the buttons. They slide right out of the buttonholes *effortlessly*. This dress desperately wants to be mine.

Of course, it fits like a glove. There's no mirror in the little curtained-off dressing cubby, but I can tell. It's snug in the right places, hangs loose where it's supposed to, and isn't too big in the shoulders or the boobs. Plus it covers my knobby knees, which doesn't suck.

"Roo? You in here?" I hear Dani say from beyond the curtain.

"Yep," I say. I slide back the curtain and step outside.

"Niiiice!" Noland says, walking around me to admire the dress from all angles.

"That dress is *adorable*," Dani says.

I scowl at her. *Adorable* is not what I was hoping for.

Noland tsks at Dani and says, "It's not adorable. It's funky-hot." As usual, Noland knows exactly how to make a moment perfect. She steers me to the huge wall mirror and nods, encouraging me to take a look.

I'm a little startled by what I see. It's me but different. It's me definitely looking like a girl in a funky-hot polka dot dress. I sway my hips a little, making the dress swish.

A fill-in-the-blank takes over—

I'm walking down the hall at school in my funky-hot polka dots. Not limping, because my feet don't hurt at that moment. Walking right by that buttwipe Ronnie Drake and ignoring him. Walking by Oliver, who gives me a semi-smile. Walking up to Julio . . .

"You are *not* getting that jacket," I hear Noland tell Dani, drawing me out of my polka dot fantasy world.

I glance at Dani, who has on an army jacket that is clearly too small to zip over her boobs unless she discovers a way to defy physics.

"I'll wear it open," Dani says.

Noland gives Dani a shake of her head that must mean *not a chance,* because Dani immediately takes the jacket off and puts it on a pile of rejected try-ons.

I glance at the pile and can't believe what's in there—a Captain America jacket just like Oliver's!

I check it out. No holes, no stains. One of the front pockets is a little torn at the seam but even I could manage to sew that up. I check the size—medium. It would totally fit me. For a second I consider buying it just because I'm sure Oliver would get a huge kick out of seeing me in it.

"Not really your style, Roo," Dani says.

I laugh. "Yeah, I know. My friend's a total Captain America nerd."

"The Captain is the coolest," Dani says matter-of-factly.

"Is it that friend *Oliver*?" Noland asks, grinning. That makes Dani grin too.

I quickly deposit the jacket back on the pile of stuff waiting to be returned to the racks. It's not like I'd have the nerve to wear it anyway.

everything's going super-awesome . . .
so naturally, i screw it all up

School was—dare I say it?—kind of fun today. And yes, of course,
I'm wearing my funky-hot polka dot dress, which both Oliver and
Nurse Jeff complimented first thing this morning.

The rest of the day, my classes felt almost magical. Not really
magical but *normal*. Like I was a normal human girl, having a normal
human day at school, interacting with other normal humans, not
hurting and feeling tragically weird and damaged. That was the
magical part for me.

I head for the music room before my Afterschool Special with
Jenkins because I absolutely need Julio to see me in this dress.

"Dig the dots, man," Julio says when I walk in.

I could have done without the "man" part but *he noticed the dress!*

"It was a birthday present to myself," I tell them.

"Shit. When was your birthday?" Lex asks, sounding like he's
legitimately bummed he didn't know. Weird.

"It was Saturday. Don't worry about it."

"Happy birthday!" Julio says.

"*Belated*," Lex grumbles. Again—super weird.

Lex offers me the chair beside him and I lower myself down gracefully.

"How about a birthday request?" Lex asks me. "Whatever you'd like."

I'd *like* for the offer to have come from Julio but it's still kind of sweet. I choose Green Day's "Holiday," even though the song has nothing to do with actual holidays.

Lex launches into the song, and Julio jumps in with Tré Cool's killer drum licks. I bop my head to the beat, singing along and thinking—I've been sung to, taken to an awesome party, gotten the best birthday gifts of my entire life . . . and then my mind drifts into a mini fill-in-the-blank, where I get one more surprise gift—a birthday kiss from Julio.

Stay in the present, I hear Oliver say.

In this present moment, I am a legit happy human girl.

But then a commotion out in the hall—yelling and laughing—takes me out of the moment. Lex and Julio hear it too and stop playing. Julio's cell makes the Snapchat *clink* sound and he whips it out of his pocket.

"Oh shit!" Julio says with a laugh, holding up his phone for me and Lex to see. The image disappears within a couple seconds, but it's there long enough for me to recognize Oliver, on the floor by the main doors, with some sort of yellowish slime down the front of his shirt. The commotion in the hall grows louder. My heart starts to pound.

"Come on!" Julio says excitedly. He and Lex race out of the room.

I get up slowly and follow them. Dread seems to propel me down the hall to the mob of kids, all shoving and squeezing in to get a better look. I slide around the crowd, hugging the wall by the elevator. I don't want to see what's happening, but I can't *not* see it. I know I should do something, *anything*, but now that I'm here, I can't seem to make myself move.

The crowd somehow parts, even though I don't want it to, don't want to see—

Oliver. Still on his knees, trying to collect his books, which are scattered on the floor. The yellowish slime isn't just on his shirt. It's on his jeans, in his hair.

Ronnie Drake and Matt Booker stand over him. Ronnie's holding a package of fruit cups.

"Come on, Olivia, eat up! Captain America says fruit salad's good for you," he sneers, pouring another fruit cup on Oliver's head and tossing the empty container on the floor with several others.

Matt Booker opens the last fruit cup and pours it over Oliver's backpack. "Make sure your little bear friend gets some, too. He looks hungry!"

The mob around Oliver gawks and laughs. Half of them have their phones out, documenting his humiliation.

I look down the hall, toward the office. *Where's Principal Piranha? A teacher? Anyone? They must hear what's going on. For God's sake, where are they?*

Oliver starts to gasp for breath as the crowd crushes in closer.

"Aw. What's the matter, Olivia?" Ronnie Drake taunts, pretending to pat Oliver on the head but he's really just mashing up the bits of fruit.

I watch as Oliver's Teflon coating breaks. The crowd, the sneering laughter, the camera phones. It's all too much. It breaks him, and he starts to cry.

"What a pathetic douche," Lex says. I didn't even realize he was right beside me.

Of course, it's right then that Oliver looks up and sees me. "Ricky . . ." he gasps.

And now everyone's looking at me.

Say something! Tell them all to go to hell. Help Oliver pick up his books, walk him outside and tell him it's no big deal, that they'll get bored and move on to tormenting somebody else.

But I'm frozen. I can't move.

"Wait? Are you *friends* with that guy?" It's Lex asking.

Oliver stares at me, waiting for my answer, *everyone* seems to be waiting for my answer. And then Ronnie Drake nods at Matt Booker, a leering grin on his face like—*let's get her too.*

The elevator doors rumble open behind me.

"School's over. You should all go the fuck home!" I say as I step back, onto the elevator.

Say you're his friend! Get off the fucking elevator and help him! Do it right now, before it's too late!

But I can't. Not with them all staring. Not with that look on Ronnie Drake's face. Not with Oliver *crying in front of everyone.* I just can't.

I let the elevator doors rumble closed on the mob, on the laughter, on Oliver.

I ride up in shock. Horrified at myself. Numb.

In Jenkins's classroom, I slide into my seat by his desk in a daze.

"Ms. Bloom?" Mr. Jenkins says, looking concerned. "Is something wrong?"

It takes me a moment to find my voice. "I just did something horrible to my best friend."

"Mr. Horn?"

I nod, fighting off tears.

"Is he okay?" Mr. Jenkins's face has gone from concerned to alarmed.

In a flash I realize there *is* something I can do. "No! He's in the hall downstairs, right by the elevator. Can you go, please? Hurry!"

Jenkins rushes out of the room.

I sit, paralyzed again. Heart pounding. Waiting. I wait forever.

Finally, Jenkins comes back. His face is a mask but I sense the anger behind it. "The hall was empty when I got down there, but I found Mr. Horn in the nurse's office. His mother's coming to get him." He sits at his desk, his eyes drilling into me. "Would you like to tell me what happened? Oliver is refusing to disclose the details."

"Ronnie Drake and Matt Booker happened," I whisper.

"You told me *you* did something horrible."

"I didn't help him."

"But you *did* help him," Jenkins says, his face softening. "You told me. You got help from an adult. That was the appropriate thing to do."

I shake my head, wiping away the tears slipping out of my eyes. *Way too little. Way too late.*

In my X-Car on the way home, I try calling Oliver's cell. Of course, he doesn't pick up. I try texting—**pls, pls, pls call me!**—but he doesn't text back.

And even though it's completely obvious he doesn't want to talk to me, I try his home phone because my skin's crawling and I don't know what else to do. I'm stunned when someone actually picks up. It's Oliver's mother, though, not him.

"Hello?" she says.

"Is Oliver there?" I ask, my heart racing. I hadn't gotten as far as figuring out what I was going to say.

"Is this Ricky?" Her voice is calm, almost sympathetic, not laced with icy daggers like I deserve.

"Is he okay?"

"He's okay," she says, "but I'm sorry, he doesn't want to talk to you. I'm having trouble even getting him to talk to me."

"Can you tell him . . ."

That I'm a jerk! That of course I'm his friend! That I am so, so sorry!

". . . that I called?"

She lets out a sigh, tells me she will, and hangs up.

And that's that. He won't talk to me. Maybe he'll never talk to me again. He probably hates me.

I hate me too.

44

failure is not an option

I wake up burning again. Okay, more like smoldering. It's not anywhere near as bad as the last time, but it's bad enough. I panic. *Why is this happening?* I haven't woken up feeling this crappy since before I started on the new medicine and my third infusion is still weeks away. I make a mental note to call Dr. Hunt's office and try to see him before then. *Be proactive*, I can almost hear Oliver say.

Oliver.

That's when I remember everything. The plan I came up with last night as I was falling asleep is to corner him in Nurse Jeff's office before school and force him to accept my apology. Now I'm not so sure if I can do it. I briefly consider cutting school. Dr. Dad doesn't watch me like a hawk anymore. He trusts me now.

Okay. So I can't cut school. But I could ask for permission to stay home sick. It wouldn't even be a scam, since I feel like crap. Of course, I have two tests today—in Spanish and world history.

I studied and I want to get them over with. Plus if I don't try to talk to Oliver today, right away, it's just going to get harder and harder and . . .

Uuuuuuggghhh!

Okay. So I'm definitely going to school.

I can either sleep for another fifteen minutes or take a shower. I decide getting under some hot water is an absolute must, so now I just have to brave getting up. I try to sit up, but it hurts, so I decide to get gravity on my side. I inch my feet to the edge of the bed, and bend my knees as I shift the rest of my body sideways. I rest there for a moment before tightening my stomach muscles, grabbing the edge of the mattress with both hands, and slowly wrenching the top half of my body upright.

Piece of cake!

Sitting there on the edge of the bed, my body seems to calm down some, like the blood's flowing better or something. Maybe I was just stiff and needed to get moving.

I test my feet. They seem sort of medium-bad.

It's a slow crawl to the bathroom, but I get there and get the water running. As soon as I step into the heavenly/hot shower, I know I made the right choice.

Right away, my joints loosen up, my muscles start responding to instructions from my brain, you know, like a normal person's would. I don't bother washing for the first few minutes. I just stand there and let the glorious geyser work its magic on me.

This would be ecstasy if I didn't have to face Oliver in forty minutes.

Oliver.

I'm on a mission, as I walk down the empty hall at school. I did my best to pump myself up on the ride over. I know he's mad—and he has a right to be—but I'm determined to get him to forgive me. Somehow.

I walk into Nurse Jeff's office and it's just me and Oliver. Nurse Jeff is off somewhere else.

Oliver glances up at me before quickly looking away, burying his face in a textbook. I try to move forward but I seem to have left my determination out in the hallway. Maybe even back in the X-Car.

Somehow I get myself over to the window, to Oliver. It's like I'm headed for the electric chair or something, but I tell myself maybe it's not as bad as it seems. Maybe he'll understand. He understands *everything*.

When I lower myself into the chair across from him, he doesn't look up, doesn't acknowledge me in any way. I glance at his backpack and see that the writing on Ned's little nametag is smeared, from the fruit cup juice I figure.

"Hi," I whisper.

Still nothing.

I take a deep breath and jump in. "I know you probably hate me—"

"I don't hate you, Ricky," he says calmly, his eyes still glued to his book. "I don't really like you anymore, but I don't hate you."

Ouch. "Would you please just let me apologize?"

Finally, he looks at me. "Okay. If it'll make you feel better. Go ahead."

"It's not about making me feel better!" I snap.

"You sure?" he says. "You did something mean and now you feel bad about it. You want to make it all better so you don't feel like such a jerk."

For a moment I'm speechless. Maybe he's right, but that doesn't make me any less furious.

"You know, you make it awful easy for people to mess with you. Maybe if you didn't give them so much ammunition, they'd leave you alone more."

"What ammunition do I give people?" he asks.

"I don't know . . . maybe leave Ned at home and cool it on the hand sanitizer and the Captain America worship?"

"I'm superstitious about Ned. I told you that. Besides, it's a reminder of how lucky I am. And you know why I use the hand sanitizer. And I *like* Captain America. For your information, a lot of people think he's cool. I'm sorry, but I'm not going to hide who I am. Unlike you, I'm not embarrassed to take up space on the planet."

"Ugh, you know what? Fuck you," I whisper because Nurse Jeff's back.

Oliver goes back to his textbook. "Great apology, Ricky."

That *did not* go as planned.

dr. dad's office aka my happy place

Going in for my dental hygiene appointment is the only time I get to be perfect.

Unfortunately, after replaying the disaster in Nurse Jeff's office all day at school—and again, here, the whole time Trish, the hygienist, has been cleaning and polishing my teeth, I'm just not feeling it. Oliver wouldn't even *look* at me in public speaking and he didn't say another word to me the whole day.

Mr. Jenkins pulled me aside after class and grilled me about what had happened, asking what Ronnie Drake and Matt Booker did, because Oliver wouldn't say anything and the school can't punish them without the specific details. But I lied and said I'd gotten there late and wasn't sure. I assumed Oliver was worried they'd retaliate. I certainly didn't want to make things even worse for him.

I try to clear my head while Trish pokes around my teeth with a pointy instrument, doing her final, post-cleaning check.

"Ow!" I say, surprised by a sharp, electric shock of pain that seemed to come from deep within one of my teeth on the bottom right side. "What did you do?"

"Hmm," Trish says. "Open wide, sweetie. Okay?"

I don't want to open wide. I want to get to the part where my dad comes in and looks at my teeth and beams that proud, half-father/half-dentist smile at me and says *perfect*. But Trish's waiting, so I open wide, bracing myself for another jolt. She pokes around, but to my relief, a second jolt never comes.

"Hang tight," Trish says. "I'm going to have your dad come take a look."

Well, of course my dad's going to take a look. He always does. But there's something about the way she says it that seems weird, seems off.

A moment later Dr. Dad waltzes in. "Well, if it isn't my own little Ricky Raccoon!" he singsongs.

I groan. "*Fifteen* now, Dad. Feel free to retire Ricky Raccoon anytime."

"Never," he says. His dorky dad persona always seems to trump Dental-Professional Mode when I'm in the chair.

He pulls up the rolling stool and picks up the same pointy instrument Trish was using. I open wide again and he starts poking around. When he gets to the bottom right, there's another little jolt and the instrument seems to stick in my tooth for a second.

"Uh, oh," he says.

It hits me *all-at-once* and panic spreads throughout my being. This cannot be happening. I refuse to even consider the possibility that this is happening.

When Dad removes the instrument from my mouth, I clamp my lips shut. He picks up some other instrument and says, "Open up, kiddo."

"No," I say, barely moving my lips.

"Ricky . . ." he protests.

"Finish up, would you? I have lots of homework to get to." Lips still sealed.

"You'll be out of here in fifteen minutes. It's tiny, but we need to take care of it."

"No!" I practically yell—even though *I still refuse to even consider the possibility that this is happening!*

Dad morphs into Dental-Professional Mode, calmly discussing things with his assistant, Melanie, who I only know because he's introduced us and not because she's ever been needed for one of my appointments. They collect a bunch of different supplies and then their focus goes back to me and my silent tantrum.

"Everyone gets cavities, Ricky," Dr. Dad says, sympathetically.

"Everyone but *me*," I growl. But then my panic and stubbornness is completely taken over by something else—devastation.

It's official. I am imperfect in every way imaginable.

I nearly leap out of the chair when Dr. Dad whips out a large, metal needle, but he tells me all I'll feel is a little pressure and it's to numb the pain. My unofficial theme song pops into my head, though dentists use lidocaine rather than novocaine these days (which I'll be sure to mention to Billie Joe if I ever meet him).

Dad and Melanie launch into this little choreographed dance, handing off instruments to each other without missing a beat. It'd be impressive if it didn't involve Dad using a whirring/buzzing drill (very unnerving) to drill a hole in my tooth, which he explains is to clear out any decay before he fills the cavity.

There it is. The C-word.

I have to hand it to Dr. Dad—or the lidocaine—since I don't really feel much . . . other than the *crushing doom of my newly minted, wholly imperfect status.*

Dad even finishes within the fifteen-minute timeframe he promised. He grabs a handheld mirror and invites me to look at my new filling. I look in the area where he was doing the drilling, but I don't see anything. It's the exact same color as my tooth. No one will ever know it's there.

But I'll know.

46

assembly from hell . . . but aren't they all?

The ninth graders are assembled in the auditorium. I made a point of not looking around when I first came in. I just grabbed a seat way off on the side and tried my best to be invisible. I'm filled with dread because I know Oliver is in here somewhere, hating me. After the debacle in Nurse Jeff's office, I texted him another apology, a sincere one this time, but of course got zero response. I've been keeping my head down, doing my schoolwork and beating myself up. I've been avoiding Julio and Lex too. I hate them for joining in with that mob in the hall. And I hate Lex for asking me if I was Oliver's friend right in that awful moment. Last but not least, I've been flat-out hiding from Ronnie Drake and Matt Booker because I'm one hundred percent certain I'm next on their *to-screw-with* list.

The buzz of conversation in the room is interrupted by a nasty squeal coming from the stage. Everyone groans and complains. Principal Piranha clears her throat into the microphone and when that motivates absolutely no one to shut up, she says, "Quiet down, everyone. Let's get started."

It still takes a minute, but eventually there's silence.

Principal Piranha gives the room one of her sickening smiles and says, "In just one month from now, you'll be moving on from the comfortable, familiar journey of middle school and embarking on the adventure that is high school."

Comfortable? Familiar? Is she fucking kidding? Never mind that I already made that stupid journey last year.

"In this life we have rituals. We have celebrations when celebrating is in order. Your achievement at the end of this school year is just such an occasion."

She pronounces it "OH-casion." (Not even Jenkins sounds that snooty.)

"Your graduation ceremony will be an opportunity for your families to celebrate your achievement, for us to acknowledge those students who have excelled in particular areas, and for all of you to cheer on your fellow classmates as we conclude one chapter and prepare for the next—together."

I cannot be the only one who just threw up in my mouth a little.

"Here to guide you in creating a ceremony of which you can all be proud is our own public speaking and English teacher, Mr. Jenkins."

My eyes snap to the stage. Weird that Jenkins never mentioned he'd be in charge of the graduation ceremony with all the time we spend together. I fold my arms, annoyed.

As Jenkins steps to the microphone, some guy way in the back yells, "Fag!"

Laughter breaks out around me. Before I even realize what I'm doing, I twist in my seat and yell, "Shut the hell up!" Everyone stares at me. Mostly they're too shocked or surprised to laugh, but some do laugh.

My heart pounds in my chest and my cheeks turn pink. I slouch down in my seat, furious, but not just at the idiots in this room, at myself too. It was so easy, defending Jenkins. It was the right thing to do and I did it without hesitation. *Why the HELL didn't I do that for Oliver?*

This time it's Jenkins clearing his throat. He looks right at me and does his raised-eyebrow thing, which he knows I'll understand— *Language, Ms. Bloom.*

Why didn't the guy who called him a fag get the Disapproving Eyebrow? But I know the answer. Jenkins holds me to a higher standard and wants me to hold myself to one too. *Fine.*

He starts talking about the ceremony and how it's going to go. How we'll march in from the back and go down the center aisle and up the steps to the right and *blah, blah, blah.* I stopped listening at *march down the aisle and up the steps* and started wondering how I was possibly going to do that, especially with my body hurting again.

Jenkins goes on about cap-and-gown fitting schedules, ordering class photos (I must have missed photo day), and graduation rehearsals, but I'm still barely listening. I've busted my ass for the past two and a half months so I could graduate, and now I'm fantasizing about ditching the rest of the school year and making it all up in summer school, where there won't be a pathetic graduation ceremony for passing *ninth grade.*

Teachers' aides stand at the end of the rows handing out stacks of bright yellow flyers to be passed down to each student. I take one when the pile gets to me and pass the rest on. The flyer lists the dates of the events Jenkins just mentioned, plus a few more, like when to order a yearbook (pass).

Everyone heads for the exits after that. My left knee is clicking and freezing up every other step, so kids are shoving past me, just like they probably will during the stupid ceremony. We'll probably be lined up alphabetically, so I'll be toward the front slowing the whole thing down.

Once I clear the doors to the auditorium, I see Principal Piranha.

"This must be very exciting for you, Erica," she says to me, trying but failing to sound sincere. "As long as you do well on your finals, you've made it."

While I struggle to keep from telling her to drop dead, a thought occurs to me. "Principal"—(*focus, focus*)—"Perdanta? Do I have to be in the ceremony? I mean, it might be kind of hard for me."

Her face gets even more sour, which I didn't realize was possible. "Participation isn't mandatory. If you decide you're not up to it, the school can mail your diploma."

"Great," I say, and then I can't help but add, "Plus, you know, I did actually get a middle school diploma last year, so . . ." I give her what I hope looks like the same sickening smile she's always giving me and then I get the hell out of there.

After geoscience I head to Jenkins's room for our Afterschool Special since I'm back to avoiding the music room.

I find him at his desk, naturally.

"Oh, Ms. Bloom," he says. "You're a bit early."

"Is that okay?" He nods, letting me know it's fine, so I take my seat by his desk.

"You know about my doctor's appointment on Friday, right?" I'm pretty sure someone from the office would have let him know, but there's no harm in checking. "It was the only day Dr. Hunt could squeeze me in."

"Yes. I was informed," Jenkins says. "Everything all right?"

I'm about to say *yes* automatically because that's what I do. But the truth is I'm not really sure if everything's all right, so I say, "I'm not really sure." He raises a concerned eyebrow, so I add,

"I'm probably fine. I'm just kind of really sore again, and I thought I should have him check me out."

"Good for you," he says, and for some reason my insides are suddenly all warm and strong and happy.

Good for me, taking charge.

"Sorry about my outburst earlier, at the assembly."

"What outburst?"

That was almost a joke. I didn't know Jenkins had it in him.

Good for him.

47

i need answers—stat

I sit in Dr. Hunt's waiting room, hoping he has answers for me when I get in the room with him. It's now been almost two weeks since I destroyed things with Oliver, had the mini-flare, and got my first cavity. I need some good news.

I managed to convince Mom that she didn't need to come with me, that I needed to get used to doing this on my own since it's going to be my life now. I did promise to call her if it turns out something unusual is going on (and made her promise to keep coming to my infusion appointments because I'm nowhere near ready to face those without her). There's just one other person waiting with me, a thirty-something guy who's reading something on a tablet. While I wait and hope, I take out my phone and open the calendar app to check how many weeks it is until Infusion Number Three (answer: two). There's not much else in my calendar other than "speech 4 Jenkins" on June 7th (*uuugghh*), "CHOP party?" on June 8th and "Graduation?" on June 10th. I could probably delete the CHOP party because there's no way I'm going now that Oliver can't stand the sight of me. But for whatever reason, I leave it in there. I seriously doubt I'll end up doing the graduation ceremony either, but I leave that one in there too.

The door to the back opens, and Martha holds it for the patient coming out, a pretty woman with shoulder-length brown hair. She looks about thirty but walks with a cane. I can't help but notice her cane, which has a pattern with all kinds of different dog breeds on it. I spot a Great Dane right away. When I look up, she's looking at me, but not in an angry way.

"Cool cane," I say.

"Isn't it?" she says, looking down at it admiringly. "I got it online."

The guy who was reading stows his tablet and hops up to greet the woman, giving her a gentle peck on the cheek before asking her if she's all set to go. I watch them leave, thinking, *cute couple*, just before Martha calls me back.

When Dr. Hunt comes in the exam room a few minutes later, I spill it. All of it. How I had another flare. How, in general, I seem to be a lot stiffer in the mornings again. How my right knee, which had gotten a lot better, is now aching every day. How my macadamia nut pinkie throbs every morning.

He listens, nodding, typing notes in my chart. When I'm finally finished with my list of complaints, he says, "As I mentioned, it's not unusual for the effects of the biologics to be a bit inconsistent when you're first starting out."

"I remember." I sigh. I want this pain gone NOW.

He clicks around on the computer and says, "I'll call in a prescription to help to tide you over until your next infusion and you can take it as needed after that. Even once you're up to speed, you'll still have some bad days here and there. A lot of my patients report having more trouble in the spring and fall because of the fluctuating weather."

"But it *will* start working really well again, like it did before, right?" I ask. Because that's what I'm most afraid of—that the pain relief I felt before is gone for good, like my friendship with Oliver and my perfect mouth.

"I truly believe it will," Dr. Hunt says. "We'll look at your labs to see if there's anything unusual but I doubt there's any reason for concern. Again, you'll have good stretches and bad stretches. Arthritis is funky."

"Funky, huh?" I laugh. That wasn't the F-word that came to mind for me.

As I wait for my X-Car, I think about what Dr. Hunt said. Good stretches and bad stretches. Maybe that's how life is, too. Maybe I'm just in a bad stretch right now. Maybe Oliver will forgive me at some point and we'll be friends again.

Maybe.

When I get back to the apartment, I grab a bottle of Snapple from the fridge, take a quick pee, and then turn on the water for a heavenly/hot bath. I pick out a giant fizzy bomb (raspberry) and slump down onto the toilet to wait for the tub to fill. But then I hear a text come in on my cell. It's back in the bedroom, so I drag myself in there. A tiny ray of hope hits me that maybe it's a text from Oliver. Dumb, I know.

The text is from Mom:

How was the appt w/Hunt?

I text back—

Ok. Will call w/details after my bath

I want to tell her more, but it's too much to text and the tub water's making that sound it makes when it's just about full. I go back into the bathroom, strip off my clothes, and slide into the heavenly/hot water.

For the next ten minutes, it's all *relief* and *calm* and *nothingness*. But then my mind starts wandering. It wanders to Oliver, but I force it to turn around and go off in another direction. I wind up thinking about the Dreaded Speech for Jenkins's class and wishing I could somehow make it about cursing, which I obviously can't do. My brain wanders back to the conversation I had with Jenkins about curse words and how they're sometimes received differently than you intend. What did he call it? A *disconnect*? Maybe other words can cause the same kind of disconnect. Ones we say. Ones we don't.

Like Jenkins said—words have power. All of them.

One tiny, little word—*YES*—and I wouldn't have ruined my friendship with Oliver.

48

literally one week later . . .
here we go again

I glance around from my last-row aisle seat and quickly realize it must be another ninth-graders-only thing. I'm still basically trying to be invisible, hiding in plain sight. Though when it comes to Julio and Lex, at this point I'm angrier at myself than I am at them. *I'm* the one who screwed up. I should have told Lex, *yeah, we're friends, and he's actually pretty cool once you get to know him.* If he and Julio were still assholes after that, *then* I could hate them for good.

At least that whole miserable episode got my creative juices flowing on the Dreaded Speech front. What I thought was going to be a speech mostly about the value of curse words (I even found some articles claiming that cursing is helpful for people with chronic pain!) has turned into a much wider discussion of word choice in general—and how much the words we choose to say or not say matter. I've written several pages already, but my speech is still *hella rough*, with three weeks left to whip it into shape.

As I wait for the assembly to start, dread sets in. With my luck, they decided to add a dance number to the graduation ceremony. I'm missing Spanish and geoscience for this—whatever it's about. Can't say I'm sad about that, especially since it means missing the long walk from Spanish to geoscience (and not having to endure a class with that buttwipe Ronnie Drake). My ankles are kind of sucky today.

I check the weather app on my phone, which has become somewhat of an obsession ever since Dr. Hunt mentioned the weather thing. In general, it's been all over the place. Cold and dry one day, hot and sticky the next. My body just keeps getting worse and my third infusion is still over a week away. I stretch out my legs since the seats next to me are empty (of course), making a mental note to be sure to put my feet flat on the floor several times during the two periods so I'm not completely miserable when it's time to get back up.

Principal Piranha finally takes the stage and starts droning on *again* about how big a deal graduation is. *Ugh. It's freakin' ninth grade!* Finally, she gets to the point—that we're here so that some high schools in the Center City area can tell us a little bit about their schools. Right after the assembly, representatives from the different schools will be in the cafeteria so we can chat and ask questions.

First up is a group of kids from CAPA, which they tell us stands for Creative and Performing Arts. They do a song and dance number that's kind of fun. But as Lex so indelicately pointed out, I'm merely an average singer. Students have to audition to get in. Scratch that.

There's a magnet school that has a technology focus (*yawn*) and others that teach you Latin and Chinese. A couple regular neighborhood schools do their spiels and I do my best to pay attention.

Ever since Oliver brought it up, I've been wondering about next year. Mom clearly thinks the plan is that I go back to live with her in the new condo and go back to West Mount Airy High. But maybe Dr. Dad wants me to stay with him? So are they going to, like, *fight* over who gets me? That would be a riot! What if I decide I don't want to go live with whoever "wins"? What if I don't know what the hell I want to do?

I realize I missed a whole school while my head was spinning. A new group is taking the stage. There's a woman and a handful of students. The last boy lags behind the others, hobbling along on crutches—not the regular, broke-your-leg kind, the ones with the cuffs that go around your forearm. His body's bent at an odd angle, and his legs don't seem to work fully.

My heart races and my skin bristles. I put my head down, shut my eyes.

Is that what I look like to normal people? Do I look that strange? That broken?

I listen as the teacher introduces herself, my eyes still shut. "I'm Natalie Birkes. I coordinate community outreach at Hayre Community Leadership Academy, otherwise known as HCLA."

My eyes shoot open. *Oliver's "no contest" school.*

The teacher gives her pitch for the school, and it sounds sort of incredible but likely impossible for me. They go on field trips all around Center City to museums and stuff—and not just for fun. It's part of the academic program. "In addition to community involvement, HCLA has a strong focus on scholarly research, writing, and oral presentation," she says. I groan at that last part, thinking of the Dreaded Speech.

Despite all the obvious ways this school isn't a fit for me, physically anyway, I have to admit—I'm intrigued. It seems like the total opposite of a boring/average high school. It's easy to see why Oliver would want to go there.

The students then take turns gushing about how awesome their school is. The first guy says his English class this year was called Hip Hop Poetry. They studied rap song lyrics, wrote their own raps, and held a fundraiser so the whole class could go to New York to see *Hamilton* . . . dang! Next, a girl talks about her community service at a kids' rec center in North Philly and how she ended up making a speech asking for additional funding at a city council meeting. I glance around me and see that most of my Glorious Grant classmates are barely paying attention. Figures these asshats wouldn't be interested. Personally, I'm beginning to wonder why HCLA isn't everyone's first choice.

The last student to speak is the guy on crutches (naturally). I'm sort of dying to hear him talk but I feel queasy too. What if people think that's what I'll end up looking like? What if that *is* what I end up looking like?

The guy makes his way to the microphone at center stage and I sink lower-than-low in my seat.

"I'm Michael Greifer," he says, "I'm a senior at HCLA." His voice sounds totally normal. I guess I was expecting some sort of speech impediment, like maybe he'd have a strange voice to match his broken body. Just thinking that makes me feel ashamed of myself. Despite the inaccurate conclusion I jumped to, he speaks easily, confidently. Like he has as much right to be up there, representing his school, as the other students, the normal ones. He talks about how he taught computer code to first graders for his service project and how much he loves being a part of the Center City community. But the whole time all I can think is—*how does he manage all the field trips? How can he be so comfortable talking in front of people? And how much shit do the other kids give him?*

I know all of the schools will be set up in the cafeteria after this assembly, where I could ask him all those questions and more. I just don't know if I'll have the guts to do it.

A couple more schools go after HCLA, but I'm too distracted to pay attention. And then Principal Piranha comes back and prompts us to "give a big hand to all the people who came to speak to us today." I look around and see people rolling their eyes, clapping half-heartedly. I don't want to be anything like them, so I clap with meaning, even though it stings my macadamia nut pinkie. Principal Piranha keeps us there, killing some time while the schools get set up in the cafeteria. Finally, about ten minutes later, she tells us we should all head that way, enticing us with the promise of Tastykakes and punch.

The ninth graders all jump out of their seats *effortlessly* and practically stampede out of the auditorium, which is perfect for me because it means I can take my time.

Luckily, the cafeteria's right down the hall from the auditorium. Unluckily, I realize I hadn't been paying attention and had forgotten to change positions and put my feet flat on the floor some of the time. *Uuughh. How could I have been so stupid?*

So now I do, I put my feet flat on the floor, and the burning is intense, without even standing up and putting real weight on my ankles. At least I'll have the place to myself and can suffer the consequences of my immobility in private. I watch the last few girls (Kendall and her Barbie friends among them) make their way out, and then there's no putting it off.

Should I swing my arms for momentum and try to stand up in one big swoosh or grab onto the seat in front of me and try to pull myself up slowly? Or maybe I could try putting my elbow (left, for sure today) on the back of my chair and levering myself up that way? Any one of the options is going to suck, so I opt for the elbow lever. My elbow burns as I position it on my seat back and lever-wrench my body up, little by little, making sure my ankles are going to support my weight with each new inch. I get my butt up onto the arm of the chair by performing contortions that might make me eligible for a circus sideshow. Once I have my balance on the chair arm, I switch to the grab-the-seat-in-front-of-me technique, and finally I'm on my feet, hurting like hell, but I'm standing.

Thank God there was no one around to see that. But I'm wrong.

"You should stay, Granny." It's Ronnie Drake, standing at the back of the auditorium with Matt Booker and a few other goons. "The nursing homes are coming in to do their presentations next."

I brace myself, my heart thudding. Maybe I deserve what's coming to me after how I treated Oliver, my only true friend at this shithole school.

They advance toward me, leering and sneering, when—

"Hey, Ricky, you coming?" To my complete shock, Kendall stands in the auditorium doorway, smiling at me. Her presence freezes the guys in their tracks, like they know better than to make a move against the Barbie Queen.

It's been over a month since I rescued her in the girls' room and she's barely spoken to me since then. But I don't wait to make sense of it. I limp toward Kendall as quickly as I can and get the hell out of there.

49

at least there are tastykakes

Kendall doesn't say a word or even look at me. She just walks *oh-so-slowly* beside me as I limp down the hall toward the cafeteria. Three hours later (okay, three minutes), when we finally get to the cafeteria, Kendall simply rushes ahead to rejoin her posse, again without a word. I still don't know what to make of it but I'm grateful.

I look around the cafeteria and see my classmates milling around, chatting with people from the different schools. Students and school personnel are stationed at each table with a sign or in some cases a fancy banner identifying which school it is. Most have brochures or other handouts. Some even have freebie pens or water bottles with the school's logo.

I inch into the room and over to the refreshments table where I snag a Butterscotch Krimpet because my stomach's been upset again, and besides even sucky situations suck less with your favorite Tastykake, right? People are mostly too busy to notice me, which I appreciate. I try to figure out which schools are where but a lot of the signs and banners are blocked by bodies. But then I spot him—the broken boy—so I know which one is Hayre Community Leadership Academy's table. Naturally, it's all the way across the room.

I set out painfully, slowly, and panic seizes me for a second.

I don't want to go stand next to that guy, like the two of us are some kind of crippled magnets, drawn together. I don't want people to think I'm like him (even though I kind of am, but not really). I don't want to be seen with him, not because he's so awful, but because the two of us together make too big a target for the buttwipe Ronnie Drakes and Matt Bookers of the world.

It takes me another two hours (okay, two minutes), but I manage to drag myself all the way to the right table. I snag one of their brochures—the same one Oliver had—pretending it's the most fascinating thing I've ever read, and casually drift toward the far end of the table, where the broken boy sits.

Michael. Not "broken boy." He has a name.

"Hi," Michael says, brightly. "Are you considering HCLA?"

"Maybe." I glance back down at the *fascinating* brochure, which reminds me that, even if I could handle all the crazy physical stuff at this school, I'd also have to handle Oliver silently hating me for the next three years.

I dragged myself all the way over here to get some answers, so I figure I'd better get to it. I lean in close and whisper, "Can I ask you a question?"

He whispers back, "That's kinda what I'm here for." And then he winks at me and I blush/laugh. I seriously didn't expect this guy to be a flirt—one more inaccurate conclusion I jumped to. "Really, what can I tell you?"

"Um . . . what's the principal like?" I'm stalling, but I can't seem to get my real questions to come out.

"Oh, he's terrific," Michael says. He waits while I try to get my tongue and lips to function.

Now or never, Ricky.

"There's an elevator, right?" I'm still whispering.

"Yeah," he says reassuringly. He seems to get it that it's hard for me to ask. "The building's completely accessible."

"Is it a big hassle to get them to give you an elevator key?"

"There's no key. Students who need the elevator use it. Students who don't, don't. HCLA uses an honor system for a lot of things. Besides, it's kind of pathetic to use the elevator if you don't need to."

It's kind of pathetic to need to, but I don't say that.

"What about all the field trips and stuff? I mean, it's a whole lot of walking, right? What if you like . . . *have problems* . . .?"

"Problems?" he says like he's not quite sure what I'm getting at.

I'm about to drop the whole stupid thing when he smiles, and I realize he's just messing with me. Flirting again.

"Listen," he says, "they'll work with you. I have CP."

I must give him a blank expression, because he explains further, "Cerebral palsy. It's a brain thing, happened right when I was born."

"You've been like this your whole life?" I ask, only realizing after-the-fact that it was probably a horribly rude question.

But it doesn't seem to faze him. He just nods and goes on: "When I started at HCLA, I sat down with a counselor and we figured out how to make everything manageable. They're really good about stuff like that."

"Well, that'll be different," I say, glancing around me, wishing Principal Piranha had overheard what Michael had just said.

"You have to learn to advocate for yourself too, you know?" he says.

Oliver arrives at the other end of the table, and I'm suddenly desperate to get out of there. "Yeah, sure," I say to Michael, turning my back to Oliver. "I gotta go. Thanks."

"Wait," he says. He scribbles something on a Post-it note and hands it to me. "You should read up on this. It's important."

I mumble my thanks, feeling Oliver's anger radiating out at me like a cloud of toxic gas, and take off as fast as my body can manage. I keep going until I'm out of the cafeteria and down the hall and into the girls' room and into the very last stall.

I lock the door and sit on the toilet. I just need to sit.

I glance at the Post-it note Michael gave me. It says "ADA info" and has a government web address. I'll definitely look it up when I get home since Michael said it's important. He seems really smart and he probably knows a lot more about living life when you're broken than a lot of other people.

I stick the Post-it note to the front of the brochure, which I really only scanned back in the cafeteria. Now I read it, cover to cover, and find out all these other cool things—about their music appreciation program and how students can take yoga and meditation instead of gym and that they have a zero tolerance policy on bullying.

Hayre Community Leadership Academy seems like an awesome school. Maybe even the perfect school.

Except for the Oliver part.

50

the other un-perfect part

Dr. Dad's face is hard to read when I bring up HCLA over dinner. I eased into it, first telling him about my day and the assembly in general. I tried to ease into talking about HCLA specifically too, but the more I told him about it, the more excited I got.

Now he's just sitting there, looking perplexed, not saying anything.

"Don't you think it sounds cool, Dad?" I ask, hoping to get him to say *something*.

He takes a deep breath. "It's just that your mother and I—"

Instantly, I'm furious. "You and Mom *what*?!" I scream at him.

"Ricky—"

"No, Dad. Tell me. What did you guys fucking decide about my life now?"

"That's enough," he says.

"No, it's not enough! You're the king of not enough! First you walk out on us like you couldn't care less, and now you can't wait to get rid of me again. Never mind that it's *my* life, which you two fucked up, and that I should maybe get a goddamn say in where I go to school!" He's about to go all *Deep-Voiced-Angry-Dad-Hulk* on me, but he stops because tears burst out of me like a waterfall. Like Niagara Falls. "I hate you!" I scream.

I limp furiously for my bedroom. He doesn't follow me. I slam my door—hooray for having a door to slam—flounce face down on my bed, and cry and cry and cry.

It's all too fucking much. All of it. My body turning on me. Mom and Dad pretending to be my parents. Oliver hating me. The jerks at school. Not knowing for sure if I'm going to graduate (I still have finals to take, which could make or break the whole thing). Not knowing what's going to happen to me, to my body. Everything.

Every. Last. Thing.

Sometime later there's a quiet knock on my door. I don't know how I heard such a faint, little knock. But I did. My face is sticky, my eyes puffy. I must have fallen asleep, because my room is completely dark and it was barely dusk when I first came in here.

Another small knock comes, and for a moment, I hope it's Dani out there. But then I hear Dr. Dad say, "Ricky? May I come in?" and I realize I'm glad it's him.

He pokes his head in, and when I don't protest, he comes into my room and sits on the bed beside me. I curl onto my side so we can see each other and talk.

I go first. "I don't really hate you. I'm sorry I said that."

"I know," he says. "But it's okay for you to be mad at me."

"Good. Because I am."

"I know my leaving your mom made your life harder than it had to be, even before you got sick."

I sigh. "True. But I still would have gotten sick either way. That part wasn't your fault."

He grasps my right hand gently. Even with my oversized macadamia nut pinkie, my hand still seems tiny in his. "It wasn't your fault either, you know."

I want it to be someone's fault. I want there to be a reason. But it's not and there isn't. It just is.

"What I was going to say before is that now that your mom's moved to a better place for you, we assumed you'd want to return to West Mount Airy High."

"That's the thing, Dad. You *assumed*," I tell him. "You decided to ship me down here and now you've decided to ship me back. You didn't ask me either time."

"Don't you want to go back to school with your old friends?" he asks.

"My *friends* didn't want to have anything to do with me once I got sick," I say.

"I didn't know that," Dad says quietly. Never mind that he's only the second person who knows it now. Or third after me, I guess. "Maybe your friends just didn't know how to react. You have to let them know you're still the same person."

"I'm not sure I am the same person."

"You're still you, honey."

"Right. But maybe I'm a new version of me. Maybe that's not a bad thing."

"You really liked that one school, huh?" Dad asks me.

I think for a minute. Was I just interested in HCLA because of that guy, Michael? Or Oliver? No. There were other reasons. Lots of them. "It's a really cool place," I tell Dad. "The students get to do a bunch of stuff in Center City."

Dad grimaces. "Ricky, I'm not sure that would be ideal for you."

"I know. I thought the same thing at first. But one of the students who did the presentation walks on crutches. He's way more . . . *challenged* than I am," I say. "He's kind of badass actually. He says the school's really cool about it. They come up with ways to make it work."

"Well, that would be a big change from Grant," Dad says with a *harrumph*.

"Right?" I say, laughing because we had the same reaction.

"Still," he says. "It might be easier for you to go to a more traditional school. It doesn't have to be West Mount Airy High."

I roll onto my back. "What am I supposed to do? Lie in bed and wait to die?"

Dad smirks. He's not buying my drama queen act. Hell, *I'm* not even buying it.

"I don't want my body to stop me from doing things I want to do," I tell him. "If that means I'm in more pain, then fine, whatever, I'll be in more pain. My whole life is *not* gonna suck just because I have stupid arthritis."

"That's a great attitude, Ricky Raccoon," he says.

"Oh my God, Dad, with the Ricky Raccoon!" I groan.

"I will never stop calling you that, so you might as well learn to accept it."

"Gee. Just like my arthritis?"

"Hopefully not as painful." I hold out my hands, like I'm weighing the two things and it's a toss up, and we both laugh. "Let's talk to your mom about it. Get her on board. The school's close to Suburban Station. You could easily take the train down from Mom's new place."

"Yeah," I say, feeling a sudden crush of emotion, a mixture of hurt and hopeful. "But wouldn't it be easier for me to just stay here with you? I mean, if you don't mind."

His face sort of contorts, like he's suddenly flooded with a mix of emotions too. "Of course I wouldn't mind," he says, taking my hand again and squeezing it in that amazing way that dads do, where the squeeze is hard enough for you to feel squeezed and loved but never so hard that it hurts, even if you have hands that hurt easily. "I'd love for you to stay if you want to."

"I want to," I say back.

third time, here's hoping I'm charmed

Martha removes the IV and tells me to press down on the cotton ball she places over the spot where the needle came out. I press while she gets a Band-Aid. The infusion seemed to drag even worse this time. I tried to study but could barely keep my eyes open even though we skipped the Benadryl again. Good thing Mom brought her book.

"How are you feeling?" Martha asks, as she sticks the Band-Aid on. "Itchy? Nauseous? Dizzy?"

"None of the above," I tell her.

"Good," she says. "Sit tight. Dr. Hunt's finishing up with a patient. You're next."

I stretch, a little more awake now that I napped off and on for the past two hours.

"Are you up for grabbing a bite once we get out of here?" Mom asks me. "Lovely Rita's is probably crammed at this hour. But I'm game if you are."

As much fun as Lovely Rita's is, I need to tell her that I want to stay with Dad for a while. Scratch that—that *I've* decided to stay with Dad. At first I was hoping Dad would just tell her. But he said I needed to do it myself and I realized he's right.

I definitely don't want to drop a bomb like that on her in a public place, so I say to her, casually, "How about we get something and take it back to Dad's?" Mom reacts exactly how I expect—she stiffens, her face is suddenly a blank mask. "He won't be there, and I thought you might like to see where I've been staying. You know—*infiltrate enemy territory.*" I flash my best *won't-that-be-fun-and-sneaky* look, but she's still stiff-bodied and blank-faced.

"Your father isn't the enemy," Mom says.

That's not what your body language is screaming, Mom.

So I try my backup tactic: "I kind of *want* you to see the apartment. Is that okay?" How could she turn down a direct request like that, right? Answer—she can't. And Dr. Hunt's squeaky shoes are approaching out in the hall, so she doesn't have time to argue further even if she wanted to try.

"I guess we can grab steaks and eat them at your dad's place."

It's my place now too. But obviously I don't say that.

Dr. Hunt only stays briefly, but his calming presence seems to help Mom relax. We're out of there in about fifteen minutes and pick up steak sandwiches at a place a block away—fried onions and mushrooms for Mom, extra cheese for me. The apartment is only one block more, so we walk there too. My feet and left knee complain a little but the pain's manageable. And this way Mom doesn't have to move her car and spend forty minutes circling endlessly to find an open parking meter.

We ride up in the elevator, and I can feel Mom tensing up again. My brain scrambles, trying to figure out a way to calm her back down, but is that even fair considering the news I'm about to break to her?

I decide it's not, so we ride in silence, getting off at the 16th floor.

"Isn't it cool the new apartment's so close to the elevator?" I say, guiding my mom to the door ten feet away. "The Batch Pad was way at the end of a long hallway."

"Not calling this one the Batch Pad?" Mom asks as I unlock the door.

Crap. That was a slip-up. "Batch Pad 2.0," I tell her.

We go in and I'm suddenly self-conscious. Dad and I moved in almost three months ago but the place is still so stark and tidy, it barely looks lived-in. Mom looks around tentatively, clutching the bag with our steak sandwiches to her body.

"Come on," I say, "I'll show you my bedroom."

As soon as we cross the threshold into my room, Mom seems to relax a little. My room looks and feels like me. It's a little messy, with some clothes on the floor and books and papers all over my desk. Mom admires my desk, and then she peeks in the bathroom (which I'm sure looks even more like me).

She grins when she sees the kangaroo cards from Dani stuck all around the mirror frame. "Ah, Dani strikes." I grin back. Mom spots the photo of Oliver next and lifts it free of the mirror frame. "What's your friend's name again?"

"Oliver." The words *your friend* sting my ears.

"He's the one who had cancer, right? Is his hair just growing back now?" Mom says, sounding concerned.

"No. It's just a haircut," I tell her. She seems relieved and goes to put the photo back. And then I blurt out, "Actually, his hair was really long and he cut it all off to donate to a charity that makes wigs for kids who lose their hair due to medical stuff. For me. I mean in my name. As a birthday present."

"Wow!" Mom says.

"I know. He's a good . . . guy." I couldn't bring myself to say *friend.*

"When do I get to meet him?" she asks.

I shrug because I really don't want to confess my sins right now. Confessing that I want . . . *that I've decided* . . . to stay with Dad for the time being is confession enough for one afternoon. "Let's go eat before the steaks get cold."

We sit across from each other at the small table outside the galley kitchen, unwrap our steaks and dig in. I didn't realize how hungry I was until my first bite and practically inhale half of my steak. For a few minutes, there's nothing but chewing and swallowing, no conversation, but I realize I'd better stop putting off what I need to tell her. So I plunge in:

"So . . . there's something I wanted to talk to you about."

Mom stiffens again, pausing mid-chew.

"There's a school down here that I really want to go to." Earlier I'd hidden the HCLA brochure in a stack of mail on the table. I slide it in her direction. To her credit, she reads it thoroughly before saying anything.

"Seems pretty cool," Mom says. "A bit ambitious with all the activities, but I'm sure you can handle it if it's what you really want."

"I do. Plus I've heard the school's supposed to be really good with accommodations."

"Well, it's a magnet school, so you don't have to worry about living in the neighborhood."

First of all—*damn,* she really did read that brochure carefully. Second of all—*double damn*, that's basically my cue to tell her the other part.

"Yeah, about that . . ."

"No. No way. You are *not* staying here with your father," she insists, startling me with her intensity. "This was always going to be temporary. I made that crystal clear to him when he suggested it."

"Wait. It was Dad's idea?"

"I said no initially. But then . . . Thanksgiving happened—"

Thanksgiving. When Mom and Dani and Noland and I stuffed ourselves silly and played Clue and drank cups and cups of hot apple cider. And I forgot to pay attention to how I was sitting and how much I was drinking and suddenly, I had to pee so badly, and when I got up everything was stiff and aching. So I wiggle-crawled my way to the steep staircase, praying I could make it to the second floor in time because there's no bathroom downstairs. But my legs and arms were burning as I pulled myself up step after step after step. And I only made it halfway before I couldn't hold it anymore. And Mom came running but she was already crying, like it was happening to her, so I screamed for her to get away from me and it was Dani who got me the rest of the way up the stairs and into the bathroom, where she helped me out of my wet jeans and started the shower for me. And she didn't say anything stupid, like "don't cry" or "it's okay," because it was NOT okay.

"I couldn't justify keeping you with me, in that house. Not after that," Mom says. "I was afraid your dad might be too distracted by his fabulous new single lifestyle to pay proper attention to you—and he proved me right when you cut six weeks of school right under his nose."

"That wasn't Dad's fault."

"Of course it was! He's the parent. He can suddenly decide he doesn't want to be a husband anymore, fine. But—sorry—he doesn't get to half-ass being a father. Ever." She stops and angry-eats a few more bites of her steak.

Crap, now what? Do I back off? Do I keep pushing and upset Mom even more?

We eat in silence for a minute, but then Mom sighs.

"It's just . . . I was really looking forward to having you back home with me," she says quietly. "I miss you, kiddo."

I get up stiffly and go sit right beside her. "Miss you too, Mom," I say.

"Do you really want to stay here?" she asks.

"How about if I split time between the two of you?" I offer. "The school's really close to Suburban Station. I could take the train down when I stay with you. I'd be, like, bicoastal. Or . . . *bi-neighborhood-al.*"

I get a small chuckle for that one, even though she still seems less than thrilled. "I guess I could try to live with that."

"For the record, I'm the one who cut school. That's on me. And, yeah, he was too stupid to notice. He was pretty shitty at being a single parent at first—"

"His choice," she interjects.

I nod. "But he's gotten better at it. And besides, I've been kind of a shitty daughter too. To both of you. I'm sorry for that."

Mom wraps an arm around me and pulls me into a hug. It feels really good.

"Teenagers are supposed to be shitty," she says. "It was just our luck you happened to excel at it."

graduation practice . . .
what could go wrong?

We're all lined up like ducks outside the auditorium for graduation practice. I'm glad Jenkins is nearby, because we're in alphabetical order and Matt Booker is right behind me, with Ronnie Drake not far from me either. I do my best to ignore them both, kicking myself for not asking to be excused from this altogether since I'm leaning even more toward bowing out of the ceremony.

It's only been two days since my third infusion but I'm beyond impatient for it to start working again. The weather cannot seem to make up its mind—pick a freakin' temperature, any temperature!—so that's probably delaying my relief further.

My left ankle's been *impossible* from the moment I woke up (maybe it got the memo about today's rehearsal and this is its form of protest?). I've basically been dragging it around school all day, because when I try to pick it up to take a step—you know, like a normal person—I get the dagger-jabbed-in-my-ankle thing.

Plus, for added fun, my right shoulder's killing me, so I've been keeping my arm plastered to my side all day. One false move and a horrible jolt of pain shoots through my whole arm. Oh, and my stomach is *horrible*.

It's been a great day.

"Quiet, please," Jenkins says, and amazingly everyone shuts up. He makes his way down the line of ducks, checking off names on a list of graduating students. I spotted Lex earlier but he's way in the back (last name: Young). Oliver's only about fifteen people behind me, but obviously he's still not talking to me. No sign of Julio with the Ss. Guess maybe he just blew this off (lucky him).

Toward the end of the line, Jenkins makes two boys change places, saying, "Snyder comes before Stanley, gentlemen." Another boy punches the Stanley one in the arm. "Dumb ass," the punching boy says, loud enough for Jenkins to hear, but Jenkins just sighs and keeps moving down the line. He alphabetizes a few more kids and then comes back to the front of the line, near where I am, eight people back.

"Okay. The music will start, and Mrs. Hershman will give you your cue," he says, indicating the teacher's aide standing beside him. "Try to keep up a steady pace. And let's begin. . . ." He actually starts humming the pomp and circumstance graduation song. Some kids snicker. No one moves. "That's your cue, people!" he says, waving frantically at Kendall (last name: Adams), who's first in line.

Kendall starts moving through the propped-open auditorium doors and on down the center aisle. To me, it's like she's running. It's only a few steps (okay, drags) before a gap opens up between me and Tiffany Benson, the girl in front of me. A few more drags, and Matt Booker starts bumping into me.

"Hurry up, Grandma," he whispers, and I try to go faster. I

really try. But as we enter the auditorium, the gap ahead of me just grows wider. "Come on!" Matt says, not bothering to whisper this time.

And then he shoves me.

I stumble forward but catch myself, grabbing the back of one of the seats, which yanks my right arm back—hard. My shoulder EXPLODES.

I scream and cradle my arm as waves of excruciating pain ripple through me. It takes every ounce of my energy to not cry because I DO NOT want to cry in front of these assholes. I cut through a row of seats to my right, breathing in big, deep gulps of air to keep the tears away. I hear commotion all around me.

"Mr. Booker, principal's office. Now!" I hear Jenkins snarl, instructing Mrs. Hershman to escort him. I think Jenkins is coming after me, but I don't look.

Instead I drag myself through the endless row of endless seats, my shoulder still radiating pain from my neck to my ribcage, and I must have wrenched my right knee when I was trying not to fall before, because now there's this sort of hitch that makes my whole leg buckle when I take a step on that side and . . . *I GIVE UP. I FUCKING GIVE UP!*

I crash into the second-to-last seat in the row and bury my face in my hands, crying now. There's no stopping it.

I feel a hand placed gently on my back. It's Jenkins. He's in the seat next to me. "Are you okay?" he asks quietly.

DO I FUCKING LOOK OKAY?

But what I choke out is, "No. I am not okay."

"I'm very, very sorry," he says.

"*You* didn't do anything," I snap.

"I should have asked you if you felt up to this."

NOBODY FUCKING ASKS ME ANYTHING!

But I take a deep breath and then another one and then I say, through gritted teeth, "Mr. Jenkins . . . I really, really want to scream right now and say stuff that you'd have to send me to the principal for. So if you don't want to send me to the principal, you probably should STOP talking to me."

He lets out a sigh. I know he's frustrated, but not with me. "Okay," he says. "Just sit here for now and rest." He gets up *effortlessly* and right before he leaves, he adds, "I need to go deal with these hoodlums and try not to say anything I'd have to send *myself* to the principal for."

Wow, another joke. I might have even chuckled if I wasn't so utterly miserable at the moment. He moves on, down the row.

"Is she okay?" I hear a familiar voice say. Oliver. It's the closest he's come to acknowledging me since that day in Nurse Jeff's office.

"Would you please go to Nurse Jeff's office and see if he's available to come?" Jenkins asks him.

I don't want Oliver to go. I want him to come over here and sit with me and hold my hand like he did that day we were watching old soap operas together. I want him to tell me how I should just ignore them and that none of the crap these assholes do matters.

But Oliver doesn't do any of that.

53

can i please, please, please just crawl into a hole and die?

I slump into my desk/chair beside Jenkins's desk for my After-school Special without saying a word. He's quiet too.

I'm so tired.

Finally, he says, "I wasn't sure if you'd come."

Seriously? Getting here was all I've been focused on ever since the nightmare in the auditorium this morning. Nurse Jeff offered to call my dad and dismiss me for the rest of the day, but I turned him down. I wanted to be here. I needed this. Desperately.

But I just shrug.

"Do you want to talk about it?" he asks.

"No." I say it quickly.

He shuffles some papers on his desk. "I was thinking. Maybe you could wait backstage and just come out to get your diploma when your name is called. We had a graduate two years ago. A young man who used a wheelchair. That's what we did then."

"I'm not in a wheelchair, if you haven't noticed," I grumble. "Who knows though? Maybe that's the future I have to look forward to."

"You could still wait backstage," he says.

"Mr. Jenkins," I growl. "Remember a moment ago, when you asked me if I wanted to talk about this?"

"Yes," he says reluctantly.

"And do you recall my answer?" I say, doing my best Jenkins impersonation.

He gives me a smirk. "We will find a way to make it work—"

"Principal Perdanta told me I didn't even have to be in the graduation ceremony if I didn't want to. Honestly, I'm probably just going to skip it."

He seems shocked, maybe even disappointed. *Great. I've disappointed him.*

"I graduated for real last year," I say. "Don't you think it's kind of stupid for me to stress out my body being in the ceremony this year when it's basically meaningless?"

"I suppose I don't see it as meaningless," he says quietly.

Oh, for God's sake!

"Fine," I tell him, "I'll think about it. I had my third infusion a week ago. Maybe it'll turn me into Super Arthritis Girl or something."

He chuckles and I do too. That's maybe the first time I've ever joked about my arthritis aloud like that. It feels a little strange but kind of cool too.

"Now can I please run my speech topic by you? I'm worried you might not like the topic I came up with as much as I do, and I'm kinda freaking out."

"I'm pretty certain freaking out is counterproductive."

I roll my eyes. "It's just a saying."

"Is it? Or do the words carry a level of resignation and defeat along with them?"

"Actually," I say, "that's kind of what my speech is about."

He does his raised-eyebrow thing. "Tell me more."

"It's a 'power of words' thing. That conversation we had a while back, about how important the language we choose is, got me thinking." I pause there. It sounds Oliver-level-dorky now that I've said it aloud. "At first I tried to come up with a way to make my speech about cursing without actually cursing but it was a dead-end." That elicits a smirk. "So then I started thinking about our conversation and about all kinds of words and how a simple little word you say or don't say can make a huge difference. So that's what I ended up writing about."

I stop then because I'm suddenly terrified that he thinks the topic is stupid and that I'll need to start over from scratch, in which case I'm doomed to fail his class and, subsequently, ninth grade.

He thinks for a moment and then says, "I really like that idea, Ms. Bloom. And you're the perfect person to explore it."

I exhale a breath I didn't even realize I was holding in.

After that, we review the homework he gave me at our previous Afterschool Special. He corrects some grammar in my response to an op-ed, and points out a sentence that could be clearer. It's easy and fun and interesting working with him, and it's easily the best half hour I've had all day. But eventually, our time's just about up.

"Since this will be our last afterschool session, let's take a look at the checklist I gave you before we began meeting," he says.

Our last session? Really?

With just over two weeks of school left, I guess that makes sense. I root around in my backpack to find the checklist.

He gives me his red felt pen. "Why don't you do the honors?"

I take the pen, look down at the list and start checking things off . . . and checking . . . and checking. "What's this one here?" I ask when I get to one I don't remember.

"Reflection on the essay about political action committees. You did it."

I check it off and then check off every last thing on the list—except the opinion piece speech. "Wow," I say, looking at all the red check marks.

"Wow, indeed," he says.

And then our final Afterschool Special is over.

I test my feet while he packs up his bag. They're not great, but I heave myself up out of the desk/chair anyway and head for the door.

"See you tomorrow morning, Ms. Bloom," Jenkins says.

"Yeah, see you," I say back. I pause in the doorway a minute. "Mr. Jenkins?"

He looks up at me.

"This is the best D I'm ever going to earn," I tell him. And I mean it.

He smiles. "It's the most satisfying D I'm ever going to give."

oliver cracks . . . a little

Nurse Jeff's office is empty when I arrive the morning after the Graduation Practice Disaster.

After I sit, I lay my head back against the window and shut my eyes, trying to rest before the day starts. I was up late studying and working on my speech, so I'm tired for a change.

I hear Oliver come in, hear the chair scrape against the floor as he pulls it out, hear it groan as he takes a seat.

"Are you okay?" he asks.

I jump at the unexpected sound of his voice and open my eyes.

He's looking right at me with those momentous blue eyes of his, which I didn't realize how much I missed until just now. He even looks concerned, like maybe he still cares a little.

"I'm okay," I tell him. "Jenkins sent Matt Booker to Principal Piranha's office."

"Yeah. I saw that. Booker's always been an obnoxious cretin, but he really outdid himself today. Hopefully he'll get expelled," Oliver says.

"Wish they'd get rid of Ronnie Drake while they're at it. At least once his broken leg healed, I didn't have to worry about him assaulting me on the elevator again."

"*What?*" Oliver asks, shocked.

I guess I'd never mentioned the incident on the elevator to him. Come to think of it, I never mentioned it to *anyone*. "He grabbed my hand and tried to get me to touch him. It was gross," I say, shuddering at the memory.

"Did you tell Principal Perdanta?"

"Did you tell her what Ronnie and Matt did to you?" I ask.

He scowls and pulls a book out of his backpack. *Ugh. Shouldn't have brought that up.* I rest my head back again, figuring he's done talking to me, but then he says, "You seem like you're limping more again."

"It's the weather," I tell him. He scowls again, so I add, "No, really. Dr. Hunt said fluctuating weather is probably messing with my body."

"Oh," Oliver says.

"Plus, he reminded me that it takes time for the biologics to start working consistently. So I might have pain off and on for a while."

Oliver opens his mouth, like he's going to say something, like he's going to protest. Instead he just says, "That really sucks."

I close my eyes again. "Yep."

We spend the rest of our time in Nurse Jeff's office in silence. Later, in public speaking, he's back to not acknowledging my existence. It's okay. I deserve it. Besides, now I know he at least gives a shit that I'm hurting again. Not sure I deserve that.

suddenly kendall's my new bestie

In the rest of my morning classes, I raise my hand when I know the answers and frantically scribble notes when I don't. My right hand starts aching so much I actually put the hideous wrist brace on *at school* so I can keep scribbling.

At lunch, I shuffle through the line, requesting a bowl of beef vegetable soup and an apple because they seemed to be the least gross choices today, and then I head off with my tray.

"Erica! Sit here. I need to talk to you." I do a double take. It's Kendall.

She waves me over to her table, pulling out the chair next to her. My cafeteria tray is stupid-heavy with the soup, and Kendall's Barbie friends are all sitting at a table across the room. So I figure *what the hell*. But I still shoot a wary look over at Kendall's friends as I sit beside her.

"Don't worry about them," Kendall says. "I told them you did me a solid."

"You did?" I say, surprised.

"I didn't go into the specifics." Kendall rolls her eyes, like that should have been obvious. Then she says, "That was awful, what Matt Booker did. Just awful."

Oh, that.

"And I was walking too fast," she goes on. "I should have walked slower."

"You were walking like a normal person," I say under my breath. Kendall is pretty much the last person I want to discuss this with.

"It's not your fault you can't walk fast!" she insists with a huff.

I stare at my soup. "I know. But I hold everybody up."

"Not if I start out slower."

I look up at Kendall, bracing myself for the inevitable *Just kidding, you fucking freak.* But she looks totally sincere.

"I get to set the pace for the whole thing. So I'll go slow, and everyone behind me will have to go slow too."

Whoa. It's like she's given this little plan of hers actual thought.

"Thanks, that's nice of you to offer," I say, "but I'm probably not going to be in the ceremony anyway."

"What? But you have to!"

"Actually, Principal Piranha said I don't." Kendall's mouth drops open, like it's some kind of big deal to her. "Why do you care, anyway?" I ask her.

"Because it's not fair!" She starts collecting her lunch trash, angrily tossing things onto her tray. "You didn't ask for your body to get all messed up. Just like I didn't ask to be wearing a D cup in sixth grade, two months after I got my nose fixed, which was mostly my mom's idea by the way. Suddenly all the boys think I'm obligated to pay attention to them now that they're paying attention to me. When I tell them *thanks but no thanks*, they call me a slut." She leans in close to me and whispers, "The truth is—I've never even kissed a boy. But does that stop people from talking about how slutty I am?"

"Really? You've never kissed a guy?" I ask in a surprised whisper.

She shakes her head no. "I never know if boys are interested in me just because they think I'm easy, so I avoid them all. It sucks and it's not fair."

"That *does* suck," I say.

The bell rings and Kendall hops to her feet *effortlessly*. "What I just told you . . . that's between us," she says, sort of half-threateningly/half-panicked.

I give a reassuring nod like—*yeah, absolutely*—and realize I now have two secrets on the Barbie Queen. As inconceivable as it seems, she sort of *trusts* me.

"If you change your mind about graduation, let me know, okay?"

"Will do," I tell her.

She takes off, leaving me with the weirdest feeling that she and I could actually be friends in some other, alternate universe. We may even be friends in this universe. Shit, she seemed so excited about helping me, I'm almost tempted to take her up on it.

Almost.

56

who knew julio was such a gossip?

I stop by the office before leaving school today to pick up a release form my parents need to sign so Grant can transfer my medical information to HCLA.

When I walk in, I see Julio sitting in the same hard-ass chair he always seems to be sitting in. I wait for my usual reaction to him, the quickened pulse, the infestation of butterflies in my stomach. But none of that happens. He's holding his drumsticks and is tapping out a beat on his thigh. A month ago that might have made me melt onto the floor. Ever since I saw him laughing along with the mob at Oliver's expense, he's just another cute boy, nothing special.

After I pick up my papers, I go over to say hi anyway.

"Dude!" he says. "Haven't seen you in like *forever*!"

Yep. Definitely nothing special.

"I've been busy with finals and stuff," I say, sitting next to him. "What are you in the office for this time?"

"They have me taking all these tests, trying to figure out how much of a dumbshit I am."

"You don't seem dumb when it comes to music," I say, feeling kind of bad for him.

"Nah. I mostly have problems with letters. They move around when I'm trying to read. Dyslexia or something." He shrugs. "I don't mind. I like hanging out in the office."

"You do?" I ask.

"Sure. There's all kinds of rhythms in here." He taps his drumsticks along with a creaky fan across the room and then switches the beat up when someone starts the copier.

"That is seriously cool," I say.

He leans in closer to me and says, "This is also a great place to pick up gossip."

"Really? What have you heard?"

He glances around to make sure no one's within whispered-earshot. "Last week, Jenkins was in with Piranha, and dude blew a gasket! He was screaming so loud you could totally hear it right through the door."

"What was he mad about?" I ask, feeling angry for Jenkins because I'm sure if he was that mad, Principal Piranha must have done something tragically stupid.

Julio shrugs. "Something about the class photos getting fucked up. Like who cares, right?"

Obviously Jenkins, I think.

"Yesterday, there was big-time drama, too. You know that dude Olivia?"

"His name is *Oliver*," I snap.

"Dude, are you sure?"

"Yes, I'm sure!"

I swear if he says "dude" one more time . . .

"Huh. I totally thought his parents just gave him a weird name. Like you know how some dudes are named Leslie?" He laughs.

"What were you saying about Oliver?" I ask, way past impatient.

"Well, remember how Ronnie Drake and Matt Booker did that whole thing in the hallway a month ago, with the fruit cups and stuff?"

"I remember," I say.

"I mean, it was funny, but they totally went too far. It was *not* cool."

Why didn't you say that at the time? Why didn't I?

"Principal Piranha grilled him for info back when it happened. Somehow she knew Ronnie and Matt were involved, but the little dude wouldn't cough up any specifics and kept saying 'forget about it.' So she had to let it drop. Everyone in the office was all worried and shit. But then yesterday, he waltzes in here on his own and completely spills his guts. Ronnie and Matt get hauled in. Their parents come. There's a big scene and now they're both gone. Expelled!"

"Wow!" I say, making no attempt to hide my delight, my relief.

"Who knows why he suddenly changed his mind?" Julio says, shaking his head.

What I'm thinking is—*I'm pretty sure I do.*

captain america to the rescue
(hopefully anyway)

It's Wednesday, June 5th, and my only "final" left is the speech—
which I'm determined to kick major ass on, for Jenkins as much
as for myself. That leaves me two nights to practice, work out any
kinks, and somehow get up the nerve to stand in front of the class
and deliver it. At least the first two seem doable.

My X-Car's crawling along Locust Street due to some sort of
hold up, so the driver tells me he's going to drop down to Pine
Street, if that's okay with me. I nod my okay, pull out my cell, and
start scrolling through old texts from Oliver—pathetic, I know, but
his texts are sort of all I have at this point.

My latest brilliant idea is to go to the CHOP party to show
Oliver that I'm trying to be a good sport about the whole being a
Sick Kid thing. I'm hoping maybe that will open the door for me to
somehow convince him I'm not the Worst Friend Ever, although
I have *jack shit* in the way of ideas on *how* to do the second part.

When I glance out the car window, I realize we've just turned onto Oliver's block. A few doors from his house, I actually see him walking with some other kids our age. One of the guys he's with is bald. A girl in the group walks with a limp. They're all chatting and laughing and I realize they must be his friends from CHOP.

As my X-Car passes them I slink down in my seat, even though I doubt Oliver would be able to see me through the tinted windows. He's wearing his Captain America hoodie, naturally.

Suddenly a brand-new even more brilliant idea comes to me.

A second X-Car is waiting for me at Dr. Dad's building when I arrive. Now that he trusts me with the log-in info and I have a phone with enough memory to run the app, I was able to order myself a trip from home to the South Street Goodwill. I just change cars and I'm on my way.

When I heave open the heavy glass doors of the Goodwill, it hits me how tired I am. *Maybe I should have waited until tomorrow?* But no, I realize. I need to do this now, so I can spend every waking hour that I'm not in class between now and Friday practicing my speech.

I don't bother checking the CDs. No time (or energy) today. Instead, I make my way back to the women's jackets and start looking through the jammed racks, scanning for one with a blue-and-white arm. They're almost all black, brown, or navy, so I'm hoping the Captain America hoodie will stick out—if it's still here (which I realize is unlikely but I'm hoping for a miracle). I scan and scan but it's just not there. I decide to check the dressing room, my hope fading.

I poke around in the piles of castoffs and of course . . . no luck.

"Can I help you find something?" a woman behind me says.

"I'm looking for this Captain America hoodie I saw here before. It's red on the bottom, with blue-and-white sleeves and a hood."

The woman offers me a blank stare. "When did you see it?"

"It was like a month ago," I say, knowing what she's going to tell me.

She says exactly what I expect—that they have a lot of turnover and never know what's going to come in and that, if I see something I really like, I should definitely get it while I have a chance. But then she says, "You might want to check the kids' section," and I'm (probably stupidly) filled with hope again.

I slowly make my way to the kids' section, which is way back at the front of the store. The cashier's up there too, so if by some miracle I find the jacket, I can buy it and leave. My pain's not so bad today, but I'm getting more exhausted by the minute.

I get to the kids' section, find the jackets, and can tell by the length of the sleeves that they're for younger kids. But then I find another rack behind the first one that has larger sizes. Unlike the women's jackets, these jackets come in various colors. I find a few potential candidates only to wrench apart the hangers and find something other than what I'm looking for.

I survey the half a rack that's left and see only three possible matches, that glimmer of hope I had ten minutes ago waning fast. At least I'll know I really tried.

I make my way to the first possibility. The sleeve's exactly right, so tug out the jacket and—OH MY GOD! A hoodie has never looked so beautiful.

Here's hoping Captain America can save the day.

58

here goes everything

It's about 100 degrees in Jenkins's classroom (okay, not really), but I'd probably be sweating even if it were below freezing. The late bell just rang, and a few students are still settling into their seats. With just a week and a half left of the school year, most of the class seem like they're already mentally in summer vacay mode. *Good.* Maybe hardly anyone will be paying attention.

Oliver sits in his regular seat beside mine and I smile when I notice his Captain America jacket slung over the back of his chair. I might be imagining things, but somehow the Arctic Frost he's been beaming my way since I first destroyed our friendship seems less intense now.

I considered wearing the polka dot dress today since we'll be getting the class photos retaken later this afternoon (or just *taken* for me, since I missed them the first time). But I couldn't wear that dress again, not after what happened the last time I had it on. Besides, the Captain America hoodie, which is tucked away in my backpack, would look even more ridiculous over a dress. Instead I kept my outfit simple, going with Dani's girly-girl jeans and a fitted white T-shirt.

I review my index cards one last time, but I'm probably as ready as I'm going to be. Dani listened to me rehearse my speech about a thousand times (okay, maybe ten) and said it was the best speech ever delivered in the history of the planet. She's slightly biased of course, but I'm happy with what I've come up with. I hope Jenkins is too.

"Good morning, ladies and gentlemen," Jenkins says, bringing the class to order. "First a brief announcement. As most of you know, your class photos need to be retaken this afternoon due to an issue with the original photos. All ninth graders will have fifth period lunch today and remain in the cafeteria until their home-room class is called by the photographer. On behalf of the Grant Graduation Committee, I offer my sincerest apologies."

Some people in class who obviously didn't know grumble while I marvel at Jenkins's restraint. I'm sure his "announce-ment" could have started with *since the incompetent turd who runs this school . . .*

"Now," he continues. "Our final speaker. Ms. Bloom, you have the floor."

I slip the jacket out of my backpack and heave myself up to my feet. A snicker comes from the back of the room.

It's okay. Let them laugh. It doesn't matter.

The classroom's dead quiet as I make my three-hour (okay, thirty-second) journey to the front of the room, clutching Captain America in one hand and my stack of index cards in the other. Jenkins positions his chair so that he can keep an eye on the class, the fierce expression on his face daring them to make one peep. I give him a quick nod to show my appreciation.

"Stand up tall and straight and address the back row," he quietly last-minute-coaches me.

I nod again, take a deep breath, and . . . put on the Captain America hoodie.

That elicits a few snickers from the class, but it's more of an amused kind of snicker rather than the insulting kind. I reach back for the hood, ignoring my stinging elbow, and put it on so that I'm peering through the goofy cutout eyeholes. There's some laughter now—some of it nasty—but looking out at my classmates, I can tell that a lot of them are digging the Captain. Of course, there's only one person in the room whose reaction I care about most.

I look directly at Oliver. He's grinning ear to ear.

I glance at Jenkins next, and somehow I know he knows what I'm doing, why I'm dressed like this.

I take a deep breath and begin.

"My name is Erica Bloom, and the topic of my speech is the power of words. Words have a lot of power, probably more than you realize. As an American—" I flex my arms so maybe the class will think that's the reason I'm wearing the Captain America hoodie, even if it's not the real reason—"I have the right to free speech, although as a ninth grader, that right doesn't always apply."

A light chuckle rumbles through the room. I take down the hood after my opening, preferring to be able to make eye contact. Besides, the hood made its point, and this way at least my head won't be sweating like the rest of me.

"Curse words have the power to get you kicked out of school. I found that out back in February, when Principal Perdanta told me that if I was caught cursing at school again, I'd be expelled. At the time, I didn't really understand why cursing at school was such a big deal. I mean, they're just words, right? Most only have four letters!"

The class laughs again and it feels good to make them laugh intentionally, rather than being the butt of their jokes.

"But according to the school rules, cursing *is* a big deal, and I certainly didn't want to get kicked out, because that would mean I'd have to take ninth grade twice, which would be colossally tragic."

The whole class groans and I smile when I think *this public speaking thing is actually kind of fun.*

"So I had to stop cursing at school because those words had the power to mess up my life. And my life already felt pretty messed up. About a year and a half ago, one little word changed my life forever: 'divorce.'"

I look out at the class and see some nods. Kendall snorts, like she has a Disaster-Formerly-Known-As-*Her*-Parents too. I realize nearly everyone is paying attention to me, which makes what I'm about to say even harder.

"Looks like some of you are familiar with that word. You're probably less familiar with the other horrible word that showed up in my life last November: 'arthritis.' Technically, it's called *poly-articular juvenile idiopathic arthritis.* I know—kind of a mouthful.

"Most of you know about my arthritis, thanks to Mrs. Hunter. She meant well when she told my whole geoscience class about it. She thought her words would have the power to make my classmates more compassionate toward me. Instead, her words empowered people to make fun of me, to call me 'freak' and 'grandma.' I tried to tell myself that it didn't matter what people said, that I didn't care, but I didn't believe my own words. A good friend told me that people would eventually get bored with me and move on to tormenting someone else. I figured he was right but the words still hurt.

"That brings me to another word: 'friend.' It's a word that can be used in a lot of different ways and mean a lot of different things.

Best friend. Girlfriend. Just friends. Old friend. It can even be a verb: '*un*friend.'"

I want to look at Oliver again, to see if that last part registered, to make sure he's paying attention. But it might make me lose my nerve.

"Up until about a month ago, I had a really good friend, maybe even a best friend, but now we're not friends anymore. It wasn't anything I said. Actually, it was something I *didn't* say. Those words have power, too. The ones we don't say. My friend was getting picked on and I should have helped him. But I was more worried about being next in line to get picked on than I was about being a good friend. So I said nothing.

"Later I tried to apologize, but those words didn't have any power. It was too late. The words I didn't say, at the moment I really needed to say them, ended up costing me my best friend—who, for the record, is kind of amazing. He's had to deal with some big, scary words in his life too, but he didn't let that turn him into an angry little brat who curses people out because he feels so sorry for himself."

I pause for a moment, my heart racing. It's dead quiet in the classroom. They're all waiting for me to continue, to wrap up my speech in some way that makes sense. So I just plunge in.

"So why am I telling you all this? Why have I spoken all these words that are so personal and have so much power instead of picking some easy topic like the history of the Philly cheesesteak? One reason is that I need a really good grade from Mr. Jenkins."

I flash Mr. Jenkins a smile and he flashes one back.

"But another reason is because I've been thinking a lot about words lately, the four-letter ones I shouldn't say because they'll just mean trouble for me and other words I should say but often don't.

I don't mean stuff like 'please' and 'thank you,' though you might want to try them out. They're actually kind of cool. I'm talking about the words I need to say even if they make me uncomfortable. 'Help' is a biggie for me. When I was in terrible pain and I felt alone and afraid, and all those curse words were coming out of my mouth, the four-letter word I really should have been saying was 'help.' Of course, that also means that when someone offers me help, I need to say 'yes.' For some reason, that one's hard too."

I see Kendall fold her arms and smile. I'm pretty sure I just talked myself into accepting her help with the graduation ceremony. *Ugh.*

"In conclusion"—I say this in a jokey way because it sounds way too formal for me to say it completely seriously—"we all have a pretty important word coming up for us next week: 'graduation.'"

"We'll all be starting at new schools next year. At my new school, I've decided I'm going to use the words that will make my life better. I'm going to ask for help when I need it. Ask a teacher to explain something again if I didn't understand it the first time. Maybe even a third. I'm going to use my words to make friends, not enemies. And when my new friends need me to stick up for them, I'm going to open my mouth and speak my mind."

The whole class seems to be hanging on my every word.

"So here's another word for you: 'invite.' I can't tell any of you what to say or how to act. But I can *invite* you to think about your words and to try to use them for good rather than evil."

I flex my Captain America arms again for emphasis.

"Well, that's what I'm going to try to do anyway. And now I only have four words left: thank you for listening."

The class claps, no one louder than Jenkins.

"Thank you, Ms. Bloom," Jenkins says. "That was exemplary."

I take my seat and I can't figure out if I'm relieved because it's over, excited because I think it went well, or completely embarrassed that I not only just said all that stuff, but I said it wearing a Captain America hoodie. Maybe I'm all of the above. I want to look at Oliver *so badly*, but I don't. I can't. Not yet.

Jenkins fills the remaining class time talking about starting high school and how we should all consider getting involved at our new schools by writing for the school paper, running for office in student government, joining or starting clubs, etc. Chances are his encouragement is falling on mostly deaf ears but I'm listening. Not that I'd ever in a million years try to be class president or something. But the school paper? Maybe. Clubs? Why not? I wonder if HCLA has a club for students with medical issues, where we could bitch and moan freely and occasionally do something productive, like share helpful ideas. For a fleeting second, I consider starting a club like that if it doesn't exist. Maybe Oliver would join it?

The bell rings while I'm still lost in thought. Most of my class-mates bolt out the door. I take my time (as if I had a choice anyway). The room's empty by the time I'm on my feet, which is absolutely fine with me.

Jenkins gives me a nod and says, simply, "See you tomorrow."

Out in the hall, I head for the elevator.

Kendall appears by my side, and says, "Great speech, especially the part about asking for help."

"Yeah, yeah," I say.

"Find me later," she adds, before heading off in the opposite direction.

I'm a few feet from the elevator when I look up and see Oliver standing there, waiting for me. He has on his Captain America jacket, hood up.

"Great jacket," he says as I approach. He's smiling.

"You like it?" I jokingly respond, pushing the elevator call button.

"Wait, you just need to . . ." He reaches behind me and gently lifts the hood onto my head. "There. Better."

We peer out at each other through the goofy eyeholes, laughing. Then he says, "So . . . you think I'm kind of amazing, huh?"

I'm suddenly blushing like crazy. "Absolutely," I say.

"Cool. Cause I kind of think you're amazing too."

The freaking elevator doors rumble open *at just that second*. I guess I'm supposed to get on the elevator and get to homeroom, but I don't want this conversation to end. So I grab Oliver's arm and tug him onto the elevator with me just before the doors close.

We ride down in silence for a moment, and then I say, "Can we please be friends again?"

"Do you really want to be friends?" he asks me.

"Yes!" I say.

He laughs quietly. "I meant *just* friends."

I'm sure my cheeks have gone full-on tomato at this point.

I'm about to tell him maybe not, maybe we could be more than friends, maybe that should have been obvious all along and I was too dumb to realize it.

But the freaking elevator doors open again!

And Principal Piranha happens to be right there in the hall. She scowls at us.

"I don't know what *this* is," she says, waving at us, at our matching ridiculous hood-up hoodies, "but Ricky is the only student who should be using the elevator. And put those hoods down. Both of you. This is a *school*, not a comic book convention."

We have no choice but to comply with her orders. I smile at Oliver, hoping my face isn't still as red as I think it might be.

"See you later," I say.

He gives me one of his little salutes.

Good God, did his eyes get even bluer?

59

team ricky

When I get to the cafeteria for lunch, I find Kendall and sit beside her, even though all of her Barbie friends are there at the same table.

"You all know Ricky, right?" Kendall says.

Her friends nod and say *hey* or whatever. I'm pretty sure they all know me as *that girl with arthritis*, but whatever. I have as much right to be here as they do.

"Hi," I say, like this is a totally normal situation.

"Your speech in Jenkins's class was *epic*," a girl sitting next to me says, who I only know as Ms. Yoo from public speaking. She's wearing jeans and a simple yellow blouse I could *almost* see myself wearing. I didn't know she hung with Barbies. She seems more regular-girl rather than hot-and-happening.

"Thanks," I say. "I was shooting for epic actually."

The Barbies laugh. With me, not *at* me. Just like in class.

"Okay," Kendall says, "we have to figure out the right speed."

I glance at the other Barbies, some self-consciousness creeping in. But I suck it up. "Some days I'm slower than others," I tell Kendall.

"Hmmm," she says, chewing on her bottom lip. She's taking this whole thing *very* seriously. "Then we'll practice two different speeds, and you can text me the morning of graduation and let me know if you want the slow one."

"More like the slow-*er* one."

She smirks at me. "Whatever."

"What are you dorks talking about?" Redhead Barbie says, barging in.

Kendall doesn't miss a beat. "Graduation. I'm gonna walk slow so Ricky doesn't have trouble keeping up."

I wait for Redhead Barbie to come back with a snotty comment that'll make me want to forget the whole stupid thing. To my surprise she says, "Oooh! I want in! I'm about halfway back. I can make sure the end of the line doesn't speed up."

"Awesome!" Kendall says. "When we're done eating, we should practice."

"Practice what?" I ask.

"*Duh*—walking. I need to get a sense of the right pace."

"Here? In the cafeteria?" *In front of everyone?*

Kendall leans in close to me and whispers, "Get over yourself."

I'm about to lash out at her, but then it's like a bubble bursts and suddenly I feel lighter. Instead of cursing her out, I laugh.

"Hey, show her your thing," Redhead Barbie says to . . . Regular Girl Barbie.

"No! Screw you," Regular Girl Barbie protests, but she's laughing.

"Come on. It's gross. She'll love it," Redhead Barbie insists.

Regular Girl Barbie rolls her eyes but then untucks her blouse a little in the front, revealing . . . I'm not sure what. Some sort of small medical device, taped to her skin.

"It's my insulin pump," she explains. "Disgusting but, like, *keeps me alive*, so . . ."

Her friends laugh and she laughs with them. I find myself laughing too.

"Personally," says Redhead Barbie, "I'm glad your disgusting little pump keeps you alive, Janice." She hugs Regular Girl Barbie . . . er, Janice.

"Love you too," Janice says. "Bitch."

More laughter. From all of us. I notice the girl across from me, a gorgeous black girl whose makeup is always so impeccable she looks ready to go to a photo shoot every day. This close I can see bumps and acne scars under her heavy foundation. The one next to her, a chubby girl with pretty brown eyes, pops a baby carrot into her mouth and I see that her fingernails are chewed down to the quick.

God. They all have their shit. It's not just me. Even if they did get the How To Be Hot And Happening instruction manual that I never got, maybe Barbieville isn't a paradise any more than Rickyville is.

"Don't look now but your boyfriend's here," Janice says, nodding toward the food line. I follow her gaze, expecting to see Oliver (and excited to see Oliver!) but . . .

"Lex? Are you kidding me?"

"He's in my AP classes. He's got a puppy love crush on you. He knows we're in public speaking together, so he's always asking me questions about you. It's adorable." Janice takes a sip of her soda. "Did you know he's only thirteen? He skipped a grade."

I look back at Lex, who's making his way to a table, noticing for the first time how young he looks.

"Nuh-uh. Ricky's into Captain America," Kendall says, grinning.

"Oliver's just a friend," I say, since officially that's still all we are, but the Barbies *oooh* and *aaah* anyway.

"Here's your *friend* now," Fingernail-Biter Barbie says.

I seriously need to learn their names!

Sure enough, Oliver's standing with his lunch tray, scanning the tables for an open seat. It's a bit of a madhouse in here today with all the extra ninth-grade bodies.

Redhead Barbie waves him over to our table and I see suspicion cloud his face. I quickly wave him over too, hoping he doesn't get the wrong idea, like maybe everything this morning was to lure him in for an ambush. I hope he knows I'd never do that.

When he gets to us, Janice hops up. "Here. Sit next to Ricky."

The Barbies all titter and I practically *die* of embarrassment.

Oliver sits down, looking a little nervous and out of place.

But I reach for his hand, lace my fingers between his, and say, "Hey, you."

He smiles and instantly looks more at ease. And I find myself suddenly crushed that we're here, in this crowded cafeteria and not somewhere, anywhere, else. Alone.

After a few minutes, Kendall finishes the last bite of her sandwich and announces, "Okay. Time to figure out our pacing." She glances around skeptically, and I'm thinking maybe this crowded-ass cafeteria isn't such a bad thing if it gets me out of walking practice. "Come on. Let's go out in the hall."

And we do. Not just me and Kendall and Redhead Barbie but a couple other Barbies and Oliver too.

Kendall lines us up, with me in front and the others in alphabetical order behind me, and gives us our instructions:

"Oliver, you'll be the first person on the team after Ricky, so you'll set the pace for the middle of the line."

Wait. We're a team now?

"Daphne and Monique come next . . ."

Redhead and Fingernail-Biter have names!

"You two need to keep the back half of the line steady and Janice will bring up the rear, nice and slow."

"You're, like, freakishly organized," I say to Kendall.

"Thanks!" she says. I'm not sure I meant it as a compliment when I first said it, but I'm glad she took it that way. "Everyone ready? Let's walk!"

I hesitate, feeling ridiculous and really not wanting to walk with all of them behind me. But then it dawns on me *all-at-once* that this strange little team Kendall's organized is kind of like my classmates shaving their heads in solidarity or having a bake sale for me.

So *screw it*—I walk.

fireworks . . . the best kind

My X-Car drops me off at CHOP and I Ricky-hustle into the lobby. I'm actually *excited* to be going to this stupid party because Oliver's up there. And yes, I'm rocking the polka dots. Oliver practically requested it, and if he can forgive this dress, I can too. And *damn* it's fun to wear!

"Give Me Novacaine" comes from my cell and, as I scramble to answer the call, I wonder if maybe I should change my ringtone. Maybe I don't want to be numb anymore. Maybe my life's no longer All About Pain.

"Hey, you," I say, because naturally, it's Oliver calling. "I'm downstairs. Be there in a sec." I stow my phone back in my purse and hop on the elevator.

Upstairs, it's an explosion of cheerfulness, with clowns and rainbows and smiley faces everywhere. For whatever reason, all the manufactured sunshine is actually working for me today. I get it. Maybe for the first time.

I reach the activities room and find the place swarming with people—some adults mixed in with kids, ranging from toddler age to early teens. Some of the kids are in wheelchairs or attached to some type of medical equipment. Pastel-colored balloons float freely in the air, their color-coordinated strings dangling, and a big banner on one wall proclaims, HAPPY SUMMER!

I'm drawn to the side of the room where the karaoke is set up. Lovely Rita's has even brought a small collection of their wacky props. A boy of about eleven is singing an R&B song. He's pretty good—and is definitely enjoying himself.

Suddenly, Oliver's beside me. He hugs me and I hug back. And we keep hugging because neither one of us wants to let go. Being in his arms, feeling his body pressing gently against mine, is intoxicating. I want to kiss him *so badly*, but this just isn't the right time or place.

He had something to do with his mom yesterday after school, so we had to settle for texting all night and still haven't gotten to finish our unfinished business from the elevator. I don't know if we'll get to finish it here either, but for now I'm just happy to be with him. I'm just happy to *be*.

Post-hug, I notice that Oliver's face is painted with peace signs and little bursts of fireworks—silly but kind of adorable, too. He hands me a bottle of water, and when I try to twist off the cap, I realize he's loosened it for me.

I feel a tiny tug on my hand and look down. It's a little girl, maybe four or five, her face painted with hearts and flowers. There's a fresh crop of blond peach fuzz covering her head, meaning this sweet little kid is probably fighting cancer.

"Your face needs pictures!" she says brightly, and then she tugs on my hand again, leading me to another part of the room.

Oliver follows us, saying, "Don't pull too hard, Gracie."

"It's okay," I say, since her tiny fingers are like feathers in my hand.

Gracie leads me to a girl with shoulder-length brown hair, probably in her late teens, with skinny arms and knobby, swollen knuckles like my macadamia nut pinkie finger. She's sitting a bit stiffly and wears wrist braces on both hands, but hers are decorated with really beautiful designs. Other than that, she looks pretty normal.

"Her face needs pictures," Gracie repeats to the teenaged girl. It's only then that I notice the collection of face paints.

The girl waves at the chair facing her. "Have a seat," she tells me. "I'm Mary."

"I'm Ricky," I tell her back.

Oliver sits cross-legged on the floor beside us and says, "I mentioned Mary to you, remember? She has arthritis too."

My automatic self-consciousness engulfs me for a moment, but it leaves just as quickly. My "secret" is no big deal here . . . or anywhere really. If it weirds people out, that's their own shit to deal with.

"It's the freakin' *worst*, right?" Mary says casually. I nod in agreement, a bit stunned by the fact that here's a real, live human being, not much older than I am, who absolutely knows what a drag it is. "How come I've never seen you at Teen Talk nights?" she asks.

I gather she's talking about the support group Oliver goes to. "I'm kind of new to all this," I tell Mary. "It's only been since November."

"Wow!" she says, her eyes wide. "You're less than a year in? Hang in there. It gets easier."

She gets started on my pictures and I ask her questions the whole time: How old was she when she got diagnosed? (Eight.) What medication is she on? (One of the biologics but a different one than I'm on.) What rheumatologist does she see? (A female doctor named Ress.) I learn that she's seventeen and is starting college early next year. She asks for my cell number and says that we should keep in touch.

"Where did you get the wrist braces?" I ask her now, because I'm dying to know.

"Aren't they great?" she says, showing them off. "My friend Jane's an artist. I got white ones on Amazon and she dyed them. I can ask her to make you a pair."

"That'd be awesome!"

Mary puts the finishing touches on my face and pronounces me done, just as someone starts a new karaoke song.

"Hey, you're into karaoke, right?" Oliver asks me. "Are you gonna sing?"

After another brief moment of self-consciousness—even briefer this time—I say, "Heck yeah, I'm gonna sing!"

"Cool!" Oliver hops up from the floor *effortlessly.*

I glance at Mary. "Doesn't that drive you crazy?"

"*So* crazy," she says.

Mary and I get up *with effort* and laugh all the way to the karaoke corner.

I scan the song list, looking for Mom's standard, "I Will Survive," thinking it'd be a good message for the kids here. But then I wonder if some of them won't survive. So I pick Katy Perry's "Firework" instead and wait my turn. A little girl and her dad are singing "The Wheels on the Bus." They're behind with the lyrics and pretty off-key—but it's an adorable performance anyway. I clap heartily when they finish and sing along when a teenage boy does an Imagine Dragons song next.

Then it's my turn. I take my place at the mike and . . . something takes over me, some sort of fearless, joyful abandon—and I sing the *crap* out of that song. I sway with the melody, picking out individual kids to sing to, encouraging them to sing and sway with me. I'm an insane hit. Seriously. And I own that shit. I finish big and the cheers from the little crowd are borderline thunderous.

Finally I arrive back at Oliver's side, breathless.

"That. Was. Badass," he says, astonished. Like he had no idea I had that in me, which is totally understandable because I had no idea either.

After so many more karaoke numbers I lose count, someone announces it's time for the sundae bar. We line up alongside the designated table and it's *insane*! Five different kinds of ice cream accompany bowls and bowls of toppings—hot fudge, butterscotch sauce, every type of candy, nuts, jimmies, fruit.

Oliver suggests we split one, and we crack up as we pile our Supersonic Single Sundae higher and higher. When we get to the end of the table, Oliver somehow manages to get two maraschino cherries to stay put on top of our mini-mountain and says, "Come on. Let's go outside."

I follow him to a patio I hadn't even realized was there. It's mostly teenagers out here, which is cool, but so was the activities room.

We sit on a nice, padded bench and start in on the sundae. (Never mind that we have absolutely no hope of finishing it.)

"You were right," I say in-between mouthfuls, "this party is crazy fun."

"Told you," he says back. "You'll come to realize I'm right about a whole bunch of stuff."

I laugh because I can tell he's joking. "I guess that goes along with being kind of amazing," I say, echoing what I said in my speech, what we said to each other in the elevator.

And suddenly, we're right back there, on the elevator, before the doors opened and we got busted by Principal Piranha, with all that unfinished business hanging in the air. I glance at Oliver and can tell he's feeling it too.

My body's buzzing and I feel lightheaded but somehow grounded at the same time and I want him to kiss me SO badly and oh-my-God WHY isn't he kissing me *right this second* but then it dawns on me—I don't have to wait for him to kiss me. I can initiate the kissing if I want to—and I really want to!

So I lean in close to him, my lips just inches from his.

"Hey, you," he says softly, stealing my line.

And then I touch my lips to his.

And our mouths open, just a little.

And it's . . . exhilarating and sexy and somehow still sweet and fun, just like it always is with Oliver. And I think, *what took me so long? And has he always felt this way? And how come I didn't realize how amazing he is earlier?*

And then I stop thinking.

good riddance, glorious grant middle school!

Dr. Dad sprang for an SUV when he ordered today's X-Car, so he and Dani and Noland and I are all styling on our way to Glorious Grant Middle School. Dani gifted me with a ginormous graduation day bath bomb and got me up an hour early so I could take a luxurious bath. So now my skin feels extra silky, but I'm a little sleepy. Definitely shouldn't have stayed up until two in the morning texting with Oliver. At least my feet are snug in my trusty ankle braces and feel halfway decent today. I texted Kendall and told her medium-slow would probably work fine.

The scene at Grant is hectic, with lots of cars dropping off students. Our X-Car squeezes into a spot and we pile out. A fancy BMW pulls up right behind us and Lex climbs out of the passenger side carrying his guitar. A woman barks at him from inside to put his gown on and wait for her there before she zooms off.

"Hey, Lex," I say, as he fumbles with his oversized gown.

"Are you playing in the ceremony?" He nods. "I haven't seen Julio yet."

"He has to go to summer school to graduate," Lex says. "So no ceremony for him."

"That's crap," I say, but it dawns on me that I must have passed all my classes, since no one told me I couldn't be here today.

"That's Julio," Lex says, with a shrug that seems more disappointed than critical. He looks different, standing there awkwardly without Julio by his side, kind of lost and lonely. I'm tempted to give him a hug, but I don't want him to take it the wrong way.

Instead I introduce him to my family, adding, "Lex is an amazing guitarist."

He blushes a little and mumbles *thanks*.

After that, Dad heads for the auditorium to save some primo seats and Dani and Noland escort me to the side entrance where the graduates are supposed to enter.

We run into Oliver the moment we step inside and suddenly everything rushes back to me—the karaoke, the kissing, last night's epic text-a-thon. (I confessed that I've basically become obsessed with Afterschool Specials and now he totally wants to watch them with me.)

"Hey, you," I say, happily caught in the trance of his blue eyes. I want to kiss him again—and again—right there, in front of everyone.

"Is this Oliver?" Dani says, crowding into our space. "I'm Dani, the big sis."

"Roo's told us *all* about you," Noland says, butting in too.

"Yeah, like what a great kisser you are," my traitorous sister adds.

"Dani!" I shriek.

"She's a pretty good kisser too," Oliver says.

A brief but horrifyingly awkward silence follows, during which I stare at the ground and pray for death. Death does not come.

Then I decide—*screw that*. I lean into Oliver and give him a soft, lingering kiss—right there, in front of everyone.

Once my lips are free, I spot Jenkins straightening out people at the end of the line and say to Oliver, "We'd better take our places."

We all walk to my spot and then Oliver gives me one of his salutes.

Cripes. Must he be so adorkable?

I salute back. *And then Dani and Noland salute too.* I smack both of them and they just laugh. "Shut UP!" I tell them.

Kendall walks by after that. "Got your text," she says. "How about I keep the pace pretty slow anyway, just in case. Sound good?"

"Sure. Sorry."

"Don't be sorry," Kendall insists. "Where's your cap?"

I nudge Dani, who dubbed herself the Official Cap Bearer. She unfolds the dorky cap, while Noland pats down my hair. Then the two of them fuss over me, adjusting the cap, my hair, my gown, while I stand there like Arthritis Barbie.

I spot Mom heading in our direction. She looks way too *proud-and-excited-parent* for a (second) middle school graduation. Even more surreal, Dr. Dad's with her, looking about the same.

"I saved us seats in the front," Dr. Dad reports.

Mom hands me a little box. "Here's a graduation present for you, honey," she says. Inside is a beautiful necklace with amethyst stones set in silver. "I got the long one, so you could put it over your head."

Arthritis Barbie likey!

We're all smiles and hugs and excitement until I spot Principal Piranha at the front of the line, handing something to Kendall.

"That's Principal Piranha," I whisper to Mom.

In no time, Principal Piranha's made her way down to me.

"Now, isn't this nice," she says in her condescending tone, handing me the same envelope she handed everyone else. "Four months ago, I never would have believed you'd be standing here, Erica. But you proved me wrong. And I must say I'm glad you decided to participate with your peers."

I bite my tongue because what I'd like to say in response might get me retroactively expelled.

"I didn't have any doubts," Mom pipes in, looking as if she'd like to hurl a few choice obscenities at Principal Piranha herself.

"You must be Mrs. Bloom," Principal Piranha says.

"It's Eagleton now," Mom tells her, "and it's *Ms.*"

Principal Piranha pinches up her face. "My apologies," she says before leaving.

Noland stifles a giggle. "Damn, Mom. You told her."

"What's in the envelope?" Mom asks.

I tear it open. "It's my report card," I say, suddenly nervous.

"Well? What'd you get?!" Dani says, trying to read over my shoulder, but I block her view. They're *my* grades. I get to see them first.

"I got an A in Spanish," I report. It's likely my only A.

"Muy bien!" Dr. Dad says.

I scan the rest of the classes, filling them in as I go along. "Algebra 1: B minus; English: B; another B for geoscience. That's generous." I snort. "C in world history, and public speaking . . ."

I stare at the report card, trying to focus. I can't be seeing what I'm seeing. . . .

"That's the class you had all those afterschool meetings for, right?" Dad asks.

"Yeah, with Mr. Jenkins," I whisper. I blink again. Nope, I'm not seeing things. "He gave me a C . . . *plus.*"

They all shriek and congratulate me, and they think I'm speechless because I'm relieved that I passed everything. None of them know the real reason.

Principal Piranha's obnoxious voice coming from way at the end of the line breaks the spell. "Time for family members to take their seats in the auditorium," she says, clapping her hands to get everyone's attention. "Let's go. It's time!"

"Let's go! It's time!" Noland says under her breath, clapping and doing a spot-on Principal Piranha imitation. Dad gives me a hug. Mom kisses me on the cheek. Dani adjusts the stupid cap one last time.

Once they're gone, Jenkins buzzes onto the scene. "Okay, graduates!" he whisper-shouts. "The ceremony will begin momentarily. I need everyone to be alert, orderly, and quiet. You'll begin entering the auditorium when Mrs. Hershman gives you the signal." He points to her standing at the front of the line. "That'll be about ten minutes from now."

Ten whole minutes?

But Jenkins appears beside me, carrying a chair. He places it beside me and gives me a look that says *non-negotiable.*

"I'm very glad you're here, Ms. Bloom."

I beam a smile at him and hold up my report card. "Got my grades."

"I see that you have." Jenkins makes his way to the front of the line, pausing by Kendall. "Ms. Adams, there's no need to rush things—"

Kendall shoots a look my way. "We got this, Mr. Jenkins."

He nods, obviously pleased, before heading for the auditorium.

The chair he brought me is good—fairly high and sturdy. I plant both feet firmly on the ground so they stay sharp.

Two whole minutes pass before I remember to wonder if people are staring at me.

Two more seconds pass before I decide I don't care.

Finally Mrs. Hershman motions for us to get ready and props the doors to the auditorium open.

I get up without much struggle as the graduation song starts playing in the auditorium. I'm having déjà vu from last year and it all seems kind of silly for ninth grade, but for some reason, I feel excited. A second later, the line starts to move.

So slow that I'm not even limping.

We inch along, like snails, clear the doors, and make our way toward the stage. Nearly every seat in the auditorium is full.

We keep inching.

Kendall starts to ascend the steps onto the stage, and instead of panicking about not being able to float up those steps *effortlessly* like my classmates . . . I can't wait to get on that stage. Kendall's going so slowly, everyone has to go up one step at a time. I make my way to the front row of chairs on the stage and lower myself into my assigned seat.

While my classmates file into the rows behind me, I glance around the stage and see most of my teachers. Even Nurse Jeff's there at the end of the row. *Wait. Where's Jenkins?* I think, in a moment of panic, but then I see him standing just offstage with a rolling cart filled with stacks of folder-like things. Our diplomas.

Principal Piranha makes some obnoxious remarks and then announces "a musical performance by Lex Young."

Lex makes his way to the front of the stage and somehow he looks bigger, more confident, than he did when I saw him outside earlier. No stage fright for him I guess.

He settles onto a stool and begins to play . . . and it's the most beautiful music I've ever heard—a classical piece of intricate and precise notes that I know must be incredibly difficult to pull off. But Lex makes it seem *effortless*. He has the entire auditorium transfixed the whole time, and it's only after he's done and everyone's applauding like mad that some of his awkwardness returns.

I catch his eye when he's on the way back to his seat and mouth the word *WOW* because—wow, that was amazing.

Next Principal Piranha introduces the "class valedictorian, Janice Yoo"—guess I could have called her *Valedictorian Barbie*. Finally, Mr. Jenkins rolls his cart to the front of the stage, joining Principal Piranha by the podium. It's time.

We all stand on cue and Principal Piranha starts to call out names—*Kendall Adams, Terrance Anders, Danica Barton*. My line moves slowly as people collect their diplomas.

When my name's called, I step up to Mr. Jenkins. I can hear Mom, Dad, Dani, and Noland hooting and hollering from the front row like crazy people.

Jenkins beams a huge smile at me. "Congratulations," he says, as he hands me my diploma and moves my tassel from the right side of my cap to the left.

I want to thank him for the C plus and tell him that he ended up being my favorite teacher, that I loved his class and won't ever forget how hard he pushed me and that I understand now why he did it and how grateful I am that he did. But Principal Piranha has already called the next person's name. I need to keep the line moving.

So I hold out my hand for him to shake. That seems proper and formal—just right for Mr. Jenkins. He takes my hand and gives it a firm shake but doesn't squeeze too tight—just right for me.

the me i am now, the real one

Nothing about me is perfect, not even my mouth anymore, but my dad, aka my dentist, says my teeth are still pretty darn exceptional.

The rest of me is okay, too. Not perfect. Not horrible. Somewhere in-between.

Like a normal human being.

Here's some other basic info on me (the me I've become):

1. I'm fifteen, and next year I'll be going to a really cool high school with my best friend—an amazing guy who's sweet and funny and brave and kind of my boyfriend.

1a. I have an amazing boyfriend!

2. My parents, formerly known as the Disaster-Formerly-Known-As-My-Parents, aren't any more perfect than I am. But they love me and they do their best.

3. I have a chronic illness. It has a long, confusing name, but let's just call it arthritis for short. Arthritis can be extremely painful and I wish I didn't have it. But I do.

4. I used to curse a lot. Now I only curse a little (okay, maybe more than a little).

5. I used to think I was cursed. I don't think that anymore. Not even a little.

Author's Note

As Dr. Hunt tells Ricky, arthritis is funky. It can affect different people in vastly different ways. The medications now on the market—the biologics—are making a huge difference in the lives of people living with arthritis today. While some arthritis patients experience periods of remission (with and without medication), I wanted to steer clear of having Ricky focus on being cured. The majority of kids diagnosed with arthritis won't go into full remission and must find ways to lead big, beautiful lives anyway. *Cursed* is for those kids and others living with chronic illnesses and/or disabilities—as well as anyone who wants to better understand what it's like to live with chronic pain.

The specific biologic Ricky goes on in *Cursed* is intentionally not named. I didn't want to indicate one medicine's value over another, as many options are available, with more coming every year. Finding the "best fit" is a project individual arthritis patients work on with their doctors.

I also took some dramatic liberties with the Dr. Blech-stein character. In reality, such a doctor would likely never be working at a children's hospital, which are outstanding institutions with extremely high standards. I fudged the truth a little here to show the stark contrast between a doctor as an adversary versus a true partner. It took me over a decade to discover the difference. It's my hope that *Cursed* can speed up that process for others.

For more information on arthritis and living with a chronic illness or disability, check out these links:

Arthritis Foundation:
https://www.arthritis.org/.

Kids Get Arthritis Too:
http://www.kidsgetarthritistoo.org/.

Americans with Disabilities Act information:
https://www.ada.gov/.

Christine Miserandino, The Spoon Theory:
https://butyoudontlooksick.com/articles/written-by-christine/the-spoon-theory/.

Stella Young, "I Am Not Your Inspiration, Thank You Very Much," TED Talk (April 2014):
https://www.ted.com/talks/stella_young_i_m_not_your_inspiration_thank_you_very_much/.

Wikipedia, "Hypoalgesic effect of swearing":
https://en.wikipedia.org/wiki/Hypoalgesic_effect_of_swearing/.

Thank you! Thank you!

Acknowledgments

I doubt any of you are expecting me to gush on about how grateful I am for having gotten arthritis as a kid since the resulting challenges ultimately made me a more empathetic person, gave me a truer sense of myself, enabled me to write this book and *blah, blah, blah.* You've all read *Cursed*, so you're crystal clear on how colossally awful arthritis can be, even though each of the benefits listed above is real—and appreciated.

Make no mistake—living with chronic pain and/or a disability is hard. I was rudely not consulted when the Universe made this decision for me. It just happened and I had to deal with it—poorly at first but I gradually got better at it.

So what's the key to navigating a life like mine? In addition to cursing a lot, which honestly does help, I've found that surrounding myself with amazing people is crucial.

I started life with a nuclear family that, all things considered, was pretty righteous—a mom and dad who always encouraged me to reach for the stars, applauded my decision to become a writer, and never once asked when I'd be getting "a real job." My absolute love and appreciation for my sister Deb is reflected in the Dani character, and I'm blessed to have another great big sis, too—Jane, a brilliant artist, who always let me hang out with her and her cool friends and took me to see The Rocky Horror Picture Show on my thirteenth birthday.

As a (kind of) grown-up, I've managed to cultivate a group of friends who help me live independently despite my disability, root for me through thick and thin (some from afar), and somehow seem to love me, warts and all, as much as I love them. Among them, in no particular order, are Sonya Senkowsky, Terry Holzman, Nick Roman, Keryn Sánchez (who restores me to sanity on a weekly basis), Gil Marder, John Kiernan, Michael Blanc, Thor Gold, (dance partner) Kurt Sutter, Tony Frietas, my like-a-sister Janice Fan, Darlene Martin, Loring Hill, my late common law brother Jim Trois, and quite possibly the most neighborly neighbor on the planet, Carole Presser. I'm sure there are others I'm forgetting who deserve to be on this list. Sorry about that. I love and appreciate you all.

Medically, I've been picked up and put back together by countless health professionals. And while I'm indebted to every one of them, there will never be another Dr. Bruce Hoffman for me—the first doctor with whom I formed a true partnership and my inspiration for the Dr. Hunt character. Dr. Richard Ress stepped into his rather large shoes when I moved to Los Angeles and was my rheumatologist for two-plus decades before he had the nerve to retire on me. Surgeons of note who saved my quality of life, if not technically my life, are Edward J. McPherson and Daniel C. Allison. I owe my still-ambulatory status to both of them. I'm also deeply indebted to the US government, without whose financial and medical assistance, I'd be uneducated, nonambulatory, and living in the cheapest nursing home I could find. Regardless of how messed up our politics can be and how imperfect our union still is, I am blessed to live in the United States.

Cultivating an amazing support system as a writer is also essential. I joined the SCBWI decades ago and my doing so is the reason I'm writing these acknowledgments and struggling to not have them run longer than the book itself. My local kid lit buddies have all been along for the ride with me—Charlie Cohen (my partner-in-snark), Lee Wind, Greg Pincus, writing cop Jeff Cox, Laurie Young, Cheryl Manning, Mara Bushansky, and the (lovely) Rita Crayon Huang (whom I can never thank enough for introducing me to private-room karaoke). Again, I'm sure I'm forgetting people. Again, I beg your forgiveness.

In addition to the many folks named above, there are a few individuals without whom *Cursed* would not have seen the light of day, the first being my superhero agent, Jen Linnan. I didn't know if a book full of f-bombs would ever sell; Jen assured me it would, that it had to because this story simply had to be out in the world. She remained passionate about finding *Cursed* the right home well after I'd begun to lose hope. She found that home with Monica Perez at Charlesbridge Teen, who had the courage to take on my potty-mouthed, angry kid and shepherd her story into one that could actually reach an audience.

Monica's many questions and suggestions brought about countless improvements, and without them there would be no karaoke scenes in the book, which would have been tragic. Joyce White's insanely perfect design for *Cursed*, inside and out, has me particularly fan-girl-gushy, and I'm grateful to everyone at Charlesbridge Teen for all their hard work. My thanks also to the following readers who were kind enough to help me steer clear of all sorts inaccuracies: Dr. Don Goldsmith, Lana Lilienstein, and Michael and Eileen Flax.

My good buddy and fellow WGA Writers with Disabilities Committee member Michael Dougherty assured me that a particular scene, which shall remain unidentified, would not be offensive. So, like, if you're offended by anything in the book, feel free to blame him.

But none of that would have mattered if I hadn't started writing the book to begin with. Back in the early nineties, the brilliant Holly Goldberg Sloan encouraged me to write about my experience of getting sick as a young teen. (Spoiler alert: I didn't want to.) Years later, in a small children's-writing workshop, I was given the following prompt: Pick an age and free-write as yourself at that age. I scribbled madly and out came Ricky—angry and funny and foul-mouthed and terrified.

Still, it was just angsty scribbles in a random notebook . . . until I showed what I'd written to my writer friend Joseph Taylor and nervously asked, "Is this something?" Thus began a journey Joe and I basically took together. He read every scene I wrote (emailing over one hundred pages back to me after I'd lost them in a hard drive crash), encouraged me to keep going, celebrated with me when I signed with Jen and was among the first calls I made after hearing we'd gotten the offer from Charlesbridge. Joe, you know as well as I do that there simply would be no *Cursed* without you. You are and always have been this book's North Star.

Do you like my mustache?